B y the time they were back in their chairs, Sir Mason Green was once again seated in the witness box. He gazed out across the courtroom, straight at Gerald.

The prosecuting counsel resumed his battle. "Sir Mason, let us turn to the theft of the Noor Jehan diamond," Mr. Callaghan said. "You have told the court that you spent the evening in question at the opera. That is correct?"

There was a long silence. Green did not respond.

"Sir Mason?"

Every eye in the court turned to the figure seated in the witness box. Green stared at Gerald, unblinking.

The judge shifted in his chair. "The accused will answer the question."

Nothing.

The clerk of the court stood up from his desk; his chair scraped across the floorboards. He approached the stand and peered up at the man seated there.

"Sir Mason, are you all right?"

After a second, the clerk's face went pale. He turned to the judge.

"I—I think he's dead!"

THE ARCHER LEGACY ♦ BOOK THREE

THE MASK OF DESTINY

RICHARD NEWSOME

ILLUSTRATED BY

JONNY DUDDLE

WALDEN POND PRESS

An Imprint of HarperCollinsPublishers

Library of Congress Cataloging-in-Publication Data
Newsome, Richard.
    The mask of destiny / Richard Newsome ; illustrated by Jonny
Duddle. — 1st U.S. ed.
        p.   cm. — (The Archer legacy ; bk. 3)
    Summary: "This final chapter in the Archer Legacy finds
Gerald, Ruby, and Sam trying to clear Gerald's name for the murder
of longtime enemy Sir Mason Green, which can only be accomplished
by finding the treasure he has been after"— Provided by publisher.
    ISBN 978-0-06-194495-6 (pbk.)
    [1. Mystery and detective stories. 2. Supernatural—Fiction.
3. Adventure and adventurers—Fiction. 4. Murder—Fiction.
5. Precious stones—Fiction. 6. France—Fiction.] I. Duddle,
Jonny, ill. II. Title.
PZ7.N486644Mas 2012   2011053290
[Fic]—dc23   CIP
                                                                    AC

Typography by Amy Ryan
13 14 15 16 17   LP/BR   10 9 8 7 6 5 4 3 2 1
❖
First published by The Text Publishing Co., Australia.
First U.S. paperback edition, 2013

For Robern and Mark, and Daphne —
professional child wranglers

PROLOGUE

The man in the beige trousers checked his watch. It was still a few minutes before three o'clock. A bit early to go in—he didn't want to look too keen. One more turn around the conservatory ought to do it. Constable Lethbridge of the London Metropolitan Police set off for another circuit of the building.

Kew Gardens on a summer's day: just about the perfect place to be in London. The sun's warmth lay across the parkland like a comfort blanket. The trees strained under their foliage. The lawns were lush carpet. There were even butterflies. And was that a wren warbling in the hedge as the constable lumbered past? Or perhaps a nightingale? Lethbridge didn't much care for songbirds—he was a racing-pigeon man. He could prattle for hours about the standard method of calculating velocities, or the complexities of the "slow clock" rule. A man and his pigeons—was there anything more natural?

Lethbridge struck up a tuneless whistle as he trudged around the large glass building. It was an odd place to meet somebody for the first time. He would have preferred the pub. He'd met the last five women from the matchmaking agency at the Dog and Partridge. They were all very nice. He always made a point of buying the first drink. Then he'd tell a few good racing-pigeon yarns. At that point the women always said they needed the ladies' room. And that would be the last he'd see of them.

Lethbridge rounded the rear of the conservatory and emitted a satisfied *hrumph*. "Good," he thought. "No back door."

The call from the dating agency had come at the perfect time. Lethbridge had just come off the red-hot end of a roasting from his boss, Inspector Parrott. It had not been a good month—for either of them. The ongoing murder investigation involving the fugitive businessman Sir Mason Green was proving a nightmare. Lethbridge was looking forward to meeting someone who wasn't going to yell at him—at least not straightaway. Maybe even, dare he hope, she might be that someone special?

He reached the front of the Princess of Wales Conservatory. The courtyard was crowded with young families, happy couples, and a few pensioners holding hands. Lethbridge felt a sudden surge of confidence—this one was going to work out. He was sure of it.

And then he saw her.

They'd spoken briefly on the telephone to arrange the meeting. She had an intriguing voice—full-bodied, rounded vowels. She said she would wear a red coat with her hair down, so Lethbridge could recognize her.

"Won't it be hot in a coat?" Lethbridge had asked.

"Being hot doesn't trouble me," she had said. "Does it trouble you?"

At that point, Lethbridge had dropped the phone.

Even ignoring the coat, Lethbridge knew in an instant that the woman in the conservatory forecourt was the one. She stood out like a beacon.

Tall.

Slender.

Dressed as if she'd just stepped from a Milan catwalk— a long red coat, black boots, chestnut brown hair brushing her shoulders.

Her skin was porcelain.

And perfect.

Lethbridge gulped.

"You must be David!" The woman was standing in front of him, a smile illuminating her face. "I'm Charlotte. So wonderful to meet you." She leaned on the *wonderful* like she was leaning on a car horn.

Lethbridge's palms broke into a sweat. He stared down at the woman's outstretched hand—manicured nails, doll-like skin. He didn't dare touch it—it would be like taking a freshly hatched pigeon by the neck.

The woman cocked her head to the side; she had a quizzical look in her eye. Lethbridge swallowed, wiped his palm on the back of his pants and thrust it into the woman's hand.

"My!" she said. "Aren't you the strong one."

She retrieved her hand and, with effortless poise, spun Lethbridge around and slid her arm into his.

"Let's go inside," she said. "It's nice and warm in there."

Lethbridge stumbled up the front steps arm-in-arm with the most beautiful woman he had ever seen. He could sense people watching her—watching them. The beautiful maiden with the handsome young policeman. He puffed out his chest. Then with his spare hand he reached around and plucked his underpants from between his bottom cheeks.

"You're a police constable, David?" Charlotte said as they wandered among the garden beds inside. "How terribly brave you must be."

Lethbridge's blood pressure shot up ten points. "Oh, I don't know about that," he said. "Just doing my job—working together for a safer London. That type of thing."

"You're too modest," the woman teased, squeezing his arm. Lethbridge's face lit up a bright pink. "Tell me about yourself, David. Tell me something . . . interesting."

Lethbridge glanced at the woman by his side. Her eyes were locked on him, as if the rest of the world had ceased to exist.

"Funny you should ask," he said, "Because I'm working on something quite interesting at the moment."

"Really?" The woman guided Lethbridge through a set of glass doors as if he was a shopping trolley. "Do tell."

"Well, I'm putting the finishing touches to an automatic closing gate for my pigeon coop. You see, when the birds come in after a flight—"

"No!" Charlotte interrupted. "Not about pigeons, David. Tell me about your real work. About stopping the bad people from hurting the innocent people. Like me." She stopped walking and gazed at Lethbridge with an intensity that set his heart racing. Her rich hazel eyes opened wide. Lethbridge was mesmerized.

He gulped again.

"Well, I have been working on the Mason Green case," he said. "Have you heard of it?"

The woman's eyes melted. "Now that sounds interesting," she purred. "Tell me everything." She placed a hand on Lethbridge's chest and eased him onto a garden bench, then slid down beside him.

A fine sweat broke out across Lethbridge's brow.

"I simply adore the atmosphere in here," Charlotte said, her eyes never leaving his. "The cactus garden is very special to me."

Lethbridge looked around. They were sitting by a rocky garden bed that contained an array of spine-covered cacti thriving in the desertlike conditions of the hothouse.

"Tell me, David," the woman said in a dangerous whisper. "Tell me about Sir Mason Green."

Lethbridge swabbed a handkerchief across his face. "Well, we've been looking for him for a while now. Wanted for murder on two continents, he is. He killed a man in India and he ordered the death of an old lady here in London. You know the one—Geraldine Archer."

Charlotte could not have been paying closer attention.

"The billionaire? The one who left all her money to her great-nephew? Now, what was his name . . ."

"Gerald Wilkins," Lethbridge said. "We're, uh, quite good friends, actually."

"Is that so?"

"Oh yes. We went on holiday together. To India. I'm spending a lot of time at his house in Chelsea at the moment."

"As a guest?"

"Um, not exactly," Lethbridge mumbled. "On guard duty. He's under twenty-four-hour protection until Sir Mason Green is arrested."

There was a glint in the woman's eyes. "You see a lot of

this Gerald, do you?" She opened her handbag and pulled out a delicate lace handkerchief. "It is quite warm in here, isn't it, David?" She dabbed the lace across her perfectly dry top lip. Then let it fall to the ground.

"Oh dear. Clumsy me," she said. "Would you be so kind?"

Lethbridge wriggled upright and levered himself off the bench. "Allow me."

He stooped down and plucked the handkerchief from the floor. And the woman rammed a syringe deep into his right buttock.

The constable's lips clamped shut and a muffled yelp seemed to escape through his ears. He remained bent over, snap frozen in place, his face blooming as purple as the cactus flowers behind him.

The woman yanked the needle out and reached down to take her handkerchief from Lethbridge's fingers. She wrapped the syringe in lace and dropped it into her handbag.

"Let's sit you down again, shall we?" Charlotte said. She took Lethbridge by the elbow and heaved him back onto the garden bench. He flopped into place like a sack of potatoes. A look of dazed stupor was plastered across his face.

"Comfy, are we?" the woman asked.

"No," Lethbridge said, his voice a dreamy wave. "My bum hurts."

The woman suppressed a grimace. "David, I have just injected you with a powerful serum. It's derived from the poison in the cactus right behind you. It has the intriguing effect of making anyone under its influence tell the truth."

Lethbridge blinked. He cast his eyes about as if he'd just landed from another planet.

"So you're not from the matchmaking service?" he slurred.

The woman managed a slight grin. "No, David. Sorry to disappoint you."

Lethbridge jerked his head to the front and blinked again. "I'm not going to get a kiss at the end of this?"

"David, I need you to concentrate," the woman said. "Tell me about your friend. About Gerald Wilkins. Does he ever leave the house?"

Lethbridge lolled his head around to face the woman.

"Nope," he said. "Can't go out. Not allowed to."

"Is he planning any trips away? Abroad, perhaps?"

Lethbridge's head started a slow descent toward his navel. His chin banged onto his chest and he jolted upright. "France!" he bellowed, as if spotting land from the crow's nest of a pirate ship.

A few heads turned their way. The woman shushed Lethbridge and placed a calming hand on his arm. "Where, David? Where in France?"

Lethbridge looked at her with uncertainty, as if he was undergoing some great internal struggle. "I don't know," he said.

"I'm sure you must have overheard something." The

woman considered him carefully. "There might be a kiss in it for you."

Lethbridge's purple hue deepened two shades.

When his answer came it was greeted with a smile of glacial warmth.

"You've been very helpful, David," the woman said. "One last thing. Did Gerald bring something back with him from his holiday in India? A little souvenir he keeps hidden away?"

Lethbridge's head bobbed like a drunken sock puppet. His lips quivered open, and his reply set the woman's eyes afire.

Charlotte gathered her things and stood up from the bench. "Good-bye, David," she said.

She turned to leave, but a grunt of protest stopped her departure. Lethbridge stared up at her.

"K-kiss?"

The woman looked at him and sighed. She straightened her coat, grabbed Lethbridge by the lapels, and hauled him to his feet. Then, as if planting a seed in a pot, she pressed her lips to his cheek, leaving behind a smear of crimson lipstick. Lethbridge's eyes beamed out like headlights.

Charlotte then shoved on his chest, sending the constable backside-first deep into the nest of cactus plants.

When Lethbridge woke, he was facedown on a hospital gurney. A nurse armed with a set of pliers was plucking cactus spines from his buttocks. The constable turned his head and gazed up through groggy eyes to find Inspector Parrott frowning back at him.

Lethbridge took in a deep breath, smiled up at his superior officer, and gave him a shaky thumbs-up.

"K-kiss!" he said.

Chapter 1

The photographers leaned against the crowd-control barriers. There were more than a dozen snappers and each one had two cameras: one at the ready and a spare slung over the shoulder. A couple of the shorter ones had brought along stepladders. They all huddled under rain jackets, slickened by showers that had scudded across London all morning, and waited.

People had started gathering outside the Central Criminal Court of the Old Bailey soon after dawn. There were newspaper reporters, television crews, and satellite vans.

But mostly there were teenage girls.

Hundreds upon hundreds of teenage girls.

Some clutched flowers. Others held teddy bears. There were scores of hand-painted placards, the colors streaked by the rain. A team of mounted police stood to one side. The horses snorted, stamping their hooves, alert to the tension in the air. More police lined the opposite side of the barriers, facing the crowd as it multiplied by the minute.

Everyone was on edge. There was some distracted chatter among the girls, but most of them were concentrating on the fifty-foot expanse of cobblestones that stood between the steel barriers and a set of wooden doors on the far side of a courtyard.

The wait was getting too much for some. A woman in her forties clutching a copy of *Oi!* magazine prodded her daughter. The woman pointed to a photograph of a blonde girl aged about thirteen or fourteen—fresh faced and aglow with a summer tan. The shot had clearly been taken without the girl's knowledge—her head was half turned and the image was slightly blurred. The caption underneath read: *Is this the boy billionaire's love match? Pals say Ruby Valentine has hardly left Gerald Wilkins's side since returning from a holiday with him in romantic India.*

The woman frowned at the photograph. "Who's she to be putting on airs and graces?" she said. Her daughter wiped the back of her hand across her nose, shrugged, and mumbled something. The woman glared at her, then back at the magazine. She tensed, unsure if she should voice what she was thinking. Then it burst out. "Why can't that be you?" the woman snapped. "Why can't you be Ruby Valentine?"

The girl stared down at her shoes. A dozen other girls nearby did the same thing.

Then a voice from the top of a stepladder called out. A photographer wearing a red vest had a camera to his eye. "Here they come!"

A murmur of excitement swept the courtyard. Bodies surged. Two of the snappers were jolted from their ladders and they tumbled into the crowd below.

A robust woman entered the courtyard through an arched walkway. Dressed in an ensemble that oozed new-season Paris with shoes entirely unsuitable for cobblestones, she waddled toward the wooden doors. She was halfway there when a spindly heel lodged between two stones and stuck fast. She stopped midstride and tugged on her foot. It wouldn't budge. She hitched her skirt above her knees and bent down to grab at her ankle when a volley of cries burst from the photographers.

"Vi! Vi Wilkins! This way, darlin'! Over here!"

Shutters snapped and whirred. The woman's head shot up, a look of horror on her face. She redoubled her efforts to free the trapped heel—pausing to straighten and wave to the cameras—before finally abandoning her shoes and completing the walk in her stockings.

As she disappeared through the doorway, three people emerged from the cloisters: a man dressed in a business suit, and his son and daughter. The boy and girl, both fair-haired and tanned, were clearly twins. The boy nudged his sister and nodded toward the crowd. She looked up and a gasp of recognition shot out from the onlookers.

"Ruby! Over here, sweetheart!" The snappers wound themselves into a frenzy. "Over HERE!"

The girl buried her head in her father's side and they hurried through the doors. A second later, the crowd got what it had been waiting for. A barrage of camera flashes whitewashed the courtyard as a thirteen-year-old boy stepped onto the cobbles. His untidy hair fell over his ears and he looked uncomfortable in a gray suit and tie. He dragged on the arm of his father, who was lagging behind him. The man stopped to collect his wife's shoes.

"Come on, Dad," Gerald Wilkins said. "Let's get inside."

"GERALD!"

The crowd was hyped to explode.

The posters declaring undying love were consigned to the muck on the footpath, trampled beneath a herd of hormonal teenagers reared on a diet of celebrity and gossip magazines. The photographers, who had held their line by the barriers, were pushed aside. Stepladders toppled and lenses smashed underfoot. Screams of "GERALD!"—and just plain screams—filled the courtyard. For a second the boy glanced up. He gave a half-hearted wave. It was enough to ratchet the hysteria to another level. A police horse reared at the shrill cries that burst from the mob. But the moment the boy crossed the threshold and a police constable stepped out to pull the wooden doors shut, disappointment fell over the crowd.

The show was over.

The photographers, reporters, and hyperventilating teens drifted away until all that remained were two girls. They leaned glum-faced against the metal railings amid a mush of crumpled cardboard and flowers.

One nudged the other.

"Come on," she said. "Let's get something to eat."

The other girl nodded. A tear rolled down her cheek. She didn't bother to wipe it away.

A long wooden table ran down the center of the waiting room. A dozen mismatched chairs were arranged around its sides. The stench of furniture polish hung stagnant in the air.

Gerald claimed a spot near the door. Ruby and her brother, Sam, pulled out a chair each and sat on either side of him. Gerald's mother headed straight to the far end of the room, to a battered urn.

She wrenched off the lid and peered inside. "This water's none too hot," she said with a sniff. "And I don't fancy it's been cleaned anytime recently. I can't see why they wouldn't let Mr. Fry come with us—he'd get a decent cup of tea out of this thing." She dropped the lid back into place and wiped her fingers on a paper napkin.

"You can't have a butler with you all the time, dear." Gerald's father squeezed past his wife and pulled down a packet of Archer-brand teabags from a shelf. "You managed well enough without him for most of your life."

Vi looked down at the chair at the head of the table and let out a sharp *ahem*. Ruby and Sam's father rushed across to pull it out.

"Thank you, Mr. Valentine," she said. "Most gentlemanly of you." She squeezed her bottom into place as if taking up residence in Windsor Castle. Then she raised a stockinged foot onto the tabletop and put her shoes back on. "The point is, Eddie," Vi said to her husband, "we have a butler now, and it seems a shameful waste not to be able to use him. Especially in frightful circumstances such as these."

Eddie ignored his wife and dangled two teabags into a pot. "Cuppa for you?" he asked Mr. Valentine. "Milk? Sugar?"

"I just hope it doesn't take all day," Vi declared, drumming her fingers on the table. "I have several important appointments this afternoon. And there's Walter to consider."

Eddie placed a mug in front of his wife. "I'm sure the hairdresser won't mind if you're late. And as for Walter—"

Vi held up her index finger in warning.

"Don't you dare," she said. "I have had enough of your negative energy. You are having a serious impact on my emotional scaffolding. You know how important Walter is to my blueprint of enhanced health."

Eddie poured tea into another mug. "Pfft," he muttered. "Blueprint of wasted wealth, more like."

At the other end of the table Gerald sucked in a deep breath. His parents had only returned from their holiday the week before and already he was wishing they'd leave for their next one.

Ruby leaned across and whispered, "Who's Walter?"

"Please—don't ask about Walter," Gerald said. He gazed down the length of the room as his mother continued to scold Eddie. "You don't want to know."

Sam reached over, took a ginger-nut biscuit from a plate in front of Gerald, and took a bite. "You've had a fun week, then?" he said.

Gerald cupped his chin in his hands. "You have no idea."

Just then the door to the waiting room opened. A small man dressed in a suit a size too large stepped inside.

"Ah, Mr. Prisk!" Vi boomed, startling the man. "How much longer are we to wait? I don't fancy paying your fees by the hour if it's going to take all day." She turned to Mr. Valentine and gave him a wink. "Lawyers, Mr. Valentine. A pox on them all, I say."

Mr. Prisk fiddled with his cufflinks. "They've just

started," he said. "You'd better come through."

Vi pushed back on her chair and stood up. "About time," she said. "Walter will be anxious if I'm late."

They followed Mr. Prisk along a dimly lit hallway and gathered in a foyer before a large set of double doors. Vi ignored Gerald's protests as she straightened his tie and patted down a tuft of hair.

"Best behavior," she said to him. "Right?"

Gerald made a point of ruffling the back of his head as they went through the doors and into Courtroom Number One of the Old Bailey.

The trial was already underway.

Gerald followed Mr. Prisk's directions and joined the others in the front row of the public gallery. The scene before him was straight from an old courtroom movie. A judge in red robes and a white wig sat at the bench, peering down at the prosecution counsel to one side and the defense counsel to the other. A jury of seven men and five women watched as a barrister in a black gown stood up at the prosecution table.

"The Crown calls the defendant to the stand."

Every eye in the court moved to the dock. A silver-haired man dressed in a navy-blue suit and regimental tie rose to his feet and stepped down from the raised wooden enclosure, then crossed the short distance to the witness box. He turned and fixed a firm gaze on the barrister.

The prosecutor straightened a pile of papers on his desk. "For the record," he said, "please state your full name."

The man in the witness box stared out at the court, as if searching for a friend in a crowd. His eyes passed across the jury, journeyed beyond the table of lawyers, cleared the packed press gallery, and came to rest on the face of Gerald Wilkins. Then the man smiled.

"My name," he said in a voice of clear authority, "is Sir Mason Hercules Green."

CHAPTER 2

Prosecuting counsel Garfield Callaghan, QC, was fast losing his patience. He had spent the previous hour questioning Sir Mason Green about his movements on the night Geraldine Archer was murdered. But he was getting no closer to the answer that he wanted.

"Sir Mason," Mr. Callaghan said with exasperation, "may I remind you of the gravity of the charges before you? Murder. Attempted murder. Conspiracy to murder. These are not trifling matters."

He was interrupted by the sound of a chair scraping across the floor, followed by the clipped tones of the defense counsel. "My lord, my learned colleague is surely aware that Sir Mason is attending these proceedings voluntarily. He surrendered himself to the authorities and is here to clear his name of these baseless accusations. There is not a scrap of evidence to tie him to these crimes other than the overactive imaginations of three juveniles—and there is considerable doubt as to whether their evidence will be admissible. It hardly seems in order that the Crown be badgering my client in this way."

"Thank you, Mr. Elks," the judge said, leaning back to adjust his robes. "You have made that point several times. Perhaps we could allow the prosecution to continue. Proceed, Mr. Callaghan."

Mr. Callaghan glared at Sir Mason.

"I put it to you that you ordered the murder of Miss Geraldine Archer, that you attempted to murder her great-nephew Gerald Wilkins and his friend Sam Valentine, and that you indeed did murder one Sunil Khan, an itinerant vendor of Delhi, India."

Before Sir Mason could open his mouth, his counsel was back on his feet. "My lord, are we now to hear accusations regarding events that may have occurred in other countries? Is the Crown's case that weak? I would argue that the charges before my client be dismissed at once."

"Thank you, Mr. Elks," the judge said. "You have saved me the effort of reminding the prosecuting counsel to restrict himself to the matters that are before this court. The jury is to disregard the matter of Mr. Khan."

Mr. Callaghan closed his eyes. He appeared to be

counting to ten. "Of course," he said. "As ever, Your Lordship is quite right."

"He is also quite hungry. This might be an appropriate time to break. Members of the jury, we shall reconvene after luncheon at, let's say, two thirty."

The twelve jury members followed the usher from the court. Most of them stared at Gerald as they filed out, keen to get a good look at the richest thirteen-year-old on the planet. Sam tapped his friend on the shoulder. "Looks like you're the center of attention," he said. "Again."

Gerald's face burned. He hated it when people paid him any attention. He looked up to find that Sir Mason Green, still seated in the witness box, was staring at him with laser intensity. Their eyes locked. And Green's lip curled in a malignant smile.

"Come along, Gerald." It was Inspector Parrott from the London Metropolitan Police. He moved across to block the view of the man who had become Gerald's waking nightmare. "Let's get something to eat."

Gerald prodded a fork at the reheated lasagna on his plate, failing to make any impression on it.

"You going to finish that?" Sam was eyeing Gerald's barely touched lunch.

Gerald slid the plate across the cafeteria table. "Help yourself." He took a sip on a straw that poked from the can of lemonade by his elbow. "I don't get it," Gerald said. "Why is Green looking so pleased with himself? He's guilty as all get-out."

"Maybe," Ruby said. "But when you think about it, he didn't actually kill your great-aunt. The thin man did that."

"On Green's orders, though," Sam said through a mouthful of mince and cheese.

"The thin man's dead," Ruby said. She flicked a sprig of parsley from her sleeve and sent a look of disgust to her brother. "He's not giving any evidence."

"But Green tried to kill Sam and me in the cavern under Beaconsfield," Gerald said. "We're all witnesses to that."

"The word of a thirteen-year-old against one of England's most respected business leaders? Who do you think the jury is going to believe?"

"Why wouldn't they believe me?" Gerald said.

Ruby let out a weary sigh. "Because, Gerald," she said, "everyone in Britain hates you."

"Hates me?"

"Because of the money. It's like you're the biggest lottery winner in the history of all history. Everyone wants to be as rich as you. It's envy."

Gerald's shoulders slumped. "But what about all those girls outside? They seemed to like me."

Sam took a long sip of his drink. "And the number of times you were mobbed by screaming girls before you inherited all that money was how many?"

Gerald screwed up his face. Life as a junior billionaire was confusing.

"What if the jury says Green's not guilty?" he said. "What happens then?"

Ruby paused for a second to stab a cherry tomato in her salad. "Then Green walks free."

Gerald dropped his head to the tabletop. "No wonder he's smiling."

The courthouse cafeteria was crowded with lunchtime diners. Barristers in robes sat alongside freshly scrubbed defendants in suits smelling distinctly of mothballs.

Mr. Prisk sipped his cup of tea. "I'm afraid, Gerald, Miss Valentine is correct," he said. "The case against Sir Mason Green relies on the evidence of you three children."

"So?" Gerald said, his cheek flat to the table. "We're hardly going to make up a story as weird as this."

"What's not to believe?" Sam said, scooping the last of the lasagna into his mouth. "Three kids accuse one of England's richest men of nicking the most valuable diamond in the world and then ordering his evil henchman to kill an old woman because she won't reveal the location of a mysterious casket that contains an even more mysterious golden rod. And then he tries to kill Gerald and me in a Roman burial chamber that's been hidden in a cavern for a thousand years. And we track him to a lost city in India, where he murders a fortune-teller and escapes with another golden rod that has the power to turn Gerald into a gibbering idiot." Sam took a sip of his drink. "I'd totally believe that."

Gerald slid back into his chair and loosened his tie. The greasy surrounds of the cafeteria were a million miles from the adventures he and his friends had experienced in India. But now he was back in London, his parents had returned from their tour of Gerald's freshly inherited luxury estates, and he was the star witness in what threatened to be a long and torturous court case—sitting in the same room as Sir Mason Green, sharing the same space, feeling those eyes drilling into his forehead.

"He'll try to kill us again," Gerald said. "If he gets off. The way he was looking at me before. There's something not right about him."

"Of course there's something not right about him," Sam said. "He's barking mad."

"It's not that," Gerald said, taking another sip of his drink. "He just seems—I don't know—too relaxed."

"You'll be fine," Ruby said. She placed a hand on Gerald's forearm. He looked down at the fingers spread across his sleeve.

"Uh, thanks," he mumbled, his voice catching in his throat. Ruby gave Gerald a gentle smile.

"At least Green is banged up for now," Sam said.

"That's another thing," Gerald said. "Why would he

give himself up to the police? You saw what he was like with the golden rod in the temple in India. It was like his life's quest had been fulfilled."

"That was a surprise." Inspector Parrott joined them at the table, carrying a ham sandwich on a plate. "He turned up at the British Embassy in Madrid and said he wanted to clear his name. Not the actions of a guilty man, you might think. Still, if he is convicted, we can call off your police guard, Gerald."

"Good," Gerald said. "Not that I don't appreciate it. But breakfast with Constable Lethbridge every morning isn't my idea of the best way to start the day."

"How is the constable, by the way?" Ruby asked. "Is he feeling better?"

Parrott shook his head. "He's as good as he'll ever be, I expect," he said. "How he gets himself into these situations is beyond me. Mugged on a blind date! Extraordinary."

Sam stifled a giggle. "Sounded pretty painful the way he described it."

The inspector winced. "I'd assign him to desk duties but he's not too keen on sitting down at the moment."

A dark-haired waitress in a tunic appeared and started stacking the lunch dishes and soft-drink cans onto a tray. Mr. Prisk consulted his watch and pushed back his chair. "Time to move back in," he said.

There was a logjam of people in the foyer waiting to get

into the public gallery. Gerald noticed three burly police constables standing outside the entrance to the men's room, across to his left. Just then, Sir Mason Green emerged through the washroom door. He was wiping his hands on a paper towel. He handed the crumpled wad to one of the policemen, who took it with mild disbelief. Then Green set off—straight toward Gerald. Caught by surprise, the police pushed their way after him, but not fast enough. In the crush of bodies, Green managed to weave past Inspector Parrott and Mr. Prisk and the court security staff, straight by Sam and Ruby, until he was just inches from Gerald.

"Mr. Wilkins, what a pleasure to see you again." Green towered over Gerald, like an avalanche about to happen.

His voice was cool.

Calm.

And completely menacing.

"We really must have a bite together after this is over. It seems to be going terribly well for me, don't you think?"

Gerald stood frozen to the spot, unable to respond. The man who had tried to kill him was inviting him to lunch?

Gerald sensed that people were struggling to get to them. Mr. Prisk was calling to the police for assistance; his mother was somewhere nearby, shouting.

But it was as if a glass dome had been lowered over Gerald and his tormentor. It was just the two of them. All the world could do was stand back and watch.

The old man gazed down at Gerald, malice in his eyes.

"You don't scare me," Gerald said, as convincingly as he could. "They'll find you guilty."

"Do you think so? I rather fancy I'll be dining at Simpson's-in-the-Strand before the week is out."

Gerald stared at Green in defiance, while trying to stop his knees from wobbling. "Nasty cold you've picked up," Gerald said. "Bit chilly down in the cells, is it?"

Green cleared his throat and coughed lightly into a handkerchief. "Yes, I suppose I am a little rough. The conditions here aren't quite what I'm used to. Perfectly frightful."

Green swatted at something on his neck. "And to top it off, blasted mosquitoes," he said. "Nothing worse than an irksome pest that won't go away." He inspected his fingers, then sprinkled the debris over Gerald's head. "Still"—Green's voice narrowed to a flintlike sharpness—"so much more satisfying when you catch them . . . and kill them."

Two policemen appeared from the crush behind Green. Hands slapped onto his shoulders and he was hauled back through the crowd toward the courtroom door. Sir Mason didn't take his eyes off Gerald the entire way.

"Gerald, are you all right?" Ruby took him by the elbow and spun him around. Gerald sucked in a lungful of air. He hadn't realized that he'd stopped breathing.

Mr. Prisk appeared on his other side. "That is well out of order," he said. "Sir Mason shouldn't be talking to witnesses. What did he say to you, Gerald?"

Gerald tightened his jaw. "It was nothing," he said, a little too loudly. "Can we just go inside?"

By the time they were back in their chairs, Sir Mason Green was once again seated in the witness box. Gerald ignored Ruby's whispered questions and tried to concentrate on what was going on. Green gazed out across the courtroom, straight at Gerald.

The prosecuting counsel resumed his battle. "Sir Mason, let us turn to the theft of the Noor Jehan diamond," Mr. Callaghan said. "You have told the court that you spent the evening in question at the opera. That is correct?"

There was a long silence. Green did not respond.

"Sir Mason?"

Every eye in the court turned to the figure seated in the witness box. Green stared at Gerald, unblinking.

Total silence.

The judge shifted in his chair. "The accused will answer the question."

Nothing.

The clerk of the court stood up from his desk; his chair scraped across the floorboards. He approached the stand and peered up at the man seated there.

"Sir Mason?" he said. "Are you all right?"

After a second, the clerk's face went pale. He turned to the judge.

"I—I think he's dead!"

Chapter 3

Bedlam. The courtroom erupted.

Reporters rushed from the press gallery, sending chairs tumbling as they made a dash for the door, stabbing at their mobile phones as they went. The usher bustled the jury out through a side exit; some jurors were on the verge of tears.

The defense counsel and his team surrounded the witness box, all talking at once. The judge and the crown prosecutor were at the bench, heads together in a hushed conference. Beneath them, all was confusion. A police constable cleared a path for a paramedic carrying resuscitation equipment. Somewhere in the tangle of bodies, the accused was lying on the floor. Court staff tried to clear the public gallery. People were standing. But no one was leaving.

The only person still in his seat was Gerald Wilkins.

Sir Mason Green was dead?

Sir Mason Green—threat, presence, shadow—dead?

Someone was pulling on Gerald's arm, tugging hard on his sleeve.

"Gerald! Did you hear that?"

Ruby's voice penetrated the fog that had smothered his brain. Gerald was suddenly aware of the clamor around him. The judge was on his feet, leaning over the side of the bench.

"Are you sure?" he was saying to the clerk.

The clerk looked back at the judge, ashen-faced. "I think it's his heart." The paramedic emerged from the scrum around the witness box. He was shaking his head.

"You're safe, Gerald!" Ruby was shouting in his ear, barely able to contain herself. Her eyes shone. "He can't get you now!"

Sam appeared at his other arm and pulled him to his feet. He punched him on the shoulder again and again.

Gerald looked at his friends as if he'd never seen them before. Who was this pretty girl holding him so tight, tears rolling down her cheeks? And why was this boy thumping him on the arm? Again and again? Why were they jumping up and down, pulling him into this strange celebration dance? The world had switched to slow motion. All was mayhem—a muffled stage play where the actors were continuing their parts even though the curtain had fallen.

Gerald looked at his mother. At the end of the row, Vi was staring into a pocket mirror and reapplying her lipstick. Satisfied with the result, she dropped her makeup into her handbag and snapped it shut. With it, Gerald's world jolted back to normal.

"Well, that opens up the afternoon," Vi said. "Time for a decent cup of tea."

For Gerald, the days following the death of Sir Mason Green went past in a blur.

Constable Lethbridge and his colleagues returned to normal duties, being no longer required to guard Gerald in his home. The media frenzy subsided as other news events sprouted and blossomed. There was an obituary in the *Times*, naturally. A full page. It went into great detail about Sir Mason's long and respected business career, his generosity, and the many charitable committees on which he served. The only mention the article made of the murder trial was about some "unproved allegations from a nouveau-riche Australian which failed to sully the reputation of a truly great Englishman." Ruby was outraged—"those stupid, pig-ignorant, ill-informed, melon-headed . . ."—but Gerald didn't care what the papers said about him. Sir Mason Green was gone. That was all that mattered.

A flurry of activity overtook life in the Chelsea town

house. Gerald's mother, even busier than usual, was organizing a party. "There's no use having a ballroom if you don't use it," Vi said to Gerald. "Now that your father and I have returned to London, it's the perfect opportunity to make our presence felt." Invitations had gone out. More than two hundred guests were expected. Decorations had been ordered, flowers arranged, menus planned.

In the days leading up to the big night, Gerald's father did his best to keep out of the way, spending most of the time at the cricket ground at Lord's. Gerald was keen to follow his father's example. So when the telephone rang the morning of the party and it was Ruby, he was happy to accept any suggestion that would get him out of the house. Even—

"Shopping?" Gerald said.

"You've got something better to do?" Ruby asked.

Gerald looked at his mother. She and Mr. Fry were going over the dinner plans. A sheaf of menus and seating charts covered the kitchen table. From the expression on Vi's face, she could have been planning the invasion of Europe.

"Where do you want to meet?" Gerald said into the phone. "And can we make it really, really soon?"

Oxford Street was alive with shoppers. The late summer that had warmed London that year was still bringing smiles to the city's inhabitants, and they were making the most of the final days before the first chill winds of autumn blew in.

At the back of a restaurant, on a side street away from the colorful shopfronts and the crowds, Gerald, Sam, and Ruby sat in a booth. A mountain of shopping bags lay at their feet. After hours of shopping and planning, they were exhausted.

The remnants of a meal of burgers, French fries, and milkshakes were spread across the table. Sam belched. "Not up to Mrs. Rutherford's standards," he said, rubbing his belly, "but it filled a hole." He let out a satisfied sigh.

Ruby turned to Gerald. "I think it's a brilliant idea—a week camping in the Lake District sounds perfect. I'll ask our parents, but I'm sure we'll be able to come."

Gerald nudged his foot against the pile of shopping bags under the table. "You better come," he said. "Or I've just bought a ton of camping gear for nothing."

Sam groaned. "I can't believe we have to go back to school so soon. This holiday's flown by."

"Have your parents decided about school for you yet, Gerald?" Ruby asked. "Are you going back to Sydney?"

"They're talking about boarding school," Gerald said. "But until they make up their minds, I'm on holiday."

In fact, life for Gerald without the specter of Sir Mason Green hovering over him was looking pretty good. He'd already placed an order for a customized snowboard and had convinced his mother to fly his friend Ox over from Sydney for a snow holiday the following January. "I'm fairly sure Geraldine kept a chalet in Klosters," Vi had said. "Possibly even two. I'll ask Mr. Prisk—it is so hard to keep up with the details." She had clasped Gerald's face in her hands and given his cheeks an extra tweak. "You are my special little man," she'd cooed. "Walter says we have to take extra-special care of you. He says you're the reinforced slab that I need to build my life upon." Gerald wasn't sure he liked being referred to as a lump of concrete.

Ruby's voice broke Gerald out of his daydream. "Aren't you even a little bit curious, Gerald? About the last casket? About why those golden rods had such an effect on you?"

Gerald stretched his arms wide and yawned. "Not even slightly," he said. "All of that ended the moment Mason Green dropped dead."

"If it was me, I'd give anything to find out," Sam said. "Just think: There are two ancient artifacts out there that have some mystical power over you, Gerald, and maybe a third one just waiting to be discovered. It was funny enough seeing what one of them did to you. I'd pay money to see what all three would do."

Gerald shook his head. "Look, it was a fun adventure and I've got a couple of nice souvenirs back at the house. But that's it. A week ago that ruby we found in India and the drawing of where the ruby casket is probably hidden were the most important things in my life. I really wanted to beat Green to that last casket, to ruin his quest. But now?" Gerald stretched his arms even wider. "Now my biggest worry is what food to pack for our camping trip."

"I guess so," Ruby said. She picked up a french fry and nibbled an end. "It'd be nice to know what that gem unlocks, though."

"I bet that's why Green gave himself up," Sam said. "To get closer to Gerald so he could steal the ruby."

"The way Green's lawyer was going, he would have got off, too," Gerald said.

"Maybe," Sam said. "But when Death comes knocking, nothing's going to turn him away, no matter how much cash you've got piled up against the door."

Ruby and Gerald both stared at Sam.

"Bit profound for you, isn't it?" Ruby said.

Sam shrugged. "Green got what was coming to him. Still, it would be interesting to know what he was looking for."

Gerald dismissed the thought with a wave of his hand. "Whatever it is, it's been buried for a thousand years or more. It can stay that way."

Sam's eyes flickered toward Ruby, then he gave another shrug. "So who's coming to this party tonight?" he asked.

"At last count it was a couple of hundred people," Gerald said. "But Mum's phoning around to try to boost the numbers. She wants it to be an 'event.' And you'll finally get to meet Walter."

"Who is this Walter?" Ruby asked.

Gerald closed his eyes and took in a deep breath. "Mum's life coach," he said. "She brought him back from America. They met at some party at Martha's Vineyard. He's supposed to help her achieve her full potential, or something."

"How does he do that?" Sam said.

"He's putting her through some course that's meant to make her vibrant and fresh and happy."

"She's sitting on a fortune worth twenty billion pounds," Sam said. "What's not to be happy about?"

"Ah, but it's not her money," Ruby said. "All the money was left to Gerald—his parents are just looking after it till he turns eighteen."

"That's another five years," Sam said. "That's forever. Plenty of time for her to play at being a gazillionaire."

"Sam!" Ruby frowned at her brother. "Don't be so rude."

"That's okay," said Gerald. "One thing I've learned from Walter is that sometimes you've got to take what comes. You can't control everything that happens to you."

"Really?" Ruby said. "So nothing is certain?"

Gerald cringed. Ever since his last day of school back in Sydney, the phrase "Nothing is certain" had been popping up all over the place.

"Very funny," Gerald said, as Ruby and Sam burst out

laughing. "All I'm saying is if the fates have it in for you, there's not much you can do to change things."

"Rubbish," Ruby said.

Gerald looked at her, surprised. "You don't think so?"

"Think has nothing to do with it," Ruby said. "I know so. And I'll show you." Ruby stood and took Gerald's hand. She dragged him over to a round table in the middle of the restaurant.

"What's this supposed to prove?" Gerald asked.

"Just shut up and follow me, okay?" Ruby tugged on his hand and led him twice around the table, then back to the booth. She plopped down next to Sam with a look of accomplishment on her face.

"So?" Gerald said. "What's a guided tour of the restaurant meant to show me?"

Ruby leaned forward and said in a low voice, "Your life is now forever changed."

Gerald started laughing. "What are you talking about? How can two laps of a table change my life?"

"Chaos," Ruby said.

"Chaos?"

"It's chaos theory. If we hadn't walked around that table we might have left this restaurant by now. For the rest of your life you are going to be a minute behind where you would have been. Every interaction you have with the world from now on—the things you see, the people you meet—will be different because of that little walk. And all the people you meet: Their lives will be different too, even if only just the tiniest bit. The same goes for the people they meet, and so on—like ripples spreading on a pond."

Gerald wasn't convinced. "So life is just one coincidence after another? There's no grand plan?"

"I'm the coincidence queen, Gerald," Ruby said with a wink. "You can trust me."

Sam picked at his teeth. "Well, it's no coincidence that this conversation is boring. We get to meet Walter tonight. Terrific. Anything actually exciting going to happen, Gerald?"

A shadow passed over Gerald's face. "Two things," he said. "And I can't bear thinking about them."

CHAPTER 4

Vi was still fussing over seating plans for the party when Gerald walked through the front door, weighed down with shopping bags.

"I'm not sure the archbishop should be sitting next to Lady Carstairs," Vi said to Eddie. "Not if the gossip magazines are to be believed."

"Why don't you move the bishop?" Eddie said. "Stick him next to Walter." Then, under his breath, he mumbled, "That ought to shut him up for a bit."

Vi bristled and straightened in her chair. "I will not have you white-anting Walter." She grabbed up her handbag from under the table and pulled out a key ring. She jangled five golden keys in Eddie's face. "See this? I am only three away from graduating from the Drawing Room of Indifference to the Library of Absolute Insight on the fourth floor," she said. "The fourth floor, Eddie! No one in Walter's course has ever got that far. He says I'm gifted."

Eddie snorted. "A gift, more like."

"What was that?" Vi skewered her husband with a rapier stare. "You know what's in the Library of Absolute Insight, don't you?"

Eddie emitted a weary sigh. "The Chalice of Inner Stability?"

"Exactly," Vi said. "The Chalice of Inner Stability. Walter says it is essential for my core structural strength. And from there it's a mere eleven stories until I reach the Attic of Ultimate Fulfillment." Vi's face flushed at the thought of it. "I'm the best student he's ever had."

"For what he's getting paid," Eddie said, "you're the only student he'll ever need."

Gerald knew when to make himself scarce. He reached the elevator just as his mother exploded.

From the tall window in his bedroom, Gerald gazed out at the line of chimney pots that ran the length of the rooftops opposite. He had a sweeping view of the rear lane and the chain of luxury terraced houses across from his own. Not a roof slate was out of place. Window boxes were carefully tended, blooms of red and yellow dotting the upper levels. Two houses down, a man in a dark suit and parade-gloss shoes swept leaves from a driveway out into the cobbled lane. Gerald watched as the man bent down to run a thumb across the toe of his right shoe, wiping away some smudge or speck of dirt. The man inspected the spotless driveway and retreated behind automatic gates as they swung closed, sealing off the outside world.

Imagine being trapped in a life like that, Gerald thought. What a drudge. Then he looked down to discover Mr. Fry, broom in hand, ejecting a pile of leaves from his driveway. The butler surveyed the result and, with a nod of satisfaction at a job well done, wandered back toward the kitchen door. He paused by the Rolls-Royce parked in the drive. Pulling a handkerchief from his pocket, he dusted it across the silver bonnet ornament, then disappeared into the house.

Gerald shook his head. Just imagine . . .

He sat on the edge of his mattress and drummed his fingers on the bedside table. He had promised himself that he would stop thinking about it; stop wondering about its meaning. He knew he had to keep it out of his mind. But . . .

One more time won't hurt, he told himself, and he opened the top drawer. From under a pile of socks he pulled out a red suede jewelry roll, secured around the middle by a leather lace.

He unrolled the pouch to reveal a ruby the size of an egg. Gerald picked up the gem in his fingertips and held it up to the window. A pink sheen washed across his face as he gazed into the ruby's heart.

"What secrets are you keeping?" he whispered. The stone seemed to vibrate like a deftly struck tuning fork. He twisted the gem this way and that, letting the sunlight play across its facets. "What are you trying to tell me?"

Gerald tossed the stone onto the bed and opened a flap on the jewelry roll. He slid his fingers inside and pulled out a folded square of paper. He was about to flatten it out when there was a knock on the door.

"Just a minute!" he called out. He shoved the gem under his pillow, sweeping the leather pouch and paper in after it. "Okay, you can come in."

The door opened and Gerald turned to find a white-haired woman dressed in a gray servant's tunic, standing in the doorway.

"Pardon the intrusion, Master Gerald, your guests have arrived." The woman stepped aside and Sam and Ruby bowled into the room.

"Thanks, Mrs. Rutherford," Ruby said as she plopped down into an armchair by the window. "Looks like quite the party you're preparing for downstairs."

The housekeeper jutted out her chin and drew the corners of her mouth down. "It is none of my doing, Miss Ruby," she said. "It seems Mrs. Wilkins thought preparing food and drink for two hundred and fifty guests was beyond my limited abilities. She has engaged the services of"—Mrs. Rutherford paused as if she had just swallowed a rancid oyster—"a caterer."

"But your cooking is fantastic," Sam said. "I thought we'd be having something spectacular."

"Oh, it will be spectacular," Mrs. Rutherford said. "If you consider rubber chicken and packaged sauce spectacular. But Mrs. Wilkins is the lady of the house and I am but a lowly cook . . . apparently."

"So what are you doing tonight if the caterer is running the kitchen?" Ruby asked.

"I believe Mr. Fry keeps a stock of very reasonable sherry in the butler's pantry for such occasions," she said.

Gerald looked at Sam and then at Mrs. Rutherford. They looked like they were about to attend a funeral.

"I don't feel like rubber chicken tonight," Gerald said. He cocked an eyebrow at Ruby.

"Oh, no," she said, cottoning on. "That sounds dreadful. If only there was some way we could have something else. Something delicious." She cast a meaningful glance at the housekeeper.

Sam's eyes lit up and he blurted out, "Make us some dinner, Mrs. Rutherford? Please?"

Ruby threw her hands in the air. "Sam! Honestly. You're as subtle as a shark attack."

A smile creased Mrs. Rutherford's face. "Master Sam,

you are my biggest fan. I'm sure I can throw a little something together for you." With an extra bounce in her step, the housekeeper excused herself and set off for the kitchen.

Gerald closed the heavy oak door and pushed the bolt home.

"Have a look at this," he said, and crossed to his bed. He took out the gemstone and the piece of paper.

Ruby sat on the mattress and flattened the page across the bedspread. It revealed an intricate sketch of a medieval castle atop soaring cliffs with waves pounding at their rocky base.

"I remember you drawing this," she said to Gerald. "In Alisha's house in Delhi."

Gerald brushed his fingertips across the surface of the page, as if reading it in Braille.

"I'm not likely to forget it," he said.

"I wonder what Alisha and Kali are up to," Sam said. "All that seems ages ago now."

"Alisha is due back in England the week after next for the start of school," Gerald said. "Miss Turner is escorting her. And the last I heard, Kali and her mum were going to join Mr. Hoskins at his bookshop in Glastonbury."

Ruby emitted a short *hrumph*. "Both Alisha and Kali are coming to England? Won't that be nice for you."

Gerald looked at Ruby through half-closed eyes. "What's that supposed to mean?"

"It means whatever you want it to mean," Ruby said. She stood and marched back to the armchair under the window and sat down. Gerald stared after her, clueless. He looked to Sam for help, but his friend just shrugged. "I gave up trying to understand years ago," he said. "So this castle is in France someplace?"

Gerald nodded. "That's what Miss Turner said. Somewhere off the coast of Normandy."

Sam took the ruby from Gerald's hand, then wedged it into his eye socket like a monocle. He bent low over the page. "Hey! This makes everything look pink."

Ruby watched her brother as he made hoots of delight. "To think we're twins," she muttered.

Gerald clamped his lips together to smother a laugh. He slid his hand between the sketch and Sam's face and plucked the gem from Sam's eye socket. The moment it fell into Gerald's palm, the ruby flared up like a lantern.

Sam's head bucked back. "Holy cow!" he said. "Look at that!"

Gerald stared at the stone—it seemed as if a fire had been lit deep in its heart. He lifted it closer to his face.

"The light's fading," Ruby said, crossing back to the bed. "Move it over the sketch again." She took Gerald's wrist and pulled his hand down until it was just above the castle. The gem flared; a surge of energy pulsed from its core. Fingers of red light stabbed across the paper, coloring the waves and the sheer rock walls.

"Let me have a go," Sam said. He grabbed the gem from Gerald's hand. The light vanished instantly. Sam let out another hoot of surprise. He dropped the stone back into Gerald's palm.

The ruby flared as bright as ever.

The three friends looked at each other.

"Gerald," Ruby said. "Do you get the feeling the third casket wants to be found? And found by you?"

Gerald's mouth had gone very dry. He swallowed. "We don't need to find it," he said. "My family and the Fraternity in India spent two thousand years trying to keep secret whatever this is all about. If it wasn't for Mason Green those two golden rods would still be buried and forgotten. Why not just leave things as they are?"

Ruby leaned forward and cupped her hand over Gerald's palm. The gem inside glowed out between their fingers like a Chinese lantern. Ruby tilted her head and peered at Gerald through upturned eyes.

"You must be curious," she said. "To find out what the big secret is. Surely you want to know." Gerald felt Ruby's fingers tighten on his own.

There was a stirring in the pit of his stomach.

"I'm hungry," he said. He broke away from Ruby's touch and rolled the gem into its leather pouch before shoving it into the back of his sock drawer. He folded up the paper and dropped it into his backpack on the floor by the bed. "Let's see what Mrs. Rutherford has cooked up."

The elevator doors opened onto a blazing row in the kitchen. Mrs. Rutherford was on one side of the room, arms crossed and scowling. Opposite her was a slender woman dressed in black shirt and trousers, her hair pulled tightly back into a ferocious bun. Between them was the kitchen table, piled high with trays of canapés.

"You can't possibly serve this . . . this . . . rabbit food to the guests," Mrs. Rutherford said, with more force than Gerald had ever heard her use before.

The woman in black shot her a dark glare. "And what would you suggest? Sausage rolls and jellied eels?"

Mrs. Rutherford's cheeks flamed red. Her nostrils flared and she turned to the penguin that had appeared in the kitchen doorway. "Mrs. Wilkins, I do not think your guests will appreciate being fed puffballs of alfalfa sprouts and raw broccoli. It is not hospitable."

The woman in black snorted. "Perhaps you'd feel more at home if we deep-fried everything in a vat of lard."

Vi held up her hands for silence, but with no effect. Gerald thought his mother might have exerted a bit more authority if she wasn't dressed as an enormous penguin. She flapped her wings in agitation.

"What's with the costume?" Ruby whispered to Gerald.

"Costume party," Gerald said. "I'm going as a mortally embarrassed teenager."

Gerald, Ruby, and Sam stared wide-eyed at Vi as she

waddled around the kitchen, trying to bring calm.

"Mrs. Rutherford!" Vi called. "Miss Rousseau! This will be the party of the year. I will not have it ruined by squabbles over the hors d'oeuvres. The people attending this event are here to be seen with me. They're not here for the food."

Mrs. Rutherford sniffed. "You've picked the right caterer, then."

Miss Rousseau's lips tightened. "Why, you vexatious old—"

Vi flapped her wings as another shouting match broke out. Just as Gerald thought he might have to restrain the housekeeper, a man stepped into the kitchen.

His very presence brought the screaming to silence.

He wore the full dress uniform of an officer in Napoleon's cavalry: navy trousers with a broad white stripe down the legs; a dark blue jacket, unbuttoned at the neck, with golden epaulets on his broad shoulders; and a red sash taut across his barrel chest. His hand rested on the grip of a golden saber slung on his belt. The man surveyed the kitchen as if it were a battlefield. A wry smile appeared on his face.

"Walter!" Vi's face lit up. "Thank goodness you're here. We're in the middle of a crisis."

"A crisis?" The man's voice was richer than Mississippi mud. "Surely not, ma'am."

Walter surged forward like an icebreaker. He flung

an arm around Mrs. Rutherford's shoulders. "How could anything get in the way of this evening's festivities? With the two finest cooks in London, how could it possibly fail? Now, am I right in assuming that you two fine ladies are having some disagreement over the menu?"

Mrs. Rutherford struggled out of Walter's embrace and straightened her tunic. "Mr. Walter," she said, her jaw clenched, "why don't you try what's on offer and tell us what you think." She held out a tray of green-topped canapés. Each piece was an artful creation but, from where Gerald was standing, none of them resembled anything he'd want to eat.

Walter cocked an eyebrow and looked over the selection. "I'm sure it's all . . . mighty fine," he said.

Miss Rousseau snatched the tray from Mrs. Rutherford. "I'll take that," she sniffed. "Please, try one of the *yeux de mouton*—they're *très magnifiques*."

Walter recoiled slightly, then picked up a pasty case filled with a glistening white ball. He sniffed it. "Interesting, um, aroma," he said.

"You have a good nose, sir," Miss Rousseau said. Walter popped the morsel in his mouth. "So many people use tinned ingredients these days."

"Oh really," Walter said, chewing away.

"I prefer fresh. Especially the sheep's eyes."

"Sheep's eyes!" Walter gagged and spat into his hand.

Gerald couldn't help noticing the look of pleasure on Mrs. Rutherford's face.

Walter rushed to the sink and poured himself a glass of water. "Very interesting, uh, texture, Miss Rousseau," he said between gulps. "Very modern, I'm sure."

"So it's settled," Mrs. Rutherford said. "I will be directing affairs in the kitchen tonight." She pulled an apron from a cupboard and tied it behind her back.

"Oh," said Gerald's mother, her face shining red inside her costume.

"Impossible!" Miss Rousseau declared.

"Now wait, wait," Walter said, trying to restore calm. "Let's just—" Then he saw Gerald.

"Gerry!" Walter called out, crossing the kitchen, clearly relieved to be diverted from the tension behind him.

"Gerry?" Ruby whispered.

"And these must be your buddies I've heard so much about," Walter said, switching on the southern charm. "The valiant Sam and the redoubtable Ruby, eh? Pleased to be making your acquaintance, I'm sure." Walter thrust a hand toward Sam. Sam offered up his own and it was swallowed in a double-fisted pump action that threatened to dislocate his shoulder.

"Uh, yeah," Sam said, wringing some blood back into his fingers. "Nice to meet you, too."

"I hear you are brave and resourceful, Sam. A friend to

51

be favored and a foe to be feared. Am I right?"

Sam's cheeks reddened. "Oh, I don't know about—"

"Nonsense! Don't sell yourself short. False modesty is the white ant of the soul. I see in you a tremendous builder of palaces in the sky, Sam. Brave at heart—that's what *Sam* means. Did you know that?"

"No, well, I—"

"And you, Ruby. The celebrity magazines weren't telling lies. You truly are a beauty for the ages. The new 'it girl,' they're saying. And one with a killer crush on our Gerry as well."

Ruby gagged as if someone had shoved a fresh sheep's eye down her throat. "I really don't think that's—"

"And I know you offer so much more than just fashionable good looks. A house with a fancy coat of paint on the outside is nothing if it's got termites in its timbers."

"I'm sorry, but are you calling me—"

"My friends!" Walter cut her off, ushering them into a group. He clamped a hand on Sam's shoulder on one side and Gerald's on the other. His voice dropped low. "My friends, you must all be brave. Brave of heart and brave of purpose. You will need to be for the challenge that lies ahead."

"Challenge?" Gerald said. "What challenge?"

Walter guided them back into the elevator. "The challenge of spending tonight at the children's table." He pushed the button for the third floor. The doors slid closed; his beaming face disappeared through the narrowing gap. "You have fun now."

The elevator shunted upward.

Ruby turned to Gerald. "What's he mean, 'the children's table'?"

Gerald blushed. "Oh, didn't I mention that?" he mumbled. Then, keen to change the subject, "What did you think of Walter?"

Sam held up his right hand. "I need to wash this as quickly as possible."

Gerald's smile lasted until the elevator juddered to a stop and the doors opened. "Come on," he said. "We may as well get this over."

He ignored Ruby's and Sam's questions until they got to a large set of double doors at the end of a corridor. He faced Ruby. "I want to apologize ahead of time and assure you this was not my idea."

"What are you talking about?" Ruby said. "Apologize for what?"

Gerald didn't answer. He turned the handles and pushed. The doors opened into an opulently decorated room set out for an evening of parlor games. Against the far wall, under a bank of tall windows, was a buffet covered with trays of food and drink. In the middle of the room stood a boy and a girl. The boy's round head balanced on his stout shoulders—there was no evidence of a neck.

The girl's red hair was pulled back into stringy pigtails. She glared at Ruby.

"What's the princess doing here?" the girl said.

Ruby's eyes shot wide.

Gerald cleared his throat with a nervous cough. "Uh, Sam and Ruby, you remember my cousins, Octavia and Zebedee?"

It was going to be a long night.

Chapter 5

Gerald held his breath. And waited.

Ruby scanned Octavia's face. She was taking in
every detail: the creases across the forehead, the narrowed
eyes, the cluster of flyspeck freckles on the nose, the sharply
upturned top lip.

The silence seemed to suck all the air from the room.
Ruby tilted her head. Then she plunged at Octavia and
flung her arms around her neck.

"Octavia!" Ruby cried, squeezing a sharp *oomph* from
the girl. "How are you? It's been too long. I haven't seen you
since . . . oh, when was it?"

Octavia struggled to free herself from Ruby's grip.
"Since you locked me and Zeb behind the fireplace at
Beaconsfield," she said, with venom in her voice.

"Really?" Ruby said. She skipped over to a table piled

high with board games and made as if she was inspecting them with rapt interest. "Has it been that long?"

Octavia squared her shoulders, her eyes ablaze. "You snot-faced little—"

Gerald coughed loudly and rushed across to put an arm around Ruby and steer her to the buffet at the far side of the room. "Sam, why don't you and Zebedee see if there are any games worth playing in that pile," Gerald said. "I need a quick chat with Ruby."

Ruby allowed herself to be dragged over to the sideboard, but her eyes never left Octavia's scowling face.

"Is there something the matter, Gerald?" Ruby asked, all innocence.

"Don't be a pain," he said. "You know what Octavia's like. She doesn't need any urging from you to turn this into a nightmare."

"All I said was it had been a while since we'd seen each other." Ruby fluttered her eyelashes at him. "Is that such a bad thing?"

Gerald gave her an are-you-for-real? look.

"What?" Ruby said. "Can't I have a bit of fun?"

Gerald looked over to where Sam was sorting through the games. Octavia and Zebedee were muttering to each other in the corner.

"I don't think tonight is about having fun," Gerald said.

"Why are they even here?" Ruby asked. "I thought your

mother and your uncle Sid were fighting."

Gerald picked up a plate of wilted alfalfa sprouts and dried-up carrot sticks from the buffet and looked at it with distaste. "Walter told Mum she needed to repair some broken fences. It's all part of the life course he's putting her through. A twelve-step personal property appraisal, or something."

"It looks like Walter has his hooks into your mum good and proper."

"I know. I'm hoping it's just a phase she's going through. Parents can be so frustrating."

Sam wandered over, a look of bemusement on his face. "It looks like we've got a choice of playing parlor games with the chuckle twins over there," he said, "or we could skip the kids' party and check out what's going on downstairs."

"Parlor games?" Ruby said. "Who plays parlor games anymore?"

The doors to the room suddenly opened. In the entrance was a tiny woman wrapped in a shawl so tight it gave the appearance of being the only thing holding her bones together. Her skin was the color of a used teabag and was stretched so thin on her frame it looked like she would split open in a high wind. On either side of her stood two of the palest children Gerald had ever seen.

"Uh, hello?" Gerald said.

The woman fixed him with a rifle stare.

"You are Gerald?" she said. It was more accusation than question.

"Uh, yes," Gerald said.

The woman prodded the pale boy between the shoulder blades, pushing him into the room. "This one is Wendell." She repeated the shove on the girl. "This one is Caroline."

The pair stood knock-kneed on the rug.

Octavia glared at Wendell. "What are you doing here?" Then, in an appalled tone, "You're not friends with the princess, are you?"

Gerald latched his hand onto Ruby's arm, holding her back. "Easy, tiger," he said.

"We live next door," the boy said in a barely audible peep. "Our parents are at the party downstairs."

Octavia crossed her arms and ran an appraising eye over the newcomers. "And what did you come dressed as? A glass of water and a wisp of smoke?"

The pair stared saucer-eyed at Octavia, not sure what to say.

"Never mind her," Gerald said, rescuing them. "She has a condition."

"What sort of condition?" Caroline asked, making sure to keep well clear of Octavia as Gerald ushered them toward the buffet.

"She gets cranky if she hasn't feasted on human blood," Ruby said.

The doors shut with a solid thud. The woman made her

way to an armchair and settled herself.

"You will play Snakes and Ladders now," she said. She extended a bony finger in the direction of the games table.

Octavia screwed up her nose. "I hardly think people of our age are going to play Snakes and—"

"NOW!"

The noise that erupted from the woman's throat rattled the windows.

Gerald led a slow march toward the table. "Excuse me," he said to the woman. "Who are you?"

The woman pulled a packet of cigarettes from a beaded case. She pushed a cigarette into the end of a black holder, which she then clamped between her teeth. She lit the end, snapping the lighter shut with a practiced flick of her wrist. The cigarette tip glowed and crackled as the woman drew in a seemingly endless breath. Finally, she expelled two jets of smoke from her nostrils.

"Do you mind?" Octavia coughed.

The look on the woman's face clearly showed that she did not. She ashed the cigarette into a bowl of peanuts on a side table.

"Your task is to play games," the woman rasped. "Shut up and do it."

The seven of them pulled up chairs around a card table. Gerald was taking the lid from an ancient box of Snakes and Ladders when the woman spoke again. "I'm a cousin of your father's," she said to Gerald. "A distant cousin. I abhor parties."

"What's wrong with parties?" Ruby said.

The woman picked a speck from the tip of her tongue and regarded it with interest. "They are a pointless exercise," she said. "Nothing of use can be learned at parties. All that chattering and all those lies. People like you should be seeking life's truths, not wrapping themselves in pretense and falsehoods."

Gerald raised an eyebrow. This woman was related to him? "What's your name?" he asked.

"Clea," the woman said. "Don't use it unless there's an emergency."

She stubbed out the cigarette and fitted another into the holder. Clearing her throat with a moist hack, she lit up again.

"What's the matter with you pair?" she said to Octavia and Zebedee, who couldn't take their eyes off her. "Not having fun yet?"

The next two hours dragged by in a smoky haze of brain-deflating boredom. Wendell and Caroline barely spoke, apart from occasional whispers between themselves; though they did brighten when Clea ordered everyone to play anagrams.

"Here's a good one," Caroline said. "*Semolina* is an anagram for *is no meal.*"

Wendell was the only one who laughed.

Octavia was staring at Ruby with snake eyes. "The

magazines say you two are in love. So, has there been any kissy-kissy?"

Zebedee started making smooching noises on the back of his hand. Octavia cackled with delight.

Gerald looked at Ruby, expecting her to erupt. To his surprise, she sat with a serene smile on her face.

"I don't read those sorts of magazines," she said. "Gerald and I are just good friends. Aren't we, Gerald?" She placed her hand on the back of Gerald's and squeezed.

"Uh, that's right," Gerald said. "You can't believe what you read in those things."

Ruby dropped Gerald's hand and latched onto Octavia's. "They tell the most wicked lies," she said, fixing Octavia with an intense stare. "It's sickening. I mean, you don't believe that story about us planning to kill Mason Green if he walked free from court, do you?"

"Er," Octavia said, looking nervously at Ruby's hand as it tightened on her own.

"I didn't read anything like—" Gerald began, but stopped when Ruby switched her glare to him. Then he realized. It was a wind-up. "Uh, that's right," Gerald said, trying not to smile. "It was a big conspiracy. I'd already hired a hit man from Bulgaria to do the job. Big money. Very hush-hush. You won't tell anyone, will you?"

Octavia looked first at Gerald, then at Ruby. "You two are nuts," she said, snatching her hand back.

From her smoke-cloaked chair, Clea hacked, "Play!"

Zebedee stared at the card in his hand, a look of total confusion on his face. "I don't get it," he said. "What are you supposed to do?"

Octavia clicked her tongue and took the card from her brother. "It's anagrams. You rearrange the letters in this word to come up with the answer to the clue. Even you can do that."

Ruby piped up. "Sure, it's very straightforward. For example, the anagram for *Octavia Archer* is *I've a crater face.*"

Sam snorted, stifling a giggle.

Octavia thought for a second. "No it isn't," she said. "There's no *f* in my name."

"Really?" Ruby said. "When Gerald saw you earlier I'm sure he said there's *f* in Octavia."

Gerald's chair bounced across the rug as he hauled Ruby by the arm over to the far side of the room. Octavia was on her feet, fists pounding the tabletop, screaming abuse at them. Her face was purple. Clea, for her part, sat back in the armchair with a look of quiet satisfaction on her face. She turned a page in a book she held and blew a smoke ring into the air.

"What are you doing?" Gerald hissed at Ruby, trying to ignore the screeches coming from Octavia.

Ruby had a glint of mischief in her eye. "Serves her right for calling me a princess," she said.

Gerald looked back at his fuming cousin. Sam was doing his best to settle her.

"Look, I'm not enjoying this any more than you," Gerald said to Ruby. "But I can't see any way out. Clea's not going to let—"

A soft *ding* cut him off. They both looked at the wood-paneled wall by the sideboard. There was a small red light next to a discreet silver button set into the mahogany. Gerald gave Ruby a quizzical look. He stretched out a finger and pressed the button. A section of the paneling about waist high slid up to reveal a cozy space behind.

"A dumbwaiter!" Ruby said.

Gerald peered into the darkened box, which was about three feet on each side. "What's it for?"

"It's like an elevator, to bring food up from the kitchen." Ruby reached inside and took out a folded card that had been propped on the floor.

"'There's proper food in the kitchen,'" she read. "Mrs. Rutherford has come to our rescue."

Gerald looked back to the card table. Octavia had her back to them, in a deep sulk. Zebedee had made a hat from the game box, and Wendell and Caroline soldiered on with the anagrams.

"Oh, that's an easy one," Wendell said. "*Astronomer* is a *moon starer*."

Clea remained in her chair with her head in her book,

smoking like a blocked chimney.

Gerald caught Sam's eye and beckoned him over. He slipped across unobserved.

"Want to get some real food?" Gerald said to him.

Sam beamed. "Mrs. Rutherford food?"

Gerald slid backside first into the dumbwaiter, tucking his knees under his chin. Ruby and Sam squeezed in after him. Gerald took an elbow to the eye and a head to the ribs in the crush. "Push a button, will you?" he said. "Any button."

Ruby was closest to the front and she pressed at the keypad. The door slid back into place, casting them into darkness. The tiny elevator moved down with a lurch.

"We should have done this hours ago." Sam's voice came out of the tangle of limbs. "I wonder what's to eat?"

The dumbwaiter came to a halt. Nothing happened.

"Now what?" Gerald said.

Ruby pushed another button. The door slid up, and they stared out at a riot in progress.

"I don't think this is the kitchen," Ruby said.

The dumbwaiter had stopped in the ballroom.

Gerald had always considered adults incapable of enjoying themselves. Always griping about unmade beds and the washing up. They seemed programmed for misery. Which was why it was taking him so long to process the scene before him.

The ballroom was going off.

It was costume madness. There were streamers and

lights of every color and hue. A band played in the corner, the brass section struggling to make itself heard above the roar of the well-fueled crowd. There was braying and screaming, shouts and hilarity. Clea would not approve.

There were pirates dancing with harem girls; an astronaut was jiving on a table with a nun; a bishop was screaming "Louie Louie" into the microphone on the bandstand. Gangsters, vampires, a bandage-wrapped mummy, kings and queens—all prancing and prowling in a melee of color and sound.

And in the middle of it all stood a stout penguin, one wing holding a glass of champagne and the other whooping tight circles above her head. The man dressed as a French cavalry officer by her side was dancing as close as he could, the golden braid on his jacket catching the light from the giant mirror ball suspended from the ceiling.

"Is that Inspector Parrott over there?" Ruby asked as she climbed out of the dumbwaiter onto the ballroom floor. Gerald and Sam followed.

"What? In the zombie getup?" Sam said.

"And I think that's Constable Lethbridge."

"Where?"

"The giant pigeon."

Gerald shook his head. "Mum invited him as a thanks for all that guard duty, but I didn't think he'd show up. At least not dressed as a pigeon."

Then Sam and Ruby screamed—a high-pitched stereo

shriek that pierced Gerald's brain. A large man in a kilt, his face painted a vibrant blue and his red beard flared out like he'd been electrocuted, had leaped in front of them, his features contorted in rage. "Death to all Sassenachs!"

It took a few seconds for the ringing in Gerald's ears to fade.

"Professor McElderry," he said to the blue-faced Highlander. "I didn't know you were coming."

The professor gave Gerald a wink and raised a full glass. "Never miss a good knees-up," he said. "You never know when it might be your last. Still"—he took a long draught—"wish they'd told me it was a costume party."

"Oh," said Sam, "Didn't you know?"

McElderry blinked at Sam, as if he wasn't sure what he was seeing. "Have I ever mentioned that you might well be the stupidest boy in the world?"

Gerald smiled. "Well, it looks like you're having fun," he shouted to McElderry above the booming racket of the ballroom. "Who's that dressed as a bishop and singing with the band?"

The professor glanced over his shoulder. On the other side of the room, a tall man dressed in white robes with a golden miter askew on his head was belting out the chorus to "River Deep, Mountain High."

"That is the bishop," McElderry said. "He really didn't know it was dress-up. Not a bad voice. All those years in the choir, I expect. Look, I'm glad I caught up with you. I've had a call from my friend at the Vatican library in Rome—you remember him."

Gerald nodded. The professor's friend had made the connection between Gerald's family seal and an ancient Roman emperor.

"He's been doing some more reading into your very interesting family, Gerald," the professor said. An explosion sounded over McElderry's right shoulder. Gerald caught sight of a penguin lopping off the top of a champagne bottle with a French cavalry sword.

Gerald let out a long breath. "It gets more interesting, does it?"

"Oh yes," Professor McElderry said. "And on both sides as well. Did you know that your mother's ancestors believed the family would one day produce someone special?"

"Special?"

"Yep. The progeny. Can you believe—"

The professor's words were drowned out by a shriek of "Gerald!" A pink-faced penguin was advancing on them.

"Gotta go, Professor! But let's talk later, okay?" Gerald said.

Gerald rolled back into the dumbwaiter. Sam and Ruby followed him. Sam fumbled with the button panel.

The professor reached into a pocket and said, "I've got something for—" But the door slid shut, cutting him off.

The dumbwaiter moved down, and the blare of the party faded behind them.

"Your mum seems to be having a good time," Ruby said to Gerald.

"Yeah. She specializes in that."

"I didn't see your dad," Sam said. "What's he dressed as?"

Gerald stared at the wall. "I can't remember."

"You can't remember?"

"That's right," Gerald said. "I cannot remember."

The door slid open and the three of them tumbled out of the dumbwaiter onto the kitchen floor.

Mrs. Rutherford looked up from the table. "You took your time," she said. "I've been battling to keep Mr. Fry away from this lot." She whipped a tea towel off a platter of steaming sausage rolls, pies, and pasties.

"Go on," she said to Sam. "Don't hold back. There's no bad manners in a working kitchen."

Sam didn't hesitate. He snatched up a sausage roll and bit into the pastry, sending a shower of flakes down the front of his shirt.

"Mmmph," he mumbled. "Del-ish-us."

Mrs. Rutherford piled a small basket with a selection of pastries and handed it to Ruby.

"Here," she said. "A little picnic for you. Fancy thinking people would want to eat parsley and sheep's bits."

Gerald thanked Mrs. Rutherford and tried not to laugh at the sight of Mr. Fry laying a clean white handkerchief across his lap before nibbling on a piecrust.

"Come on," Gerald said to Sam and Ruby, "let's take this back to my room."

The elevator stopped on the fourth floor and they were halfway up the hallway toward Gerald's bedroom when they saw her. The woman was dressed in a black catsuit, complete with triangular ears on her head and a mask covering her eyes. She was at the end of the corridor, one slender leg out the window and about to step onto the neighbor's roof.

Gerald couldn't understand it. What was a party guest doing climbing out a window?

But then his eyes caught a flash of red in the woman's hand. A corner of leather poked from her clenched fist. The jewelry roll from his bedroom. The ruby!

"What are you doing?" It was all Gerald could think to say.

The woman glanced down at the leather pouch in her hand and shoved it inside a pocket.

"I thought you might be otherwise detained, Gerald," she said in rounded tones. "This changes things a tad."

Gerald balked. How did she know his name? And what did she mean "otherwise detained"? Then he saw a glint of silver in her hand. Something shiny. Something sharp.

Without warning, the woman flung out her fist. In the blur of movement, Gerald sensed something coming at him, fast. He dived to the wall, crunching hard into the flocked velvet wallpaper. A dart shot past his ear, missing him by centimeters. Gerald slid to the floor and took a second to recover from the impact. "She's got the ruby," he called out.

Sam lunged for the woman, but she was already out the window. Gerald joined Sam at the sill and caught a glimpse of the woman, slinking around a chimney pot and away into the night.

"She moves like a cat, too," Sam said.

Gerald rubbed his shoulder where it had hit the wall. "She must have come in with the other guests," he said.

Ruby's voice came from back in the hallway. "You two need to see this." She was standing by a potted palm tree. As they watched, the deep green of the trunk turned a mottled gray, then it sagged to the floor. Ruby pointed to its base, out of which stuck a silver fountain pen.

"Somehow, I don't think that was dipped in ink," she said.

Sam went to pluck out the pen but his sister pulled his hand away. "Wasn't Inspector Parrott downstairs? I think we need to get him. Now."

Gerald stared at the tree—it looked like it had been gassed. "Wait on," he said. "I want to check something." He raced down the hall to his bedroom and came out a second later, carrying his beaten backpack.

"The drawing of the castle is still here," he said. "The ruby is the only thing missing."

"How would anyone know you had it?" Ruby said.

"Beats me. But she somehow knew where to look. Let's go get the inspector."

Gerald jabbed at the lift button, glared at the still-closed doors, then made for the stairs. They rounded the landing to the third floor, and were about to launch down the final dozen stairs to the second floor when Gerald skidded to a stop. Sam and Ruby piled into the back of him.

Gerald gazed down, surprised to see his mother in her penguin outfit standing outside the closed doors to the ballroom. Walter was close by and they were talking with two uniformed police officers. For a second, Gerald thought they were party guests. But by the look on his mother's face, he knew something was wrong.

Vi caught sight of the movement on the stairs and turned her head. "Oh, Gerald," she said, her distress showing through her penguin makeup.

"Mum?" Gerald said. "What is it?"

Vi put out a hand and leaned on Walter for support. "The police," she began. "They want to talk to you."

"What about?" Gerald's gut tensed.

The taller of the police officers took a step forward. His expression was as hard as granite.

"It's more than just a chat," he said.

Vi sniffed back a tear. "Oh, Gerald," she sobbed. "They are going to charge you with the murder of Sir Mason Green!"

CHAPTER 6

Vi hung up the phone in the main drawing room and poured herself another glass from the dark green bottle.

"Mr. Prisk is on his way," she said. "Gerald, you are to say nothing until he arrives."

Gerald sat with Sam and Ruby on a long leather couch, growing more frustrated by the second. The thump of the party sounded through the floor from the ballroom below.

"This is ridiculous," Gerald said. He turned to the policeman who was standing by the windows. "I keep telling you. You should be looking for the woman who stole the ruby. And how am I supposed to have killed Green anyway? He died of a heart attack in front of a hundred people. You were there, Inspector Parrott. You saw it. Tell him."

"I must say I'm surprised by this," Parrott said, looking

as serious as he could while dressed as a blood-splattered zombie. "Gerald has always"—Parrott checked himself— "has mostly been very cooperative with the police in this matter. Constable Lethbridge and I have full faith in him." Lethbridge, still dressed as a pigeon, went to say something but his voice caught in his throat, and he only managed to make a soft cooing noise. Parrott glared at him, then turned back to the police officer. "Exactly what evidence do you have, Inspector Jarvis?" Parrott asked.

The tall policeman clenched his jaw. His voice sounded like he gargled gravel every morning before breakfast. "I have received certain information and I am confident Constable Nelson will turn up specific evidence in her search of the young man's bedroom. We are well advanced in our investigation." He cast a dubious eye over Parrott and Lethbridge. "If we need the services of a six-foot-tall budgerigar, I'll give you a call."

"Pigeon," Lethbridge said.

"What?" Jarvis's mustache bristled like a privet hedge full of rabbits.

"I'm a pigeon. Not a budgerigar."

Parrott hissed, "That will do, Constable."

Lethbridge flapped his wings and mumbled to himself. "Never a budgerigar . . ."

Gerald stood up. "And while we're wasting time here, the thief is getting away with the key to the ruby casket."

The door to the drawing room opened and a young policewoman entered. She was carrying an evidence bag. Gerald could see that it contained a small plastic tube. "It was right where you said it would be," Constable Nelson said to Inspector Jarvis.

Jarvis's eyes flickered. He took the bag and held it up to Gerald. "Do you recognize this?" he asked.

"No."

"It was found in your bedroom closet. I have reason to believe it is part of a blowgun used by you in the assassination of Sir Mason Green."

"That's outrageous!" Vi was furious. "How can you possibly—"

"We have forensic evidence that Sir Mason died from a drug-induced heart attack," Jarvis said. "A drug that was administered by a tiny dart to the neck. From the anonymous information I have received, I am confident that DNA testing of this blowgun will reveal that the person who fired that dart, the killer, is none other than you, young man."

Every eye in the room turned to Gerald.

"But that's impossible," Gerald said. A fine sweat broke out on his forehead. "Like I'd try to kill him."

"Really?"

The voice made Gerald cringe.

Octavia.

Gerald's cousins had appeared in the doorway.

"That's not what you and the princess told me," Octavia said. "That was quite a story—about hiring a professional killer to take out the old man."

Gerald couldn't believe what he was hearing. "That was just a joke," he said. "Surely you didn't believe—"

A large hand clamped onto Gerald's shoulder.

"Gerry," Walter said, beaming down at him. "The first step in emotional renovation is to admit that your personal blueprint is flawed. There's no use denying your structural shortcomings if all the evidence points to wood rot in your soul."

"Walter," Vi said. "Surely you don't think Gerald is capable of murder?"

The cavalry officer turned to face the penguin. "All I'm saying is it's important that a person capable of murder does not influence your own renovation, my dear."

"Bleeding nonsense!" Eddie was on his feet and advancing on Walter. He exerted all the influence that might be expected from a man dressed as a prima ballerina. His pink tutu brushed against Walter's leg. "I've had enough of you and your new-age gibberish."

Inspector Jarvis fixed Gerald with a tight stare. "Time to come with us, son."

Vi choked back a gasp. "Not my little soldier," she sobbed.

Walter patted her arm. "It's for the best, Vi," he murmured. "A greenfield start for your reconstruction."

Eddie stepped up and grabbed Walter by the collar, swinging him around. "That's enough!" the ballerina shouted, and threw a wild punch. It missed by a foot.

Gerald saw Constable Nelson move across the room toward him. This was the only chance he was going to get.

He dived in close to Ruby and Sam. "The kitchen," he whispered. "In two minutes."

Then he grabbed his backpack and bolted for the door.

Constable Nelson tried to reach Gerald but instead ran into the melee of off-target fisticuffs that was going on between Walter and Eddie. Gerald was halfway to the door, vaulting an armchair to avoid Inspector Jarvis. He wrong-footed Octavia and only had Zebedee to beat. His cousin squared up and blocked the doorway. Gerald didn't miss a step. At full speed he planted his right hand on top of Zebedee's head and shoved hard. Gerald's feet shot up the doorframe and he whirled clear over his cousin's head and into the passage outside.

He knew he would have to be quick. He tugged the straps of his backpack to notch it tight and bolted for the stairs. Shouts of "Stop!" followed him down the stairwell.

The party in the ballroom was still booming. Gerald dived into the middle of it. He dodged between dancing pirates and milkmaids, vampires and executioners, and made straight for the dumbwaiter on the far side of the room. Halfway across the dance floor he charged into a blue-faced Scottish warrior.

"Professor!" Gerald shouted above the din. "Something's come up. I have to go."

"Go, Gerald?" the professor shouted back. "Where to?"

"Away. Look, if I ring you, promise me you'll answer? No matter what you hear about me?"

McElderry's eyes darted up and focused on the two police officers who had just barged into the ballroom. Gerald followed his gaze with alarm.

McElderry planted a hand on Gerald's shoulder and pushed him lower. The bustling dancers closed in around them.

"I wanted to give you this," the professor said. He pulled his hand from his pocket and opened it. In his palm rested a band of gold.

"It's the signet ring with your family seal on it I found in the burial chamber under Beaconsfield," McElderry said. "The one belonging to Gaius Antonius." He pushed it onto Gerald's finger. "I thought you should have it." He gave Gerald a clap on the shoulder.

"Whatever mischief you're up to, young Gerald, I'm sure your great-aunt would approve." The professor gave him a wink, then stood up and plowed across the dance floor. "Who's that trying to get out the window?" McElderry bellowed, waving his glass at the police and pointing in the direction farthest from Gerald.

The ballroom was still heaving with partygoers, the band still raising a riot. Gerald grinned and ducked his way through the dancing throng toward the dumbwaiter. The door slid open and he clambered inside. He reached out to press the button when a hand shot in and grabbed him by the wrist.

"Dad!" Gerald cried.

Eddie Wilkins stared at his son through watery eyes. "Gerald," he began. "I need to tell you something."

Gerald saw the police almost at the windows where the professor had sent them. They'd soon realize they were in the wrong place.

"Dad," Gerald said. "This isn't the time."

Eddie looked into his son's eyes. "I know I haven't been around much lately, what with all the travel. And then there's your mother, of course."

"Don't worry about it, Dad," Gerald said, pulling back on his arm. "It doesn't matter."

"But it does matter, son." Eddie's face tightened. "It matters a lot."

Gerald tugged again on his arm but his father held on tight. "Dad, please let—"

Gerald stopped. A French cavalry officer had emerged from the crowd to appear over his father's shoulder.

"You've snared the little termite," Walter said, slapping a broad hand on Eddie's back. "Well done."

Eddie dropped Gerald's wrist and spun around to face Walter. Their noses were centimeters apart.

"Don't call my son a termite."

Gerald watched as his father drew back his shoulders and chest-bumped Walter. The impact caught Walter off guard, sending him back an unsteady step. Walter's hand fell to his sword. For a second, Gerald thought he was about to draw the weapon.

But with a bellyful of champagne and only watercress and eyeballs for dinner, Walter was still off balance. The sword was half out of its scabbard when Walter took another step backward, into the path of a waiter carrying a tray of glasses and an ice bucket with a bottle of champagne in it. Walter hit the floor and the tray tumbled on top of him.

Gerald couldn't see clearly from his spot in the dumbwaiter, but he guessed that the hollow clonk he heard was the bottle connecting with Walter's head.

Gerald looked at his father with a new appreciation. Eddie straightened his tutu and turned back to his son. "Gerald," he said. "Whatever happens, do the right thing. Know yourself and do what's right. Follow what's in here." He grabbed Gerald's hand and punched it above his heart.

Octavia's voice cut through the mayhem. "There he is! Over there!"

Gerald looked across to the ballroom doors to see his cousin, face set in a scowl, pointing right at him.

He lunged out and gave the burly ballerina a hug. "Look after Mum," he said to his father. Then Gerald rolled back inside as the dumbwaiter door slid shut.

Gerald lay cocooned in the tiny elevator as it descended, the sound of his heart thumping in his ears like a bass drum. When the door opened he rolled out onto the kitchen floor. Sam and Ruby were by the table. They held the backpacks from their shopping trip that day. Mrs. Rutherford was tucking a parcel into Sam's pack.

"Some food for the road," she said in a businesslike fashion. "Miss Ruby has told me all I need to hear. So hop to it. Mr. Fry is waiting in the Rolls."

Gerald threw his arms around the housekeeper's neck and squeezed. She closed her eyes and squeezed back. "Your great-aunt said you would be tested one day. It looks like that day has come."

"Thanks, Mrs. Rutherford," Gerald said. "For everything."

Tears welled in Mrs. Rutherford's eyes. She dabbed them away with a corner of her apron. The sound of boots approaching clattered down from the hall above.

"You best be going. I'll hold them off as long as I can."

Gerald gave her one more hug, then followed Sam and Ruby out the kitchen door and down the stairs to the back drive. Mr. Fry was in the driver's seat of the Rolls, engine running.

"Where to, sir?" Fry asked as they piled into the backseat.

It was the first time Fry had sounded remotely sincere since Gerald had met him.

"Are you ready for a helicopter flight?" he asked the butler.

The car sent up a spray of white pebbles as it turned out of the drive.

"Where are you going, Gerald?" Sam asked.

"France," Gerald said. "Want to come?"

Chapter 7

They skimmed past the last lights on the edge of the coast and headed across the English Channel; the only sound was the dull *fwup* of helicopter blades slicing through the night air.

Gerald's head rested on the kid leather of his seat in the Sikorsky S-76 chopper as they beat a path toward the French coast. A thousand thoughts battled for dominance, but Gerald knew one thing for certain: Someone was trying to frame him for the murder of Sir Mason Green. He screwed up his eyes. Just when he thought his worries were over.

"So who is she?" Ruby's voice cut through his brooding. "The woman in the catsuit. She knew exactly where to look for the ruby."

"I don't know. But I bet she planted that blowgun in my room."

Sam undid his seatbelt and slid onto the floor between Ruby and Gerald. "Whoever she is, she must be searching for the third casket," he said. "Those golden rods must be worth a fortune—it's not like Gerald would be the only one wanting Mason Green dead."

"Thanks a lot," Gerald said. "Now you're making it sound like I did kill him."

"That Inspector Jarvis sure wasn't listening," Ruby said. "He's convinced you did it."

Gerald stared out the window into the gloom. A bank of clouds lay dark and bruised ahead.

"Where are we going?" Sam asked.

Gerald pulled the drawing of the castle out of his backpack and unfolded it on his lap.

"Do you remember that map on Mason Green's desk in the Rattigan Club? The one that showed the paths taken by each of the three brothers when they smuggled the caskets out of Rome?"

"Yep," Sam said. "The diamond casket went to Glastonbury, the emerald one to India, and the ruby one was somewhere on the coast of France."

"Thank you, geography boy," Ruby said. "So we're actually going to look for the ruby casket?"

"Exactly," Gerald said. "I think the woman who stole

the ruby killed Green, and now she's trying to frame me for it."

"So the best way to find her is to find the casket?" Sam said.

"What? We fly along the coast of France till we spot this castle?" Ruby said. "Seems a bit random, doesn't it?"

"Actually, Mr. Fry says he knows where it is," Gerald said. "It's Mont Saint-Michel. Miss Turner told him."

"Miss Turner?" Sam said. "How is Mr. Fry's squeeze going?"

"He gets phone calls from Delhi every day," Gerald said. "I think they're meeting up when Miss Turner brings Alisha out for the start of school."

Sam laughed. "Old Fry has a girlfriend! That's too funny."

Ruby sat back in her seat with a thump. "Well, it's nice that some people get a happy ending," she said. She turned and stared out the window.

Gerald and Sam looked at each other. "What's the matter with her?" Gerald said.

Sam shrugged. "Girls," he said, as if that explained everything that was unknowable in the world.

The intercom crackled through from the cockpit. Mr. Fry's voice was tense. "I think you ought to hear this," he said. There was a click and then the gravel voice of Inspector Jarvis filled the cabin.

" . . . I say again, all airports across the UK have been

placed on alert. There is nowhere you can go where I will not find you. You must surrender now or face the direst of consequences. I have sought permission to use force and will not hesitate to use that authority."

No one spoke while the words sank in.

"Have you responded?" Gerald asked.

"No," Fry replied. "They seem to think we're still in the country and I see no need to let the rotten beggars know where we are."

"Mr. Fry!" Ruby said. "Are you feeling rebellious?"

There was a pause, then, "An accusation against the young master is an accusation against the house of Archer. He may be undeserving, ill-disciplined, and irritating in the extreme, but I don't believe he is a murderer."

Gerald let out a hollow laugh. "Tell us what you really think, St. John," he said.

"Can't they see us on the radar?" Ruby said.

"I am flying too low, Miss Valentine. They have no idea where we are."

"Nice work, ace," Gerald said. "How long till we're there?"

There was a frosty silence for a second before Mr. Fry replied: "We will be approaching Mont Saint-Michel in twenty minutes. Would young sir like me to land or tip him out from a reasonable height?"

The Archer corporate helicopter skimmed close to the waters of the channel, skirted the Cherbourg Peninsula, and traced a path beyond the islands of Guernsey and Jersey. Sam was the first to catch sight of their destination. About a mile off the coast, at the end of a narrow causeway that jutted into a sweeping bay, the island of Mont Saint-Michel was lit like a fairy-tale castle.

Waves crashed against the broken rocks along the shoreline, infusing the air with a fine mist. Floodlights captured the spray, making the island glow against the dark waters of the bay.

"It's just like your sketch," Sam said to Gerald. "Amazing."

Three noses pressed against the glass as the helicopter swept closer. Sitting on top of the huge granite rock that soared out of the bay was a medieval castle, its stone turrets and battlements winding up the monolith until they peaked in a colossal spire that pierced the night sky. The edifice looked as if it was carved from a single block of gray stone, as ancient as creation.

"That is the most amazing thing I've ever seen," Ruby said. She wiped a clear patch in the window where her breath had fogged it up. "It's like we're stepping back in time."

Mr. Fry guided the helicopter in a broad sweep around the top of the castle. They gazed down on a corkscrew of narrow laneways that wound their way up from the city gates to the top of the mount. The place appeared to be deserted.

"I'll have to put down on the mainland," Mr. Fry's

voice sounded through the intercom. "Too windy to risk the causeway."

Minutes later, Gerald, Sam, and Ruby were standing on French soil, at the start of a narrow ribbon of elevated roadway that stretched into the bay—the only way onto the island. Ruby wrapped her arms across her chest, bracing herself against the chill of the sea breeze.

"I'll secure the chopper," Mr. Fry said. "I understand there's a hotel on the island. I suggest you go ahead and book some rooms there. I'll follow shortly."

Gerald pulled his backpack onto his shoulders as Mr. Fry started the process of tying down the chopper's rotor blades. "You should go back to London," Gerald said. "Right away. Tell them I ordered you to fly around in circles to put the police off our track while we took a train to Scotland, or something."

Mr. Fry paused in his efforts. He looked at the Archer corporate logo on the side of the helicopter—an archer at full draw set against a blazing sun. "Young sir," he said. "Your great-aunt may have thought me worth little more than a set of teaspoons, or so it would seem from her will, but in your hour of need, the name of Fry—St. John Fry—will not be doubted. I shall stay the course."

Fry stood tall, his broad-chested physique silhouetted against the lights of the island. Waves slapped against the side of the causeway and the wind whipped across the marshland behind them.

"Wow," said Sam. "Way to go, St. John."

The waves sent plumes of spray across the roadway as Gerald, Sam, and Ruby made their way to the island. Water reached high on either side as they neared the castle gates. Gerald shifted his pack on his shoulders and stared up at the sheer stone walls that loomed over them.

"I thought Beaconsfield looked creepy at night," he said. "But this is something else."

They ascended a ramp toward the fortified entryway, past a huge French flag snapping in the wind. Gerald suddenly realized they were in France and a jolt of excitement shot through him. They were on the hunt again. And despite everything—the accusation of murder, the escape from London—he found himself alive with the prospect of fresh adventure.

He glanced at his watch. "Almost midnight," he said. "There'd better be a room at this hotel."

They passed through the city gates—two enormous wooden portals that looked like they'd stood sentinel over the castle for centuries—and under a portcullis, its rusted spikes pointing to the ground. A cobbled laneway wound ahead of them. It was so narrow people leaning from the high windows on either side of the street could have shaken each other by the hand. A line of street lamps, like orbs of yellow mist suspended in the air, lit the way. Finally, they

saw a shingle hanging above a doorway: *Hôtel de St. Michel.*
Light filtered out through glass panels in the door.

Gerald pushed his way inside. A bell above the door
tinkled.

A dark wooden counter filled the tiny reception area.
From behind it, a man stirred. He peered at Gerald over the
top of his newspaper with an eye wary of late night arrivals.

"Oui?"

"Uh, *bonjour, monsieur,*" Ruby said.

"Bonsoir, mademoiselle," the man replied. His eyes darted
from Ruby to Gerald to Sam.

"Oh yeah," Ruby stammered. "Evening. Um, *avez-vous
une chambre pour la nuit?*"

"You want a room?" the man said. "Just the three of you?"

"We've got a, um, guardian," Gerald said. "He's just
coming."

"He had to lock up the helicopter," Sam said.

The man's eyebrows shot up. "Helicopter?" he said.
"You came here in a helicopter?"

Ruby flashed Sam a furious look. "No, of course not.
How would we ever get a helicopter?" she said.

The man rubbed a hand down his chin. "I thought I
heard something. Just before."

"No, no—just my brother's idea of a joke," Ruby said.
She leaned over the top of the counter and whispered to the
man, *"Mon frère est un imbécile."*

The man studied Sam through his glasses, then gave a nod. "Evidently," he said.

"Hey!" Sam said. "I understood that."

The man ran his finger down a ledger on the desk in front of him. "I have a room available," he said. "But it is not cheap."

Gerald pulled out his black American Express card. "That's not a problem," he said.

The man eyed the card narrowly. "From young runaways arriving late at night in helicopters, I accept cash only."

Gerald returned the stare, then peeled off a handful of fifty-euro notes. "I hope this will cover breakfast too," he said.

The man thumbed through the wad of cash, his eyes lighting up. "For this, *monsieur*, I will lay the eggs myself."

Sam looked like he was about to vomit.

The man gave them a large brass key and Gerald led the way up the narrow staircase to the fifth floor. By the time he jiggled the key into the lock and stumbled into the tiny room, he didn't know which was feeling heavier: his legs or his eyelids.

"What about Mr. Fry?" Ruby yawned, plopping down on the bed by the window. "Should we have got him a room as well?"

"He's big enough to look after himself," Sam said. He flopped onto another bed.

"Do you think that guy downstairs suspected anything?"

Gerald said. He collapsed onto a couch and kicked off his boots.

"The way he was eyeing off your cash, the last thing he's going to do is report you to the police," Ruby said. "By breakfast, he'll be your best friend."

Gerald bit into his croissant and had the uncomfortable feeling that Ruby's prediction from the night before was coming true. The old man from the hotel reception had topped up Gerald's hot chocolate twice already and was hovering, ready to oblige, at the merest hint that Gerald needed something.

"I wish he'd go away," Gerald said to Sam over the table in the crowded dining room. "He's creeping me out."

"He's probably hoping for an enormous tip."

"Yeah? Well, here's a tip: Don't overcharge for broom cupboards and call them hotel rooms. And which one of you was snoring? Sounded like someone attacking a tin roof with a chainsaw."

"That'd be Ruby," Sam said. "She'd wake the dead."

Ruby snapped shut a guidebook that she'd picked up from reception on the way through to breakfast. "You may get a chance to test that theory if you don't be quiet. Now, if you two have finished, maybe we should concentrate on finding the casket and getting the police off Gerald's back. Okay?"

Gerald and Sam mumbled agreement.

"According to this book, the castle is actually an abbey,

an ancient church. It was built over a thousand years ago. The battlements have kept invaders out for centuries."

"So the casket could be hidden anywhere inside the town or the abbey?" Sam said. "Terrific. Shouldn't take us more than a zillion years to find it."

"Don't be a clot," Ruby said. "Gerald, what was the name of the third son? The one who smuggled the ruby casket out of Rome?"

"It was Lucius Antonius, wasn't it? Quintus was the father. Gaius took the diamond casket to England, and Marcus took the emerald one to India."

"And when was that?"

"About 400 AD, Professor McElderry reckoned."

"What's that got to do with anything?" Sam said.

"Well, if this abbey and all its spires and walls only started construction around 1000 AD, what was here when Lucius popped by on his little holiday six hundred years earlier?"

Sam blinked at his sister. "A bare rock?"

"Top of the class, Poindexter. I bet Lucius hid the casket in a cave, and then this lot was built on top of it."

"So how do we find it under a jillion tons of stonework?" Sam asked.

Ruby pointed to the backpack at Gerald's feet and snapped her fingers.

"What did your last slave die from?" Gerald said as he

kicked the pack across to Ruby.

"Insolence," Ruby said. She pulled out Gerald's sketch.

"This shows the island from the bay side," she said. "See? The road back to the mainland is behind it."

Sam chewed on a bread roll. "So? Gerald drew that when he was in one of his bizarre trances. It could mean anything. Or nothing."

"Maybe," Ruby said. "But Gerald's trances always seem to point somewhere useful. I say we head out to the other side of the island and look at this exact view."

"How do we get out there?" Gerald said. "We'd need a boat?"

"You can walk." The words sliced through their conversation like a razor. "Some more hot chocolate, *monsieur*?" The man from the reception hovered at Gerald's elbow, a milk-stained pot in his hand.

"Um, thanks," Gerald said. "That'd be great."

Steam fingers curled up the flow of chocolate as it poured into Gerald's mug.

"The tide is out so you can walk into the bay," the man said, refilling Sam and Ruby's mugs in turn. "But take care. When the tide turns, it comes in at the speed of a galloping horse. And there is quicksand." His voice dropped. "It clutches at your legs like the devil himself has reached up to steal your soul and leave your bones to the gulls. People have been caught. And drowned."

Ruby smirked. "Quite the tourist trap, then," she whispered to Gerald.

"I don't get it," said Sam. "Last night there were waves crashing against the walls. You couldn't walk anywhere. We saw them from the chopper."

He let out a sharp yelp and grabbed at his shin.

Ruby forced a laugh. "My brother and his jokes."

"*Très drôle*," the man said, without a flicker of a smile. "*Monsieur* will find that the tides here are about the largest in the world. At low tide you can walk halfway across the bay, if you are game." He checked the clock on the wall. "You have two or three hours before the water comes in again."

The man drifted back to the kitchen.

Sam shot his sister a filthy glare. "What'd you kick me for?"

"You don't think three kids turning up after midnight is suspicious enough that you have to go on about the helicopter as well?" Ruby said.

"Speaking of which, I wonder where Mr. Fry is," Gerald said.

"Sleeping in, if he's got any sense," Sam said, rubbing his shin. "We better get moving if we're going to beat that tide."

As they walked out through the reception, the old man bobbed up from behind the counter. "Will you be staying another night?" he asked, one hand resting on the till, a look of hopeful greed on his face. "I can have the room serviced straightaway."

Gerald glanced at the others. "I'm not sure," he said.

"Your friend. Your . . ." the man paused, "your guardian. He asked me to tell you he had to check on the car. He'll be back later."

"Car?" Sam said. "We don't have a—" Sam caught sight of his sister's coiled right leg just in time to check himself.

"He is not friendly, your guardian," the man said. "Not one for conversation."

"No, I guess not," Gerald said.

"And the breakfast? It was to your liking?"

"It was okay."

The man's eyes darted down to his hand by the till, then back to Gerald.

"It was good? Yes?"

The telephone rang. Gerald put his hands in his pockets—and left them there. "We might see you later," Gerald said to the man, and opened the door to the narrow laneway.

Ruby was the last one onto the street. As the door swung closed, she caught a glimpse of the man speaking on the phone. He had a sour look on his face.

"Maybe you should have tipped him," Ruby said.

The first of the day's tourists were making their way up

to the abbey. A monk in a flowing blue habit gave Gerald, Ruby, and Sam a cheery *bonjour* as he walked by.

"For some hot chocolate and a stale lump of bread?" Gerald said.

"My French is pretty rusty—but when he answered that phone call, I think I heard him say something like: *récompense*."

"So?"

"I think it means reward."

Gerald looked through the glass of the hotel door. The old man was still on the phone, staring right back at him.

Bare feet squelched into wet sand, sounding like a triple-headed sludge pump across the bay. Gerald sank almost to his knees and strained to extract his foot from the boggy silt to take another step.

"This stuff's like my mum's pea soup," he said.

"It really grabs hold of you," Ruby said.

Three trails of foot holes, like mortar strikes in the tidal flats, snaked back to the island. Gerald, Sam, and Ruby, their boots hanging by knotted laces around their necks, were finding it hard going as they trudged further into the drained swamp that was the Bay of Mont Saint-Michel at low tide.

Gerald stopped to take a bottle of water from his backpack. He sank a little deeper. "We're hundreds of meters out. This must be getting close," he said. He took a drink and passed the bottle to Sam.

Ruby held the sketch up. The position of the spire, the steep stone walls, the curve of the bay, the pitched roofs of the abbey and the fortified town below—it was like she was staring at a photograph taken from right where they were standing.

"Well, Gerald, it's your party," she said. "Do you recognize anything? Feel anything?"

Gerald took the sketch in both hands and concentrated. He studied the illustration, then the real thing. There was an uncanny accuracy, even down to the swooping gulls.

"Nothing," he said. "Not a clue. Maybe if I had the ruby."

Sam peered over his shoulder. "The only real difference is that in your drawing the tide's in. Those waves are tossing up a fair bit of spray."

"Maybe we need to try again at high tide," Gerald said. "Find a boat and come back." He went to take a step but his legs were held tight in the boggy sand—he overbalanced and toppled onto his hands, sinking into silt up to his wrists.

"You might not have to wait that long," Ruby said. "I think the tide is already coming in." She clamped her hands behind her right knee and tugged. The rising water spilled into the gaps around her legs and filled the holes with a sandy soup.

"Uh-oh," Gerald said.

They stared out at the center of the bay. Where just minutes before there had been a broad expanse of silt and sand baking in the late morning sun, there was now a smooth sheen of water, reflecting the sky like an enormous mirror.

"I'm stuck!" Ruby said. She heaved on her legs, grabbing at one knee and then the other. "I can't move."

Sam took a step toward his sister, straining to get his feet above the marshy silt.

"Don't struggle," he said. "It'll just suck you in harder. Here, grab my hand."

Ruby reached out and clasped her brother by the wrist.

"When did you become a quicksand expert?" she said.

"Um . . . watching Tarzan movies," Sam said.

"Terrific."

Gerald lifted himself upright and was shocked to find the water was up to his calves. "The guy at the hotel wasn't kidding," he said. "This is rising fast."

He drove his knees to one side, then the other, trying to break the suction that gripped his legs. He threw himself down again. This time the water was almost up to his elbows. Muttering a string of curses, he strained forward and finally slid out from the sand to lie facedown in the water. He rolled over and edged closer to Ruby, grabbing her other hand.

"Try to lie down," he said. "Then slide your legs out."

Gulls twisted and looped above them, their guttural cries sounding across the bay. The panic welled in Gerald's stomach. Sam was now lying in the water too, and he yanked his sister backward until she sat down with a splash. "Hurry up," he said. "This is no time to be a princess."

Gerald and Sam tugged on her arms and finally Ruby's legs slipped out. She was a sodden, sandy mess.

Gerald glanced back to Mont Saint-Michel—about a quarter mile away. "We're going to have to run," he said.

They set off with a flurry of spray and silt. Gerald had seen the lifesavers running through the shallows at Bondi Beach countless times, lifting their feet above the waves to escape the drag of the water. He knew he couldn't stop or the sand would grip him again. It was sprint or sink.

They covered the final hundred yards to the cliff as if all the hounds of hell were on their heels. Gerald collapsed onto a flat rock and sucked in huge breaths. Sam and Ruby fell on either side of him. They were wet, covered in sand, and exhausted. But they were safe.

Gerald raised himself onto his elbows and gazed back at the bay. It was full of water. From sandpit to swimming pool in a matter of minutes.

They were sitting at the end of a low promontory that jutted out a short distance from the cliff face behind them. The sandy shoreline that wrapped around that side of the island had disappeared under the rising tide. Waves pushed up on either side of the rock shelf, breaking onto the base of the cliffs.

They were getting cut off.

"We need to get higher up," Gerald said. "I don't fancy getting washed back out there again." They laced on their boots and set out for higher ground.

Thick vegetation to the left and right forced them to scramble straight toward the cliff. Far above, the walls of the town stood over them.

"What do you reckon that mark on the rocks is?" Sam said, pointing to a stain that ran along the escarpment ahead of them. "High water?"

Gerald looked up at the horizontal line above them. If that was where the tide was going to stop, they were in big trouble unless they got there first. His mind shot back to his sketch with the waves crashing against the base of the cliff. He glanced over his shoulder—rows of breakers were rolling across the bay.

The first one struck seconds later. A curl of water flattened them to the rock shelf and drenched them through.

"We're going to get smashed!" Ruby cried over the roar of the waves. "We've got to get higher."

But the cliff face ahead of them was sheer—there was no way up.

Another wave crashed on top of them. Sam slipped and fell hard. Ruby grabbed him by the wrist to stop him being pulled back into the bay.

Gerald pointed to a tangle of vines growing up one side of the cliff. He was almost too exhausted to speak. "Over there," he said. "There might be a way up."

He stumbled to his left and tried to make his way onto the thick matting of greenery, inching higher and higher. He reached back and hauled Ruby up next to him. Sam was only a few feet behind.

Like sailors in the rigging, the three of them started scaling the net of vines, desperate to escape the pounding surf.

But before they could get clear, a wave rose from the bay, far bigger than any that had come before. It crested over them, blocking the sun.

Then it crashed down, swallowing them whole.

Chapter 8

All was a blur. Gerald blinked to clear his vision, but he could make no sense of what he saw. Light beams shone through a dull grayness that seemed to surround him. He ran a hand over his eyes and wiped away a smear of moss and bits of leaves.

Was that someone calling his name?

He was looking up at something that looked like his foot. And was he lying in water? Of course there was water. They'd been smashed by a huge wave.

They.

Where were Sam and Ruby?

Gerald let his head flop to the right. Ruby was on her side, facing him, coughing up water. Gerald realized he was lying on a steep slope, his feet above his head. He struggled across to Ruby on his hands and knees.

"You all right?"

Ruby responded with another round of liquid hacks. "What happened?" she asked.

Gerald took in their surroundings. They appeared to be on a narrow bank at the bottom of a deep cavern. Behind them, a large pool of black water lay like a hibernating bear. Steep walls, covered in moss, soared up on all sides. High above, to one side, there was a small opening surrounded by greenery. That was where the light was coming in.

"The wave must have washed us through that hole," Gerald said. "That green stuff must be the vines we were climbing on."

Ruby jolted upright.

"Where's Sam?"

Gerald shook his head. "He must still be up there."

"Or washed away," Ruby said. "Oh, Sam . . ."

Gerald didn't know what to think. "He's a good swimmer," he heard himself say. "He'll be all right."

Ruby yelled out for her brother. The only reply was a torrent of water gushing through the opening high above.

"The tide must still be coming in," Gerald said. "And judging by the state of these walls, it looks like this cave will fill up."

Ruby scrambled as far up the slope as she could, then slipped on the moss and slid back to the bottom.

"This is hopeless," she said. "If the water fills this place it'll be like a washing machine. How can we swim against that?" Ruby looked to Gerald. "I want to find Sam," she said.

There was a rumbling overhead and more water surged into the cave, sweeping the legs out from under Gerald and Ruby and washing them into the pool at the back of the cavern.

Gerald stumbled to his feet, waist deep in black water. Ruby rose up next to him.

"What are we going to do?" she asked.

Then there was a noise behind them: something breaking the surface of the water. Something was rising out of the dark center of the pool.

Ruby grabbed Gerald's arm and spun around.

A body burst out of the water with a roar. Ruby's scream cut the air like the back of an axe.

It was Sam.

"Hey, you two," he said as he bobbed in the water. "You'll never guess where I've just been."

Ruby shoved Gerald aside and waded deeper into the pool toward her brother.

"You pea brain!" she yelled. "You utter dolt." She then threw her arms around his neck and held him tight.

Sam grinned at Gerald over Ruby's shoulder. "Sisters, eh!"

Ruby unpeeled her arms. Then she smacked Sam across

the back of the head. "Where have you been? I thought you'd drowned."

Sam rubbed his skull, fixing his headlamp back into place.

"You two seemed okay after we got washed down here, so I went exploring," Sam said. He tapped the light with a finger. "Good thing you got the waterproof ones, Gerald."

The camping gear. Gerald had forgotten about his backpack. He slapped at his shoulders and was stunned to find the pack was still there. He scrabbled around inside it, pulled out a flashlight, and strapped it to his head. Ruby was already shining her headlamp beam into the gloom.

"Exploring?" Ruby said. "This pool is all there is down here."

Sam adjusted the lamp and trained the light onto his sister's face. "That's where you're wrong, genius."

A rumble sounded from above and another surge of water shot though the cave opening. It hit them like a bomb, pushing them beneath the surface.

"Right," said Sam when they came up for air. "We're going to have to do a little more swimming."

"Swimming?" Ruby said. "Where?"

"It's not far," Sam said. "Trust me."

The look on Ruby's face made it clear that trusting Sam was the last thing she was going to do.

Sam led Ruby to the middle of the pool, up to her

armpits. "Just take a big breath and follow me, okay?"

"What if I run out of air?" Ruby said, staring horrified at the surface.

Sam thought for a second. "That would be a bad thing."

Before she could give it any more thought, Sam grabbed her hand and they both disappeared beneath the water.

Gerald glanced up at the sound of another wave approaching. An avalanche of water was rushing down at him. He took a breath, and dived.

Gerald was vaguely aware of the surface above him being bombarded by the pounding waters flowing in from the bay. But his senses were focused on the shaft of light that probed the darkness ahead of him. He kicked down. He could just make out the two fingers of light coming from Sam's and Ruby's headlamps below. They were tracing the edge of a sheer rock shelf, deeper and deeper into the pool. Gerald's ears howled in protest as the pressure ground into them, squeezing like a clamp on his head.

Then he lost sight of the others.

His flashlight sliced into the gloom but all he could see was rock wall plunging ever deeper. There was no sign of Sam or Ruby. They'd gone.

Gerald kicked on, driving himself deeper. And then the rock shelf disappeared. All he could see was bottomless space. His lungs tightened; he was running out of air. Panic rose in his gut. What was going on? His friends had vanished. He had a head-spinning sense of disorientation. Which way was up?

Then Gerald thought to blow out a bubble. His eyes followed its smooth ascent. And his sense of place was restored. He had swum under the rock shelf. He turned his head for the surface and kicked hard. Just when he thought his lungs would collapse, he burst into the sweet salt air.

Sam and Ruby were sitting on a sandy bank at the edge of the pool. Gerald crawled out of the water and flopped beside them. They were in a vast grotto. The ceiling soared high above, lost in the stalactites and shadows.

"We should be safe from any high tide in here," Sam said, his voice echoing into the space around them.

"Won't this just fill up like the other cave?" Ruby asked.

"I reckon that rock shelf we swam under is a bit like an S-bend in a toilet," Sam said. "The water level will get as high as the other cave, but this one goes higher up into the island, so we can climb above the tide."

Gerald let out an empty laugh. "We're in a toilet? Seems about right for how I feel at the moment."

He adjusted his headlamp. Their little beach opened up to an enormous cavern. A rocky platform rose gently behind them.

"Let's see where this goes," Gerald said, and he clambered up onto the platform.

Ruby swept her light in a broad arc, catching details of

crags and fissures in the walls of the stone cathedral around them. "I wonder if anyone has ever been down here," she said. She glanced across at her brother. "Hope there aren't any rats."

Sam's jaw tightened. "There's no need for that," he said.

"You're being very brave," Ruby said. She skipped ahead to catch up with Gerald. "I'm very proud of—"

This time, Ruby's scream almost ruptured Gerald's right eardrum.

"What is it?" Sam raced to join them. Ruby was clamped onto Gerald's back like a petrified koala. Three beams of light converged on a point on the ground. They lit a human skeleton.

It lay on a stone tablet where the rock ceiling dipped low, its feet closest to them.

"It's all right," Sam said to Ruby, placing a hand on her shaking arm. "I think he's dead."

Ruby unwound herself from Gerald's shoulders. "Hardly anyone likes you," she said to her brother, doing her best to still the quaver in her voice. "You know that, don't you?"

Gerald inched closer to the skeleton for a closer look at the nest of bones. The body was lying on its back, with its right arm stretched behind its head, as if pointing to something deeper in the cavern. The dull gray of the bones suggested it had been there a very long time. Then the lamp caught a glint on the extended hand.

"There's something on one of the fingers," Gerald said.

He dropped to his knees and crawled closer.

"It's a ring," he said. "A gold ring."

Then Gerald gasped.

"What's the matter?" Ruby asked, poking her head out from behind Sam.

"The ring," Gerald said. "I think it has my family seal on it."

"No!" Ruby said. "How can that be?"

Sam squeezed in beside Gerald, shining his light onto the hand. "Three arms locked in a triangle around a sun," he said. "Looks like it to me."

Gerald reached out to take the band of gold, but it was stuck on the curled finger, clenched and locked in place by a thumb. And it wouldn't budge.

"Hold on," he said. "This isn't bone. It's more like stone."

"Fossilized," Sam said. "All that silt from the bay. All those high tides. A thousand years ago the water must have reached in here and covered him up." Sam rapped his knuckles on the skull, which emitted a hollow clonk. "Looks like Ruby's not the only petrified thing down here. This guy's made of stone."

Gerald tugged hard on the finger and with a final grunt of effort it snapped off, releasing the ring into his hand. He buffed it against his shirt and held it next to the one on his left hand. Under the yellow beam of the headlamp, the rings gleamed in the surrounding dark.

"Identical," Gerald said. He slipped the ring onto the

little finger of his right hand; it almost clung to his skin. "A perfect fit," he said.

"I guess this must be Lucius," Sam said. "Maybe the ruby casket is buried nearby."

"It's all rock," Ruby said. "Not much hope of burying anything here." They hunted around the stone platform but there was no sign of any place where a casket could be hidden.

"Unless he snuck in a jackhammer, I don't think we'll find any buried treasure in this place," Sam said.

Ruby looked doubtfully back at the pool they'd swum through. "Maybe it's at the bottom of that thing," she said. "And I'm not volunteering to go have a look."

Gerald sat next to his fossilized ancestor and rubbed the cold stone skull. "Come on, Lucius," he said. "Give it up. Where did you put the casket?"

"How do you think he died?" Ruby asked. She had edged a little closer to the skeleton but was still keeping a careful distance.

"High cholesterol?" Sam said. "What do you think? He was trapped down here, stupid."

"Well, if he was trapped here, what makes you think we can get out?" Ruby said. "Or hadn't you thought of that?"

Sam's face went blank. "We can swim back to the other cave," he said.

"And what? Get pounded by the tide twice a day until

someone on a relaxing stroll through the quicksand hears our cries for help? Brilliant suggestion."

Gerald looked at the broken stone finger in his palm. Then at Lucius's outstretched arm. A wrinkle of a thought unfurled in Gerald's brain.

"What are we going to do, Gerald?" Ruby said.

Gerald didn't respond. Instead, he tried to fix the broken finger back into place.

"Gerald?"

The fractured knuckle wouldn't stick. Gerald clambered closer, his shoulders up against the low rock ceiling as he tried to wedge the fragment back on.

"What are you doing?" Ruby asked.

"Strange way to lie if you're about to cark it, don't you think?" Gerald said, concentrating on repairing the skeleton's hand. "If I was starving to death, I'd probably curl up in a ball. There. That's got it." Gerald nodded with satisfaction. "Good as new."

"What are you talking about?"

Gerald looked down at his handiwork. "It's almost like he's pointing at something." He then banged the back of his head on the low rock ceiling.

Sparks filled his eyes at the pain stabbing into his brain. Gerald's cursing filled the chamber. But it stopped abruptly when his flashlight lit the spot where he'd struck his head.

"Will you look at that," he said in wonder.

Carved into the surface of the rock, just above Lucius's outstretched hand, was a string of symbols: 10ɸvǝᐯ.

"The number ten, a circle with a line through it, a Y, an arrow, and a triangle," Gerald said. "That's what was written on the envelope that Great-Aunt Geraldine left for me. Remember? The one that the thin man stole from the house in Chelsea. This is definitely Lucius. And he's left us a note."

"But what does it mean?" Ruby said.

Gerald had no idea. But his great-aunt had thought it was important enough to write down. He rubbed his hand across the lump that was now bulging out from the back of his skull. The smack against the ceiling wasn't the only thing giving him a headache.

"Uh, Gerald," Sam said, his voice floating up from below the stone platform. "We have a problem."

Gerald turned to face Sam. There was something different about him, but Gerald couldn't quite place it.

"My light has just gone out," Sam said.

There was a moment's silence.

"Did we pack batteries?" Ruby asked, tearing her pack from her shoulders and rifling inside.

"I don't remember buying any," Gerald said. He cast the beam from his flashlight onto his outstretched hand. It was dimming before his eyes.

"Mine's fading now!" Ruby said. She looked at Gerald,

lighting his face in the dying beam. "What are we going to do?"

Gerald fished around inside his pack and pulled out a small box on the end of a knotted lace. "A flint," he said. "I knew we'd bought one." He pulled out a metal pin the length of a match and struck it along the side of the box. A spark burst into the air.

"We can light a fire," Gerald said. Relief flooded through him. It would be impossible to find a way out without any light.

"Gerald," Ruby said. "We're in a cave. There's nothing to burn in here."

In an instant, the relief that had lifted Gerald was gone. Ruby was right. They were in a dank cave that hadn't see the sun in a thousand years. He watched as his headlamp faded to nothing.

And the cave was lost to an all-consuming darkness.

Chapter 9

Gerald tried to control his breathing. But in the black cloak of nothingness that had wrapped itself around him, it was almost impossible.

"Sit down," he called out to Sam and Ruby. "Try not to move around."

Gerald couldn't see a thing. He pressed his hand to the end of his nose but his eyes couldn't register any movement. The darkness was complete.

He tried the flint but the spark just hurt their eyes and revealed nothing. Gerald blinked, trying to clear the arcing burn from his retinas.

"I guess this is how Lucius sat it out." Sam's voice sounded from somewhere to Gerald's left. "In the dark. Like this."

"Shut up, Sam." Ruby was somewhere to Gerald's right.

It was probably just as well she wasn't any closer to her brother.

Gerald closed his eyes. He had no idea what to do. Should they risk trying to swim out through the pool? But with no light they'd never find their way under that rock shelf. It was hopeless.

He opened his eyes.

And took a sharp breath. Was his mind playing tricks?

Or was the skull of Lucius Antonius glowing?

"Can you see that?" Gerald whispered.

"What?" Ruby asked.

Gerald crawled to the skeleton. He reached out to touch the skull and the back of his hand lit up in a faint blue glow. Gerald stared in wonder, then tilted his head upward.

"There's a hole up here," he said. "In the ceiling." He carefully stood up, keeping his hands above his head to feel for the rocks above him. He tapped his fingers around a square opening that must have been hidden in shadows when they were first examining the cave. "I reckon I can climb this. Sam, give me a leg up."

After a flurry of hand slapping in the dark that almost cost Sam an eye, Gerald was boosted into the tight shaft carved into the stone. "There's hand notches cut into the sides," Gerald said. "Someone's made this easy for us." He stretched out a hand and curled his fingers into a notch.

After five minutes of sweat-coated effort, Gerald's head popped out into a large chamber. He dragged himself over a low stone wall that ringed the top of the shaft like a wishing well set into the floor. Light filtered into the chamber through windows high in the walls. It took a few seconds for Gerald's eyes to adjust. When they did, he let out a low whistle.

He leaned over the wall and called down to the cave below. "It's safe for you guys to come up now. And Ruby?"

"Yes?" her voice echoed up the shaft.

"You have to promise me something."

"What's that?"

"That you won't scream when you get up here, okay?"

There was a long pause. "Why would I want to scream?"

"Well, there's a few bones up here, that's all."

There was another pause. Then Ruby's voice filtered up through the hole in the stone floor. "Sam wants to know if there's any rats."

Gerald grinned to himself. "No, Hercules," he called down the hole. "You'll be all right. Ruby, give Sam a leg up, then he can reach down and pull you up by the hands."

Soon, Sam's head emerged through the hole in the floor. He looked around and his eyes opened wide.

Gerald gave him a hand over the wall. "Uh, Ruby," Sam called down to his sister. "Maybe you should close your eyes for the last little bit."

Ruby's voice sounded up from below. "Don't be ridiculous. How bad can a couple of bones be?"

Her head reached the surface. "Don't just stand there," she said to Sam. "Give me a hand." Gerald and Sam reached down and yanked Ruby up into the chamber. She landed lightly on her feet. "Thank you," she said, brushing herself down. "Now where are—"

She stopped midsentence and turned a slow circle, taking in the full majesty of the enormous hall surrounding them. Every wall, every section of the ceiling, every frame of every window, was laid out with a pattern fashioned entirely from bones.

Human bones.

An alcove to their left was decorated with a mosaic constructed from hundreds of skulls—a vast bank of sightless eye sockets trained right on them. Arms and legs lined the architraves, feet and hands formed sweeping patterns of flowers and swirls. Tibias, ulnas, humeri . . . thousands upon thousands of them in Gothic splendor. Ruby took it all in with a slack-jawed silence.

"Ruby?" Gerald said gently. "Are you all right?" He swapped an anxious look with Sam. "Ruby?"

The screaming only started when Gerald put his hand on her shoulder.

Pigeons lofting in the upper window ledges were shaken from their nests by a shriek of such unparalleled clarity that it made Gerald's teeth hurt. Ruby's mouth extended like a bullfrog and the glass-splintering sound that escaped seemed to go on forever. The more Sam tried to calm her, the more wound up she got. She batted away his hands and screeched in primal terror at the skulls, which seemed to echo back like some choir of the damned. It was a good minute before she ran out of steam.

In the silence that followed, stray pigeon feathers wafted down from the rafters to rest on their heads. Gerald held out a tentative hand to Ruby.

"I did try to warn you," he said.

"Yeah. Cheers," Ruby said in a hoarse whisper. "A few bones. That really helped. Thanks."

Gerald took her by the elbow. "There's a door at the far end," he said as soothingly as he could. "Let's find a way out."

Ruby nodded. "Yes. Out would be a good idea." She allowed herself to be guided past piles of bones, stacked end on end like cordwood up the walls. They walked by long tables constructed from femurs and clavicles, chairs with skulls at the ends of the armrests, even a hat stand with a spray of ribs coming out the top.

"Who would do this?" Ruby whispered, her eyes tracing the white-boned artistry that surrounded them. "It's obscene."

"I've heard of places like this," Gerald said, leading them into a long corridor. "Catacombs. Houses of the dead. These skeletons probably date back a thousand years. I don't think there are any fresh ones."

"But who would use human bones to make a sculpture?" Ruby said.

Sam shrugged. "It's good to have a hobby."

They rounded a corner and Gerald suddenly stopped in his tracks. Sam walked into the back of him.

"What are you doing?" Sam said. "Can't you—" He stopped protesting when he saw it. The corridor made a sharp turn to the right. And on the wall facing them was a mosaic unlike any they'd seen so far.

"My family seal," Gerald croaked. "With real arms."

Halfway up the wall, at the center of an elaborate design of bones, was a triangle of arms, clutched at the elbows. But instead of a sun at the center, there was a single skull, its vacant eyes staring at them.

"What's that doing there?" Ruby said.

Gerald glanced down at the gold rings on his fingers. Did he feel a spark of electricity coming from them? The bands pulling tighter against his skin? He flexed his hands.

Sam was already at the wall, his nose right up against the skull at the center of the mural. "What do you think?" he said. "Is the ruby casket behind here?"

"Could be," Gerald said, joining him by the nest of bones. "Booby-trapped, do you think?"

Sam inspected the jigsaw of body bits and pursed his lips.

"Only one way to find out," he said. He poked two fingers into the eye sockets of the skull, and pulled.

The head popped out like a cork from a bottle. There was an unnerving silence as they waited for something to happen.

Nothing did.

Finally, Sam spoke up. "Looks good to me," he said. "Here, Ruby. Hold on to this." And he tossed the skull to his sister.

Ruby caught the head on her chest. She looked down to find two empty eyeholes staring up at her.

A strange gurgling noise came from Ruby's throat. She looked to Gerald, panic in her face.

"It's all right, Ruby," he said. "It can't hurt you. It's just a piece of bone."

Ruby opened her mouth and gargled a response. She swallowed, and said quietly, "That's right. Just a piece of bone."

There was a sudden knocking sound behind them. Gerald spun around. The wall of bones was starting to vibrate, clattering together as if caught in an earthquake.

"Uh-oh," Sam said. "Bone slide!"

The wall collapsed on top of them. Hundreds of leg and arm bones tumbled across the floor, sending up a cloud of dust. By the time the debris settled, Gerald, Sam, and Ruby were waist deep in skeleton bits.

Sam gave a rueful grin. "Whoops," he said.

Ruby stood frozen in place. A rib was teetering on one

shoulder. A jawbone complete with teeth rested on her head like some Halloween tiara. She still held the skull in her hands. A look of manic insanity was etched into her face.

Gerald kicked his way through the litter to get to her. He plucked off the rib and jaw and tossed them aside, then took the skull and dropped it onto the pile behind him. Without saying a word, he led Ruby out of the bone avalanche.

She turned her head to face him, the manic smile still in place, her eyes like Ping-Pong balls. "Thank you, Gerald," she said slowly. "That was very kind of you."

Gerald raised an eyebrow. "Uh, don't mention it. Are you okay?"

Ruby blinked a dozen times and her cheek twitched. "Of course. Why don't you go and help Sam?"

"Okay. As long as you're sure."

"Oh, I'm sure."

Gerald cleared a path to where Sam was standing. They both looked back at Ruby.

"I think she's in shock," Gerald said.

Sam knocked the last of the bones away from the wall. "It's better than the screaming. Hey, check this out."

Set into the blank stone wall was a squat vault, about the same size as the dumbwaiter in Gerald's house in London. Its interior was lost in shadows. Gerald reached inside and felt around. His hand fell on something and he pulled out a large book bound in red leather. Pressed onto the cover in gold leaf was the Archer family seal.

Before Gerald had a chance to flip it open, Sam emitted a cry of delight. "I think it's the casket!" His arm was sunk up to the shoulder in the vault. He strained and dragged a long stone box halfway out of the hole. Gerald shoved the book into his pack and gave Sam a hand.

"This has got to be it," Gerald said. Together, he and Sam hefted the casket out of the wall. They struggled with it to a clear space near where Ruby was standing. The sight of the ancient stone chest seemed to jolt Ruby out of her trance.

"It's identical to the others," she said. Then she shot a glance at her brother. "And don't for one second think I won't be getting even with you for that skull."

Gerald dropped to his knees and ran his fingers over a carving of an archer in the middle of the casket lid. There was a hollow in its muscled abdomen. "The ruby would fit in there perfectly," he said.

He looked at Sam and Ruby. "We've got some bait now. That cat woman won't be able to resist this. Time to call Inspector Parrott and let him know what we've found."

Sam looked down at the chest by his feet. "Can't we just break it open and take whatever's inside?" he said. "It weighs a ton."

"Can't risk it," Gerald said. "It's bound to be another of

those golden rods and you saw how Green handled the last one. It was like it was made of hundred-year-old crystal. We'll need the key."

"So we have to carry this?" Sam said.

"Just like Hercules," Gerald said. "Come on. It can't be far to the outside."

Sam and Gerald each took an end and started a slow walk down the corridor.

"How do you think the casket ended up in that wall?" Ruby asked. "This place would have been built centuries after Lucius brought it here."

"I'd say it was the same people who dug that shaft down to the cavern where we found the skeleton," Gerald said. "Maybe some of the original monks found the casket next to Lucius and moved it to higher ground. It must have been stuck behind those bones for hundreds of years."

Ruby shivered. "Let's not mention the bones," she said. "Ever again."

Gerald swallowed a grin. It was good to see Ruby mostly back to normal.

They turned a corner and Gerald slapped a hand up to his throat, as if swatting at a mosquito. He lost his grip on the end of the casket and it crashed to the floor. The sudden lurch forward tore it from Sam's hands and his end dropped with a thud. An indescribable pain shot into Gerald's chest. He opened his mouth but nothing came out.

"Gerald?" Sam said. "What's the matter?"

Gerald spun to face them, his hand still at his neck. A trickle of blood ran from between his fingers.

"Gerald?"

His eyelids peeled back. He couldn't breathe. His free hand shot out and grabbed Ruby by the arm.

His knees buckled; they wouldn't hold him. He took a step backward to lean on a wall. His body shuddered. His legs collapsed, and he slid to the floor.

"Gerald!" Ruby cried.

There was a movement from the shadows ahead. Then a slender woman with a wave of dark brown hair stepped from an arched doorway and into the light. She held a narrow tube in one hand.

"Hello, Gerald," she said. "I see you've found my casket."

Gerald's breathing came in short spasms. His lungs were incapable of filling themselves.

The woman strode across to them, leaned down and plucked a tiny dart from Gerald's neck.

"Now listen to me very carefully," she said. "Or you are going to die."

Chapter 10

Gerald lay propped against the wall with his legs out-stretched on the floor. Shallow breaths fluttered in his chest. Ruby was on her knees, clutching his hand.

"Push the casket over here." The woman snapped her order at Sam. He obeyed without a word, heaving the box across the stone floor.

She was all efficiency—dressed in commando chic: body-hugging black trousers and shirt, laced boots and a leather pouch attached to her belt. A long cylinder was slung over her back and strapped across her chest. She knelt by the side of the casket and ran her hands over the surface, a smile playing on her face.

"My uncle was right about you," she said. "You are use-ful idiots. You and your friend Constable Lethbridge."

Gerald struggled to take in a breath. "Mason Green . . . your uncle?"

Ruby held his hand tight. "Don't try to talk," she said. "It doesn't matter about Green." Then she turned to the woman. "What have you done to him? What was in that dart?"

The woman glanced up from the casket. "Charlotte," she said.

"What?"

"My name is Charlotte. I have given Gerald a strong dose of a deadly toxin, which, if left untreated, will cause his central nervous system to collapse. He has about ten minutes left to live."

A cry caught in Ruby's throat. "No! You've got to help him."

Gerald coughed weakly. His skin was the color of mortician's wax. "Cold," he whispered. "I'm cold." He blinked—he was losing focus at the edges, as if he was looking down a long tube. But he could make out the tears that were running down Ruby's cheeks. He gripped her hands, her fingers burning hot in the ice of his grasp. He held on, as hard as he could.

Ruby stared into Gerald's eyes, and he could see what she feared, that the light in them was starting to fade. "You can't let him—" She swallowed her words. "There must be something."

Charlotte pulled a red leather roll from the pouch on

her belt and untied the binding. She unrolled the package to reveal a large gem. Even in the dull light of the catacombs, the ruby glowed.

"There is an antidote," she said, as calmly as if she were discussing the weather. She picked up the ruby and placed it in the indentation in the casket lid. The gem sat in place as naturally as a queen on a throne. Charlotte gripped the stone in both hands and twisted. The carving of the archer swiveled like clockwork. "I could give it to you," she said. She curled her manicured fingers under the edge of the lid, and pulled. The top came free and she laid it on the floor. "But first, you need to tell me something."

Gerald felt a heavy weight pressing on his chest. Pins of light were sparking in his eyes. He strained to raise his head so he could see what Charlotte was doing. "Is it . . . golden rod?"

His voice was so weak it barely reached the woman hovering over the casket.

"Yes, it is," Charlotte said, lifting a gilded bar into the light. "The third of the holy three."

Gerald's head flopped back. His grip on Ruby's hand began to weaken. "I knew it . . ."

"Do something!" Ruby screamed.

The cry jolted Charlotte from her fascination with the relic in her hands. She shrugged the cylinder from her shoulders and slid the rod into its padded interior, locking a cap on the end. "I will give you the antidote if you tell me what you know about the Tower of the Winds."

There was a stunned silence. Gerald could make out the words but they made no sense to him. He'd never heard of any such place. He tried to respond but the energy deserted him.

"We don't know what you're talking about," Sam said. He took a pace toward the woman but stopped midstride.

"Not so close, Mr. Valentine," Charlotte said. She pulled a glass vial from the pouch on her belt. "If I drop this, your friend's life goes down the drain. I'm sure you don't want that on your conscience." She glanced at her watch. "He still has five minutes or so. I mixed the batch myself. I studied chemistry at Cambridge, you see."

"Did you learn how to kill your relatives there as well?" Ruby said.

Charlotte let out the type of laugh you might hear at a polite cocktail party in a ritzy hotel. "Do you mean that old fool at the courthouse? He'd outlived his use. It was easy enough shooting a dart into him while he was talking to you, Gerald. Almost as easy as getting your DNA from the drinking straw in the cafeteria."

"You were the waitress!" Sam said.

"You are the clever one, aren't you? Yes, I slummed it for a morning. Then it was a simple task of planting the evidence in your bedroom. And since your friend Constable Lethbridge had kindly told me where to find the ruby, my job was basically done. A phone call to the police to let them know where the blowgun was hidden, and I had successfully eliminated a burdensome old man and framed you for the murder. Leaving me free to claim my birthright. A good day's work, I think."

"Lethbridge told you?" Gerald's voice was barely a whisper.

"The antidote," Ruby said. "Please."

Charlotte stared at the tear-stained face before her, then at the wretched boy collapsed on the floor. "You know nothing of the Tower of the Winds?"

"I'd do anything to save Gerald," Ruby pleaded. "You have to believe me. I'd tell you if I could."

Charlotte rolled the vial in her hand, then launched it across the room at Ruby. "Catch!" she said, and set off down the corridor at a run.

Ruby's eyes fixed on the glass tube as it sailed through the air. Gerald lifted his head to see it spinning slowly toward the floor. Ruby dived forward and thrust out her right hand. But she was too late. The vial clipped her thumb and she missed it. A cry fell from her lips.

Then Sam's hand slid underneath, and the fragile container plumped into his palm as if alighting on a cushion.

"Quick!" Ruby called.

Sam lifted the vial to his eyes. Inside the tube rattled a yellow stick the size and shape of a fountain pen. "What do we do?" he asked.

Ruby took the vial and unscrewed the end. The yellow

stick slid into her hand. She stared down at it, helpless. "I don't know," she said. "I don't know."

Gerald's vision had narrowed to a pinhole. His chest had turned to concrete; his breathing was almost nonexistent. But his eyes were focused with gun-sight precision on the object in Ruby's hand. He'd have only one shot at this.

He harnessed his energy and lunged forward, snatching the stick. He shoved one end into his mouth and clamped his teeth around a rubber stopper to wrench it free, revealing the tip of a needle. Then, with the last of his strength, he drove the needle hard into his thigh.

The pain piercing deep into his leg was intense, but it was forgotten as the concrete around his lungs crumbled and sweet air flooded into his body. Gerald fell back against the wall, a sharp sigh of relief shooting the robber stopper from his teeth straight between Sam's eyes.

"Hey!" Sam said, ducking too late. "Watch it."

"Gerald?" Ruby was hovering above him. "Are you all right?"

Gerald sucked in more air and his vision started to clear. He nodded.

"How did you know to do that?" Sam said. He lifted the yellow stick from where it had tumbled from Gerald's hand. An inch-long needle extended from one end.

"First aid at school." Gerald concentrated on filling his

lungs. "Allergies. People can go into shock. And those things set them right."

He shunted himself upright. It was amazing how quickly the antidote was working. He could feel it filtering through his body, loosening his joints.

"Can you believe she killed her own uncle?" Ruby said. "That's so vile."

"Yeah," Sam said. "Killing your relatives. What a thought." Ruby glanced sideways at him, then lashed out with a flick to the back of his head.

"What was that for?" he protested.

"Just keeping you in your place," Ruby said.

Gerald wiggled his fingers. Every movement reminded him just how good it was to be alive. "You know what I think?" he said. "I bet Green told her all about the golden rods and whatever treasure they lead to so she could track it down even if he went to jail. But she got greedy and, when it looked like Green might get off, she killed him to keep the treasure for herself."

"Sounds possible," Sam said. "Interesting family."

"Are you okay to move, Gerald?" Ruby asked.

"I think so," he said. Sam and Ruby helped him to his feet and he steadied himself against the wall for a second. He looked down at the open casket on the floor and limped across to scoop up the ruby from the lid.

"Did you notice what that woman had around her

neck?" Gerald asked, staring at the gem in his palm.

"No," Ruby said. "I was too worried about you."

Gerald stuffed the gem into his pocket. "A necklace," he said. "A plain leather necklace."

"So?" Sam said.

"There was a gold ring looped through it," Gerald said. "I saw it when she was lifting the rod out of the casket. I think it had my family seal on it."

Gerald, Ruby, and Sam emerged through a crawlspace at the back of a small chapel. Light streamed through stained-glass windows in the stone walls, and a shelf in front of the altar held dozens of flickering candles. They went through the main doors and found themselves on a narrow terrace above the cobbled street they had wandered along earlier.

"I'm starving," Sam said. "I could go for some lunch."

Gerald sat on the wall overlooking the street. He was still a little shaky. "Okay, how's this for a plan?" he said. "Let's go back to the hotel and get something to eat. Mr. Fry should be there by now. Then we might as well call Inspector Parrott and let him know what's happened. If Charlotte is trying to find some Tower of the Winds, that information might help him track her down."

"What about Inspector Jarvis?" Ruby said. "He's not going to believe Charlotte planted the blowgun in your bedroom."

"Then we'd better avoid Inspector Jarvis," Gerald said.

"Come on. I'm with Sam. I'm starving."

They wound down a set of stairs carved from the ubiquitous gray granite of the island and squeezed onto the main walkway. The street was packed with tourists, jostling their way up the steep hill toward the abbey. Gerald put his head down and pushed against the flow. After struggling for fifty yards he stepped into a shop doorway. Ruby and Sam followed him.

A little farther down the roadway, there was a commotion. Shouts rang out above the crowd. Then came three sharp blasts on a whistle.

Gerald moved onto the step of the shop entrance, trying to see what was going on.

"Uh-oh," he said. "It's Mr. Fry."

Ruby craned her neck to see over the crowd. She pulled down on Gerald's shoulder, trying to inch taller. "What's happening?"

"There are two French policemen down there. I think they're arresting Mr. Fry."

"What?"

"They're outside the hotel. Mr. Fry's not looking too happy about it. He's arguing up a storm."

"The man from the hotel," Ruby said. "He must have reported us." She turned to Sam. "You and your talk about helicopters."

"Oh sure, blame me," Sam said. "You're really going to help Mr. Fry by doing that. Nice work, Ruby."

"What are you talking about?"

"Can you two quit it?" Gerald said. "There's someone else down there, arguing with Fry."

"Who is it?" Sam asked.

"It's Inspector Jarvis," Gerald said.

A clearing had formed around the butler and the police. Gerald could see Jarvis prodding his finger into Mr. Fry's chest. They were having a heated argument.

"Fry's not backing down," Gerald said. "He's giving it right back to Jarvis." Gerald smiled to himself. "Good for you, Mr. Fry."

Ruby finally managed to step up beside Gerald and she poked her head above the crowd. "Look, Constable Lethbridge is down there too."

"That's one thing in our favor, then," Sam said. "What do we do? Go tell them about Charlotte?"

"Jarvis doesn't look like he's in the mood to listen to stories about a cat woman and poison darts," Gerald said. "And we've just lost our transport out of here."

"So what now?" Ruby said. "Lie low for—"

A piercing whistle blast cut her off.

Gerald's eyes shot down the roadway. Inspector Jarvis was looking right at him, pointing a finger like a sniper's rifle. A burly French policeman was shoving through the tourists toward them.

"He's seen us," Gerald said. He grabbed Ruby by the shoulders and pushed her into the stream of people moving up the hill. "Quick!"

Sam fell in behind as they dashed in and out of tour groups, all the time moving higher and higher toward the abbey on the summit. The crowd started to slow and swell like water behind a dam.

"There's a ticket office up here," Gerald called back to the others. "If we can get in front of this group, the police will be jammed in tight."

Sam edged ahead of Gerald, elbowing his way through the crush. "Too easy," he said. "Follow me." He put his head down and shoved between the people in front of him. "Pardon me!" he yelled. "Lady with a baby! Coming through."

The crowd parted far enough for them to weave through to the front of the ticket queue. "One day someone's going to notice there's no baby," Ruby said. "Three tickets, please, uh—*trois billets, s'il vous plaît.*"

Gerald paid for the tickets and they dived through the lower entry to the abbey compound. Inside, the crowd was thinner. Gerald, Ruby, and Sam were in an outer court-yard, at the bottom of a complex of gray stone walls and pathways leading up to the spired peak of the medieval abbey far above.

"Which way?" Ruby asked.

Gerald scanned their surroundings. There wasn't much option.

"The only way is up," he said.

They dashed up a steep flight of stairs hemmed between stone walls. High above, a wooden walkway spanned the narrow gap to link the two buildings.

"This place is awesome," Sam puffed as he climbed the stairs. "All we need now is the Three Musketeers and a sword fight."

Gerald paused to catch his breath. Up ahead he saw two monks, deep in conversation as they descended the stairs toward them. Each wore a long blue cloak that brushed the tops of his sandaled feet and was held at the waist by a knotted cord, from which swung a large metal key. The shorter of the two monks stopped his descent and fumbled for the key at his side. Still chatting to his companion, he unlocked a wooden door set into one of the walls. He pushed the door ajar, then continued with his companion down the steps.

The shrill police whistle sounded from the entrance hall below. Gerald shot a glance down the stairs.

"We better hurry," he said.

As they passed the monks, the shorter one gave Gerald a smile and, with a tilt of his head, indicated the open door. Gerald stumbled to a halt. Had the monk just tipped them off to a possible hiding place?

A wink from the other monk gave Gerald his answer.

"Quick," he said to Sam and Ruby. "In here."

Gerald shouldered the heavy oak door and bundled

through the opening, straight over the edge of a narrow landing. It was an eight-foot drop to the wooden floor. He hit it and rolled onto his back just in time to see Ruby, spread-eagled in midair, plummeting down to land square on top of him.

The impact squeezed Gerald's ribs like a piano accordion. He just managed to reinflate his chest when Sam arrived, plunging down to sandwich Ruby between them.

Under the combined weight of the Valentine twins, Gerald let out a moan and his head flopped back onto the floorboards. "They really need a railing on that top step," he said.

They had fallen into a cellar. A dozen stairs ran down the wall from the doorway. Sam scrambled up the stairs to push the door closed.

Through a squat window at street level, they could see the feet of passersby outside. Within a minute, several sets of police boots clattered past.

"The police are going to be crawling all over this place," Sam said. "I guess we're stuck in here for a while."

Ruby was still lying on top of Gerald. Their noses were centimeters apart, and for a second they just looked at each other.

"You want to get off now?" Gerald asked.

"Oh, of course," Ruby said, rolling away. "Sorry."

Gerald raised himself to his elbows. "I'm not sure I

can take any more adventure today," he said. "It hurts too much."

He crawled over to a table in the center of the cellar and hauled himself onto a stool. He peeled the backpack from his shoulders and dumped it by his feet.

"That monk on the stairs," Ruby said, "do you think he opened the door to help us?"

"He couldn't have been more obvious," Gerald said. "He invited us in."

Sam dropped onto a spare stool at the table next to Gerald. "Unless he turns up in the next two minutes with a hot meal, who cares? I need food."

"Can't you think of anything but your stomach?" Ruby said. Then she bit her bottom lip. "Actually, now that you mention it, I am pretty hungry."

Sam suddenly sat upright. "The parcel from Mrs. Rutherford! All those pies and sausage rolls." He grabbed his pack and shoved his hand deep inside.

Sam's expression morphed from delighted anticipation to complete disgust. He pulled out a collapsed mound of paper, pastry, and meat, and slopped it on the table. "I guess I shouldn't have taken it swimming," he said, looking utterly miserable. Then he sneezed. "I guess I shouldn't have taken me swimming either. Don't suppose you've got chocolate in your pack, Gerald?"

Gerald upended his backpack onto the table. The

headlamp tumbled out, as did the flint on its leather cord and a water bottle. There was a small first-aid kit, a pen, a pocketknife, and . . .

"A pack of gum!" Sam said. He had two sticks in his mouth before anyone could move. After chewing hungrily for a few seconds he noticed the stares from Gerald and Ruby.

"Oh," he mumbled. "Um, anyone else want some?"

Ruby snatched the pack from her brother's hand. "Just appalling," she said.

She held out a piece for Gerald. "Would you like some of your gum, Gerald?"

But Gerald didn't notice the offer. He was staring at the book that had fallen from his pack. It was bound in red leather with the imprint of his family seal clear on the cover.

"I'd forgotten about this," he said as he flicked through the gold-edged pages.

"It's all in French," he said. "There's a surprise."

Ruby looked over Gerald's shoulder as he thumbed through the pages. "I can't understand a word of this," she said. "It must be hundreds of years old."

Gerald rested his forehead in his hands. He felt as if his brain had changed into a pound of cotton candy.

Ruby closed the book and drummed her fingers on the cover. "So what do we know? Lucius died flat on his back, and his dying thought was to point to a bunch of symbols he'd scratched into the rock—the same symbols that Geraldine wrote for Gerald."

"And Charlotte wanted to know about some place called the Tower of the Winds," Gerald said. "She was happy enough to gamble my life on finding out about it."

"And what about this book?" Sam said. "Books weren't even invented when Lucius was wandering around here. It would have been all scrolls and quills back then. How do you explain Gerald's family seal being on the cover of a book? And the book being locked away with a thousand-year-old casket?"

"It's got to be the monks," Gerald said. He looked at Ruby. "That travel guide you were reading at breakfast. Did it say anything about the monks?"

"Yes, there's been a religious order here for over a thousand years," Ruby said. "But that still doesn't explain—"

Gerald held up his hand. "How's this for an idea? Lucius arrives here from Rome with the ruby casket. Back then the place is basically a bare chunk of rock in the middle of the bay. Maybe he's sick. Or injured. Who knows? Maybe Mason Green's assassin ancestor—what was his name?"

"Octavius Viridian," Ruby said.

"Right, Octavius Viridian is on his tail. For whatever reason, Lucius can't go on. So he crawls into a cave to hide the chest. The order of monks who have set up shop here find him and hear his story: He's on the run from the

Roman emperor with a treasure that needs to be protected. You can imagine the Romans weren't too popular around here. So the monks decide to help him."

Ruby cocked her head. "So, like the cult in India, they dedicate themselves to keeping the casket hidden. And then, centuries later, when they build the town and the abbey, they move the casket out of the grotto and hide it behind all those"—Ruby shuddered at the memory—"bones."

"Bones arranged in the shape of my family seal," Gerald said. "And they stick this book in with the casket." He took the volume back from Ruby and ran his fingers over the cover. "It must be important. If we find out what this book's about, I'd say we're one step closer to the secret and one step closer to catching Charlotte."

"So who do we ask about the book?" Sam said.

"Those monks who opened the door for us," Gerald said. He pushed back on the chair and crossed to the narrow window by the door. The pathway was cast in late afternoon shadow. Only a few pairs of feet climbed the stairs past them.

"They're all old people's walking shoes," he said. "No police boots. But let's give it a few more minutes."

Gerald gathered up the camping gear and the book and arranged everything in his pack, then he draped the flint on its leather cord around his neck.

Ruby broke the last stick of gum into three and handed

around the pieces. "Dinner," she said.

They chewed in silence, apart from the occasional sneeze from Sam. Once the last of the flavor had been extracted from his gum, Gerald checked his watch. "Right," he said. "Let's go find us some monks."

He climbed the stairs and opened the door a few centimeters. "No use going back down to the entry," he said. "There's bound to be police there."

"So we head up to the abbey?" Ruby said.

"When hunting for monks," Gerald said, "go where the monks go."

The door creaked open and they squeezed through the gap onto the path outside. The stairs were deserted. The sky had turned a mottled blue as the afternoon melded into the late summer twilight.

Gerald was aware of the clomp of their boots on the worn stone stairs as they climbed toward the lower sections of the abbey. They came to an arched doorway at the top and poked their heads through.

A sparsely furnished reception room. There was no sign of anyone.

No tourists.

No police.

No monks.

A door stood ajar in the far wall and they crossed the room to the opening. Beyond it was a broad terrace that looked out over the bay. Set back to one side were the imposing walls of the abbey. The gothic spire that crowned the roof soared high over them.

There was no one about. Even the seagulls that had swooped and cawed while Gerald, Sam, and Ruby had slogged across the sand flats were nowhere to be seen.

The wind had dropped. The sun was just a memory. The brow of a full moon was rising out of the bay.

It was as if they were the last people on earth.

"Where is everyone?" Ruby said. Gerald sensed the concern in her voice. "It's so quiet."

"Let's look inside," Gerald said.

They crossed the terrace and climbed the steps to the church doors. Gerald pushed on one and they peered inside. Together, they let out a whispered chorus of "Wow!"

They stepped into the nave of the church and stood in gape-mouthed wonder. The stone walls on either side were lined by slender arches and soared seventy feet in the air to a huge vaulted ceiling. Moonlight filtered through the high windows, catching remnants of incense and bathing the interior in an eerie half glow.

"I feel very small in here," Ruby said. Her voice bounced off the stone floor.

"Shh!" Sam hissed. Then he sneezed.

Ruby narrowed her eyes to a death stare, but for once she kept her mouth shut.

They crept along the center aisle past rows of pews toward the chancel at the far end of the church. Gerald and Ruby were halfway along when the peace of the church was shattered by a splintering crash. Then another. And another.

Rows of pews were smashing over like a line of dominos, each one knocking into the one in front. In the cavernous church, the sound was like a battery of field guns. Next to the first of the fallen pews stood Sam, a "whoops" look on his face.

The last pew crashed onto the flagstones. The clatter curled up and out the arched windows high above like a cloud of bats scouring into the night.

Sam stood rooted to the spot, frozen in place by the silence that had descended over them.

Ruby glared at him. "You idiot," she said.

The silence was short-lived. From outside the church came the sound of running boots.

Police boots.

"This way," Gerald called, bolting toward the semicircular chancel. Fluted pillars loomed high out of the surrounding shadows like forest trees around a clearing. Incense wafted from two brass burners suspended nearby.

"Come on," Gerald said, and the three of them dived into an alcove on one side of the altar. They disappeared into the darkness, but they were boxed in. The only way out was back into the church.

And there was no question of going that way. A second after Sam slid next to Gerald, three men burst in from the northern transept.

Gerald flattened himself against the back wall of the alcove. His throat tightened. In the eerie moonlight, just a few feet away from them, stood Constable Lethbridge, a French policeman and . . . his mother's life coach.

Walter had joined the manhunt.

Chapter 11

Gerald was sure the thump of his heart rattling the bars of his rib cage would give them away. The pounding reverberated in his ears, growing more urgent with each beat. He didn't dare move his head to see what Sam and Ruby were doing on either side of him. All he could do was stare out from their hiding place into the body of the church.

Walter was different.

Gerald had only ever seen him with Vi. On those occasions, he was as smooth as a fox rolled in velvet. It was all opening doors and gracious manners, witty asides and casual laughter. Walter could not be more considerate. Did Vi need somewhere to sit? Could he fetch her a cup of tea? Or champagne, perhaps? He'd treated Gerald's mother like royalty. Nothing had been too much trouble for Walter.

But not now. Not with Gerald on the run.

The look on Walter's face was that of a man who had not slept in the past two days. Until that moment, Gerald had given little thought to the man. He had been just another of his mother's fripperies, picked up after Gerald inherited his great-aunt's fortune. First the Botox, then the spray-on tan, now the life coach. But Walter's expression revealed he had much more on his mind than helping Vi draft a blueprint for her life. His face betrayed a focus that bordered on desperation.

"They must be in here," Walter said. His eyes scanned the shadows, grazing right past Gerald's hiding place.

"These pews have been pushed over." The French policeman's voice sounded out from the nave. "They must have come through this way."

Lethbridge stood beside Walter. He was looking directly at the alcove where Gerald, Ruby, and Sam were cowering.

"Maybe a dog knocked them over," the constable said.

"Don't be ridiculous," Walter said. "It was them. They're here somewhere." He took a step closer to the alcove. "I can feel it."

Lethbridge suddenly jabbed his finger toward the doors at the far end of the nave. "Over there!" he cried. "I think I saw someone run outside."

Walter's head turned toward the doors. "Are you sure?"

"Oh yes," Lethbridge said. "Very sure."

Walter took off toward the entry, collecting the French policeman on the way. In seconds, they were out the door and into the night.

Lethbridge watched them leave. He then wandered toward the alcove and knelt to tie his laces.

"You three have created a ruckus and that's for sure," he said. Lethbridge lifted his head and looked straight at Gerald.

Gerald's breath caught in his throat. "You can see us?" he said.

"Good eyes," Lethbridge said. "From spotting pigeons on cloudy days. Those little gray and white beauties blend in when the weather rolls in. One time we were near Gloucester when—no, I tell a lie, it was Tewkesbury. Just off the M50 it was. Anyway, the weather turned nasty and, would you believe it, I had to—"

"Constable," Ruby interrupted. "We don't have the time."

"Oh, yes," Lethbridge said. "Pardon I. Look, what do you lot think you're playing at? Inspector Jarvis is furious."

"I didn't kill him," Gerald whispered from the shadows.

"There's plenty who think you did," Lethbridge said, still fiddling with his boots. "Your mother's friend out there is leading the charge."

Ruby shook her head. "What does she see in him?" she said.

"I think it's more what he sees in her," Sam said. "If

148

Gerald's in jail for murder I bet his parents get full control of everything."

"The DNA test came back positive," Lethbridge said. "That blowgun they found in your room is the one used to kill Sir Mason Green, and it had your saliva on it."

"That's because the woman who broke into the house to steal the ruby planted it there," Gerald said, ignoring Ruby's plea to keep his voice down. "I'm being set up." Then a memory flashed into his head. "Hold on. You were the one who told her the ruby was there, you great numpty!"

Lethbridge's face went pale. "Not Charlotte?"

"You know her?" It was Ruby's turn to ignore Gerald about the volume.

Lethbridge stiffened and sniffed back a tear. "I thought I did." His left hand rubbed at his backside.

"This is getting weird," Sam said. Ruby shushed him as well.

"Are you going to arrest us?" Gerald asked.

Lethbridge shook his head. "I don't know how you're going to convince Inspector Jarvis. He's like a dog with a bone on this one."

Gerald swore to himself. "We've got to find Charlotte. It's the only way." Then he looked back to the constable. "You better catch up with Walter and your French mate before they realize you've spent the last five minutes tying the laces on a pair of elastic-sided boots."

A sharp voice shot into the church, like an arrow into a bull's-eye.

"Are you all right, Constable?"

Walter's brash accent seemed out of place in such a solemn setting. Gerald shrank back into the shadows. Lethbridge froze like a four-year-old caught with a handful of biscuits.

Gerald held his breath as his mother's life coach materialized over Lethbridge's shoulder like a wraith from the shadows.

"Seen something?" Walter asked, his eyes sweeping the corners of the chancel like a bloodhound denied his dinner.

It was then that Sam sneezed—a nostril-blasting *watshoo!*

Ruby flung her hand across Sam's nose and mouth.

Lethbridge's eyes sprang wide, then he too let fly with a moisture-soaked *witasheeoo!*

Walter studied the back of Lethbridge's head for a second. Gerald saw that Ruby was cutting off her brother's air supply. Sam batted her hand away.

Walter's eyes narrowed. "Bless you," he said.

"Thanks," said Sam.

Gerald had to restrain Ruby from smothering Sam on the spot. But it was no use.

"I knew it!" Walter cried, and he thrust an arm into the alcove. He gripped Gerald's shoulder like a vise, and dragged him across the flagstones. "Come out, you criminal."

"Let me go!" Gerald screamed. A jolt of pain shot down his spine. He kicked out, trying to connect. But every time he moved, Walter tightened the vise. Gerald was sure his collarbone would snap at any second. It was agony.

"You're coming with me," Walter said. "Back to face justice, you little wrecking ball."

Gerald kicked out again, but missed.

"Your mother doesn't need her treatment to be bulldozed by you," Walter said, wrenching another cry from Gerald. "She's at a very delicate stage."

"What?" Gerald said. "Hasn't she given you enough of my money yet?"

Walter's face darkened. He drew back his hand and was about to strike, when Lethbridge grabbed him by the wrist. Walter had rounded on the policeman, his face ablaze with rage, when there was a colossal *bong*. Walter's eyes rolled back in their sockets and his knees gave out. He sank to the floor, revealing Ruby standing behind him, one of the large brass incense burners swinging from a chain in her hands. She looked extremely pleased with herself.

"Holy smoke," Lethbridge said.

"Look, I'm sorry, Constable Lethbridge," Gerald said, "but we're not coming with you."

Lethbridge glanced at the still-smoking incense burner in Ruby's hand. "Fine by me," he said nervously. "But where are you going to go?"

"Even if we did know, I'm hardly going to tell you, am I?" Gerald said. "But you believe me, don't you? Charlotte is the one you should be after."

"What I believe don't count for nothing," Lethbridge said. "Inspector Jarvis is the one you need to convince. And he'll be on your tail."

A low groan came up from the floor. Walter was stirring.

"You best be getting on," Lethbridge said. "I'll look after this one."

A shrill whistle blast pierced the church. Two French policemen appeared at the doors.

"Thanks, Constable," Gerald said. "I owe you."

Gerald vaulted over Walter just as he was sitting up, and a boot connected with his temple, sending the life coach slithering back to the flagstones.

Sam led the way out the northern transept. They emerged in the moonlight and found themselves in the cloisters surrounding a grassed rectangular courtyard. Doorways led off in half a dozen directions, and Sam disappeared through one on the far right. Ruby and Gerald plunged after him.

They burst into a dining hall with enough long wooden tables and benches to seat a thousand people. Gerald had no idea whether the French police were close behind them or had taken a different door, and he wasn't going to wait to find out.

A spiral staircase at the end of the dining hall disappeared to a lower level. They took the steps two at a time. The police whistle seemed to come at them from all directions. They plowed ahead.

They reached the bottom of the stairs and stopped. They had lost the moonlight, and the way forward was shrouded in shadow.

"Now where?" Ruby whispered.

"Headlamps?" Sam said, shrugging his pack from his shoulders.

"No batteries," Ruby said. "Remember?"

Just when Gerald thought they might have to retrace their steps, he caught a spark of light from the corner of his eye.

"Over there." He pointed. "Is that a lamp?"

Deep into the gloom, a flickering yellow light seemed to beckon them. Gerald tugged the straps on his backpack and set off across the room.

They found a hurricane lamp suspended from a stone column that had the girth of a sequoia. The lamp spilled a pool of golden light onto the floor. Then, further on, a doorway was suddenly illuminated in a similar hue.

"Come on, Hansel and Gretel," Gerald said to Sam and Ruby. "Someone's leaving us a trail."

They picked their way through the darkness from lamp to lamp, through a maze of interconnecting rooms and dungeons deeper into the stone forest.

"Is it the monks doing this?" Ruby whispered, sticking close to Gerald's elbow. "Leaving these lamps to mark the way?"

"Well, I don't think it's our evil stepmother," Sam said. "Have you noticed that once we reach a new lantern the one behind us goes out?"

"How would they even know who you are?" Ruby asked.

"Maybe the guy who opened the door for us saw my ring and figured Lucius is my ancestor. Word would travel pretty quickly in a place like this."

"Do you have any idea where we are?" Ruby said. "They could be leading us anywhere."

"I guess we just have to trust whoever's doing this," Gerald said. Deeper and deeper they crept, through arched openings and down damp corridors. Occasionally there was a distant blast on a whistle, but nearby the only sound was the clomp of their boots across the stone floor. Finally they stopped under a lantern by a pair of heavy wooden doors.

"We go through?" Gerald asked.

Sam looked over his shoulder. "It's darker than midnight back there. I don't think we have much choice."

Gerald pulled on a door handle and the portal creaked open. A gust of sea air hit their faces. They were in an outer walkway, high up and overlooking the southern side of the island. Far below, a ribbon of lights marked the causeway that led back to the mainland.

"That's our way out," Gerald said. "Now we've just got to get down there."

A flurry of movement caught his attention. A swirl of dark cloth disappeared around a corner of the ramparts.

"Over there," Gerald said. "It's one of the monks." He darted to the corner, positive that he had seen a cloaked figure skirt around it. But when he got there, the corridor was deserted.

"I'm sure there was someone," Gerald said. "Someone must have been leading us this way. The monks must have recognized me: They must know about my link to Lucius and the casket. But why lead us to the heights of the abbey when we need to find a way out?"

And then he saw it.

A ramp—a stone ramp, not quite a yard wide, sloped steeply, very steeply, down the side of the castle, all the way to outside the city gates.

Ruby took one look at Gerald and bucked up.

"It's not going to happen," she said. "I am not going to climb down that thing. You know I hate heights."

"Come on, Ruby," Sam said, peering over the lip of the castle wall and down the narrow buttress. "The police will be watching the gates. It's the perfect way to get around them."

"No way," Ruby said. "I won't do it." She folded her

arms across her chest. "After what happened on the Tor at Glastonbury I swore I'd never risk a climb like that again. And I won't."

Sam looked to Gerald, silently urging him to do something. Gerald thought for a second, then took Ruby by the shoulders and spun her around to face him.

"You know I'm a good climber," he said. "I'll go first, then you, and then Sam. I'll catch you if you fall."

"Fall!"

"But you won't fall," Gerald said. "Because I'll be with you. All the way." In the pale moonlight their eyes connected.

Ruby looked at Gerald for a long time. Then she pulled him into a close hug. "Only because it's you," she said, her cheek resting on his chest.

Gerald stared mortified over Ruby's shoulder at Sam, a "what's this all about?" expression on his face. Sam looked like he'd just discovered his sister was an alien with two heads and a set of gills.

"Uh, we should probably get going, then," Gerald said, giving Ruby an awkward pat on the back. Ruby unwrapped her arms and had a quick peek down the length of the ramp. "I'm not happy about this," she said.

"You'll be fine," Gerald said. "It's like climbing a ladder. One step at a time. Just don't look down."

He sat on the ledge and looked out into the night.

They were a long way up.

Gerald rolled to his stomach and eased his legs over the edge. The ramp was constructed from stone blocks, with a worn track either side of a central slab. The monks must have used it to haul things up to the abbey. It would beat carrying stuff up all those stairs, he thought. There was a deep notch between each block, perfect for fingers and toes to find purchase. It should be an easy climb down.

Gerald stopped after a few feet and called up to Ruby. "Your turn now," he said. "Face the wall and take it slow. Use the cracks between the blocks like rungs on a ladder. It's easy as."

Ruby nodded and lowered herself over the edge. Gerald could sense her fear.

But, step by step, Ruby edged down the ramp, keeping her eyes fixed on the rocks in front of her. Gerald waited until she was only a few blocks above him, then he set off again.

The breeze had strengthened and was starting to whip across the fortifications. Gerald tested each block with his foot, pushing down to make sure it would take his weight. Everything seemed secure.

Then a searchlight swept across the wall just below his feet.

Gerald froze.

"Ruby," he called. "Stop climbing."

He craned his neck. Ruby was caught between rungs. One leg was stretched down with her toes wedged into the notch between the blocks. The other foot was still jammed into the stone above.

"What is it?" Ruby whispered. "This isn't very comfortable."

"A searchlight," Gerald said. "Coming from the top of the abbey." As he spoke, a broad beam of intense white light swept just a few feet beneath them, picking out every crack and weed in the rock face.

"We have to hurry," Gerald said. "Ruby, when I say go, you have to come down to me as fast as you can. Okay?"

Gerald heard a grunted reply. The timing had to be perfect. He watched as the spotlight reached the far end of its arc, paused, then came again. This time the light was higher, scouring a path right toward him. He scrambled farther down the ramp, like a spider down a drainpipe. His boots knocked out rocks and pebbles, sending them into the void and scattering against the wall below like buckshot. Gerald glanced up to see the searchlight sweep across the blank space between him and Ruby.

"Okay, Ruby," he called up. "Your turn. On the count of three. One—"

Ruby fell.

Her lower foot slipped out of the notch and she lost her grip. Her boots landed in the smooth tracks on the sides of the ramp and she set off in a scrambling slide down the wall. The searchlight on its return arc grazed the top of her head as she shot down the ramp, hands flailing in search of a hold.

Gerald had no time to process what was coming at him.

He braced his feet deep into a crevice and wrapped his knees around the stone slab as if it was a rodeo horse. A split second before Ruby tumbled into him he pushed off with his hands, forming a safety net with his torso and arms. He batted her feet off the tracks and she landed into the cup of his lap with a thud. Gerald groaned with the strain on his legs and flattened himself to the wall, wrapping himself over Ruby like a spider's web.

For a few seconds, the only sound was the wind buffeting against them. Gerald could feel Ruby's heart pounding through her back.

His head was right next to hers; her blond hair was brushing his cheek. "You okay?" he whispered into her ear.

The screech of a passing seagull drowned out most of Ruby's reply, but Gerald was left in no doubt about how much rock climbing she would be doing in the near future.

They made it to the ground and watched Sam avoid the probing searchlight as he scrambled down to join them.

"That was a bit of fun," he said. "Anyone want to do it again?" He looked at Ruby. Her disheveled hair was draped across her face and her shirt was a ragged mess of cuts and tears. "What happened to you?"

Ruby blew a long stream of air through her nostrils like a dragon trying to start its fire. She told Sam her thoughts in words of one syllable.

Sam's eyebrows shot up. "You're not the trembling maiden now, then," he said.

Gerald tried not to laugh. "The tide's out far enough. If we keep to the side of the causeway we can run in shadow. They won't be able to see us from the top."

They crept along the rocks away from the ramp and toward the road that linked the island to mainland France.

They'd only gone ten steps when Sam stopped. "Hey, look at this," he said. He pointed to a large wire cage, easily big enough to hold the three of them. It sat on a concrete platform next to a control box and was linked to the abbey high above by a cable and winch. "Maybe the monk wanted us to use this?"

Ruby's eyes bulged.

The seagull swooped overhead again, its cry just in time to mask her response.

Chapter 12

Gerald woke with a jolt. He straightened in his seat and wiped a trail of drool from the corner of his mouth. He'd been slumped on Sam's shoulder. Sam snuffled a protest at being disturbed and rolled over against the armrest.

The bus was speeding along a motorway, making good time in the predawn traffic. Through the window Gerald could make out a cloudless sky lightening in the east. He blinked and rubbed the heels of his hands into his eyes. Rolling his shoulders as best he could without bumping Sam, he tried to get the blood flowing again.

Across the aisle the rumpled form of Ruby lay curled across two seats, fast asleep. A light snore buzzed over the drone of the bus engine.

The only light in the coach was the glow from the

dashboard. Gerald glanced down the length of the bus at the rearview mirror above the driver's head and the green-blue reflection of the man's face. The driver had seemed relaxed enough at picking up three thirteen-year-old foreigners at two in the morning from the roadside bus stop. But now Gerald wasn't so sure. Was the driver flicking his eyes up to the mirror to keep tabs on them? Gerald had an uneasy feeling.

He looked at his watch. Probably another hour before they reached Paris.

It had taken two hours to walk the five miles from Mont Saint-Michel to the small town near the motorway. Gerald, Ruby, and Sam were the only ones at the bus stop when the coach pulled in. Ruby had been adamant that they should go to Paris.

"All we've got is that old book and something about the Tower of the Winds," she'd said. "There are as many bookshops in Paris as bakeries; a bookshop is the best place I can think of to find out something about this book."

Gerald hadn't been so sure. But it was better than any suggestion he could come up with.

He watched as Ruby stirred in the bus seat. She struggled upright and wiped a hand across her face. Her hair was plastered over her eyes and stuck up at the back so she looked like a turkey. "Wozhappenin?" She blinked as the

first sunrays appeared over the horizon.

"You're not a morning person, are you?" Gerald said.

Sam propped his head on the armrest. "I'm starving," he said, not bothering to open his eyes.

"There's a surprise," Ruby said.

"No, I'm serious. If we don't get food soon, I'm going to start on these seat cushions."

"We can get breakfast in Paris," Gerald said. "But we'll have to go easy on the money. We can't risk using the credit card. You can bet Jarvis has issued an alert through the banks." He glanced at the rearview mirror. A set of eyes seemed to be staring back at him. He lowered his voice to a whisper. "We have to keep our heads down."

Sam's stomach rumbled. "Just as long as this head has something to chew on," he said, "I really don't care."

They arrived in Paris and took the metro to the Latin Quarter, joining the crush of students and workers making their way to the university and the shopping precinct.

"We came here last summer," Ruby said to Gerald as they settled into a booth in a tiny café. "Dad loves exploring the bookshops around here."

"The only reading material I'm interested in is the menu," Sam said, reaching for the plastic folder on the table. They ordered hot chocolates and croissants, and an enormous ham omelet for Sam.

Half an hour later, feeling light-headed after gorging

on pastries and jam, Gerald, Sam, and Ruby lounged back in their seats.

"That feels better," Sam said, a hand resting on his belly. "At least till lunchtime."

"Where's the book, Gerald?" Ruby said. "Let's have another look at it."

Gerald pulled the red leather volume from his backpack and laid it on the table among the cups and plates. The gilt edging on the pages glittered in the sunlight that filtered through the café windows.

Ruby opened the cover. The first page had been torn out and the other pages were covered in tiny, close-set type. "I can't follow any of this," she said.

"There must be something important in there," Gerald said. "Otherwise, why would the monks have hidden it with the ruby casket?"

"If only one of those monks had tapped us on the shoulder and told us what was going on," Sam said.

Gerald ran his fingers through his hair, which was still matted from the saltwater drenching in the grotto under the island. "I get the feeling we're going to have to figure this out for ourselves."

The waitress came over and started clearing away the breakfast plates. A cup tumbled over in its saucer as she lifted it, dribbling chocolate over the book.

"Ah!" she cried. *"Je suis désolée.* I am so sorry." She deposited the dishes on another table and picked up the book, dabbing at it with a cloth.

"It's all right," Gerald said, reaching out for the volume. "I can do it."

"*Non, monsieur.* It is my fault. I will clean it." As she fumbled with the spine, the book fanned open, and Gerald almost choked on his tongue. As the pages parted a fraction, an image appeared for an instant across the length of the gilt edges.

Gerald stared dumbstruck at the picture that had formed seemingly from nowhere. Then the waitress flattened the book again and the image disappeared, hidden behind the curtain of gold.

"There," she said. "Like new."

Gerald waited for the waitress to return to the kitchen before he said anything.

"Did you see that?" he whispered.

"See what?" Ruby asked.

"All I saw was someone doing themselves out of a tip," Sam said.

Gerald ruffled the book, twisting the spine until the cover slid back and the page edges receded.

"This," he said.

The gold edging fanned open and a vivid color illustration morphed into view.

Sam's mouth dropped open. "That's incredible," he said.

"Keep your voice down," Ruby said to Sam. A few diners had turned to look their way. Gerald, Ruby, and Sam hunched in close over the table.

The illustrated fore edge of the book stood out with stark clarity.

"It's the inside of a room," Gerald said. "With a bunch of art on the walls."

"An art gallery, maybe?" Ruby said.

"What do you think this is?" Gerald pointed to a gold line that spanned from the top of a wall on one side of the room to the bottom of the opposite wall.

"There's some writing," Ruby said. "Do you still have that pen?"

Gerald felt around inside his pack and handed the pen to Ruby. She took a paper serviette and wrote something on it. "Close the book," she told Gerald, before beckoning the waitress to come over. Gerald straightened the spine and the painting disappeared.

"That is so cool," Sam said.

"Quiet, dopey," Ruby said. "Excuse me," she said to the waitress, "can you tell me what this means?" Ruby handed the serviette to the young woman who looked at the scribbled writing.

"*La Tour des Vents?*" the waitress said. "It is the Tower of the Winds."

There was an electric silence around the table.

They declined more hot chocolate. Gerald counted out

some money for the meal and they bustled out to the street, walking and talking over each other in a stumbling jumble of feet and words.

"The Tower of the Winds!" Ruby couldn't keep her voice down. "This puts us one step ahead of Charlotte."

"The clue wasn't in the book," Gerald said, trying to contain his excitement. "It was *on* the book."

"But why would they hide the book and the casket together?" Sam asked.

"It has to have something to do with Lucius," Ruby said. "Or some story he told those original monks who helped him."

"What? And centuries later some other monks decided to paint a picture about it in a book? I don't know."

"That has to be it," Gerald said. "Something Lucius told them. Something about the ruby casket."

"So the room in the illustration—is it inside the Tower of the Winds, do you think?" Ruby said. "Is that where all this has been leading?"

"Charlotte wanted to know about it, so it must be important," Gerald said.

"There might be another clue hidden there," Sam said. "If we can find it, we find the final treasure."

Gerald stopped walking.

Sam and Ruby continued on a few paces before coming to a halt. Ruby looked back at Gerald.

"What's the matter?" she asked him.

"I'm only interested in finding Charlotte so we can hand her over to the police and get me off their most-wanted list," Gerald said. "I'm not looking for any buried treasure."

There was an awkward silence.

Ruby brushed past her brother, flicking him an annoyed glance on the way, and put her arm through Gerald's. "Of course," she said. "That's what we all want."

"I think we need to be really definite on this," Gerald said. "Charlotte and her dead uncle may have been obsessed by some priceless treasure, but I'm not. Great-Aunt Geraldine wanted me to find her killer and we did that. I just want some normality back in my life, okay?" He looked first to Sam, and then to Ruby.

Ruby was still clinging to his arm, smiling at him. "Of course," she said again, and squeezed his hand for emphasis. Her smile seemed to go on for longer than was really necessary.

"Yeah, okay," Gerald said. "How do we find this Tower of the Winds?"

"Why don't we ask somebody?" Sam said.

Ruby tilted her head and studied her brother for a second. "You know what? That might be the smartest thing you've ever said."

Sam managed to look pleased and insulted at the same time.

"We're in a neighborhood with more booksellers per

block than anywhere else on the planet," Ruby said. "One of them is bound to know something."

The next four hours were spent proving just how wrong Ruby could be. Gerald, Ruby, and Sam stumbled out of yet another bookshop, footsore and frustrated, and no closer to finding anything of use.

"This is getting us nowhere," Sam said as they stood disconsolate on the sidewalk.

"We've got to think of something else," Gerald said. "Why don't we phone Professor McElderry?"

"Oh, sure," Ruby said. "And you don't think Inspector Jarvis has tapped the professor's phone? The police would be on to us in a heartbeat." She looked across the narrow laneway. "There's one more shop over there," she said. "Let's give it a try."

Gerald dragged himself across the street.

A bell on a spring above the ancient wooden door jangled as they entered the shop. After the bright sunshine outside, it was like stumbling into a cave. Heavy curtains were drawn across the windows and a strong odor of tobacco smoke seemed to leech out of the woodwork. The tiny space was crammed with wooden bookcases, the shelves in turn stuffed with moldering volumes of all sizes. What light there was came from tall lamps dotted around the store like mushroom tops in a fairytale forest. A haze of dust motes danced in their yellow light.

Ruby wrinkled her nose. "What a smell," she said. "It's as stale as Sam's sock drawer."

"No wonder," Gerald said. "Everything looks about a million years old."

"Including the owner," Sam whispered. "Check her out."

A woman as vintage as any of the books on display perched birdlike on a tall stool behind a counter at the rear of the shop. Her skin, her clothes, and her hair were all stained the same nicotine sepia. Her head was bowed over a book and a cigarette smoldered between her fingers.

She didn't lift her eyes from the page.

"*Oui*?" It was a greeting to make an Eskimo shiver.

Gerald gave Ruby a shunt in the back. "Your turn to ask."

Ruby stumbled as she lurched toward the counter. "Uh, hello," she said, righting herself as she reached the woman. "*Bonjour.*"

The woman at the counter raised her head and looked at Ruby over a pair of brown-framed glasses that were attached to a chain around her neck.

"Yes?"

"Um . . . we're trying to find out about this book," Ruby said, holding up the red-leather volume. "And someplace called the Tower of the Winds. Have you heard of it?"

The woman put the cigarette to her lips and drew in an impossibly deep lungful of smoke. She studied Ruby over the rims of her glasses, paused, then expelled the pungent contents of her lungs into the air.

"Do I look like the tourist bureau?" she rasped.

"No, of course not," Ruby said. "Anything but. Though, that's not to say it's not a welcoming place you have here. It's very nice. *Très bon*, even. It's just that we're looking for the Tower of the Winds, and it's mentioned in this really old book and we thought you might know something about it. Not that you're really old. Though of course you are, but, um, in a good way . . ." Ruby's voice petered out to a smile of embarrassment.

The woman glared at Ruby. Then she snapped her fingers and pointed to the book.

"'Old in a good way'?" Sam whispered in Ruby's ear after she'd handed the book to the woman. "Nice."

Ruby pressed her lips together and Gerald could see she was struggling to stay quiet.

The woman bent her face close to the cover, paying particular attention to Gerald's family crest. She flicked a lamp on and it shone a yellow spot on the countertop.

"Where did you get this?" the woman asked with practiced indifference.

"It was a gift," Gerald said quickly, stepping up beside Ruby. "From some, uh, old friends of my family."

The woman shot him a skeptical glance, then expertly twisted the spine to reveal the illustration.

"As I thought," she said. "Fore-edge painting. Possibly

eighteenth century. An artistic folly: a little bit of fun and nonsense. But this one has so much detail." She opened a desk drawer and rummaged inside, finally pulling out a magnifying glass. She tipped the edge of the book forward. "You notice the imagery used here: the clock face on the ceiling, both hands pointed to twelve. A time of transition, moving from one state to another. The white line across the floor, dividing the room in two. Representing the division between good and evil, perhaps? A line that should not be crossed. The text here, identifying this as the Tower of the Winds. The frescoes—forest scenes, ancient buildings—reproduced with such precision, such *joie de vivre*." She closed the book and ran her fingertips across the cover. "It is a particularly fine piece."

"But do you know anything about the Tower of the Winds?" Gerald asked.

The woman lowered herself from the stool and crossed to a cabinet by the rear wall. She removed a key from her pocket, unlocked a sliding door, and pulled out a worn manuscript tied with a red ribbon. "This may give us some answers," she said.

She placed the manuscript on the counter and returned to her perch. A cloud of dust was liberated into the air as she untied the ribbon. She ran her bony finger down the page. "Ah," she said, flicking further into the manuscript. "Now this is interesting."

Gerald craned his neck, trying to see what the woman

was looking at. She leaned over the papers, blocking his view with her folded arms. "Now perhaps you could tell me exactly how you obtained this book?" she said, fixing Gerald with a penetrating stare.

"We didn't steal it, if that's what you mean," Gerald said, trying to look innocent. "It was a gift. Like I said."

The woman didn't blink. "Who said anything about stealing?" She stroked the cover again, trailing her stained fingers across the leather. "I assume you're interested in selling?"

Gerald titled his head. "No, not really. It's a family heirloom."

The woman arched an eyebrow. "Well, in that case," she said, "we won't be needing this." She pulled the manuscript together and started tying up the ribbon.

Gerald clenched his fists. He didn't have a choice.

"All right," he said. "We'll sell it." A sinking feeling rocked in the pit of his stomach. "Now, what does it say in there about the Tower of the Winds?"

The corners of the woman's mouth raised a centimeter. She opened the pages of the manuscript again. "The Tower of the Winds," she stated, "is a little-known annex of the Vatican Museum in Rome. It dates from the sixteenth century and was originally used for taking astronomical measurements."

"Astronomy?" Sam said. "Planets and stars?"

"Thank you, genius," Ruby said. "Top of the class."

The woman pulled the pages back together and tied the ribbon.

"Hold on," said Gerald. "Is that it?"

"That," the woman said, reaching for her cigarettes, "is it."

Gerald snatched the book back from the counter. "Then I'm not selling," he said.

The woman regarded him evenly. She placed another cigarette in her mouth and struck a match. "If I was on the run, I would not wish to be weighed down by such an item," she said. She lit the cigarette and blew a pall of smoke in Gerald's face.

"On the run? What makes you think—"

The woman flipped over a newspaper on the counter. Gerald couldn't understand the headline on the front page, but the large photographs of him, Sam, and Ruby told a clear enough story.

"I will do you a deal," the woman said, drawing in another lungful of smoke. "I will purchase this book from you. And I won't ring the police."

Gerald tightened his grip on the book.

"I don't think there's any other option, Gerald." Ruby was at his elbow, her hand on his shoulder. "And we could do with some cash."

Gerald gritted his teeth. After a lifetime of not giving a toss about his family, now, for some reason, anything that was linked to his personal history was of immense importance. The rings on his hands seemed to tighten around his fingers as he held the book to his chest.

The woman lifted a beaten tin box onto the counter and opened the lid. "One hundred euro is a fair price," she said, and held out a wad of folded notes.

Gerald looked at the money. Then he closed his eyes and handed over the book. Sam took the cash and slipped it into his pocket. "Nice doing business with you," he said. "Come on, Gerald. Let's go."

Gerald was almost at the door when he stopped and turned back to the old woman.

"There is one other thing," he said.

The woman was engrossed in the book and didn't bother to look their way. "The night train to Rome leaves from Gare de Bercy," she said. "You should make it if you go now."

The bell jangled above their heads as Gerald, Sam, and Ruby filed back onto the street.

"So we're going to Rome?" Ruby said.

"If that's where the Tower of the Winds is, then I guess so," Gerald said.

They walked back to the main road and the metro station. There was a large map of the area on a poster outside the entrance.

Ruby studied the grid of city blocks and interconnecting

rail lines. "The Gare de Bercy is just across the river," she said, with a satisfied nod. "An easy trip on the metro. We should get there in plenty of time."

They turned to climb the stairs down to the subway but found a station worker sliding a metal screen across the entrance. "*La station est fermée*," the man said.

"Closed?" Ruby said. "Are you kidding me? What for?"

The station worker ignored them and disappeared down the stairwell.

Sam groaned. "Now what do we do? I don't want to walk all that way."

"We could take a cab," Ruby said. "But that costs money. And the traffic is ridiculous. It could take forever. What do you think, Gerald?"

Ruby looked to Gerald, but he was staring down the street. There was a mischievous glint in his eye.

"Maybe there's another way," he said.

Gerald brushed past Ruby and Sam and walked to a row of bicycles lined up in a rack on the side of the street. Cars and scooters whizzed past the sidewalk. "They're rental bikes," he said. "It only costs a euro and there'll be a bike stand at the train station for sure. It's cheaper than a taxi and probably quicker."

A minute later they each held the handlebars of a gunmetal-gray bicycle with a natty basket attached to the front.

"Right," Ruby said. "See if you can keep up." She pushed

down on the pedals and took off into the stream of traffic.

Gerald was still adjusting the height of his seat and was caught off guard. He leaped on and surged off in pursuit. "Come on, Sam," he called back over his shoulder. "Don't let her get there first."

Gerald was having the time of his life. He was in one of the most exciting cities on earth with two of his best friends, in hot pursuit of a goal he could hardly fathom. The sun was on his face and a sense of freedom infused his bones, like he'd been pumped full of helium and might soar into the Parisian sky.

Ahead of him, Ruby was already weaving in and out of lanes choked with cars and lorries and scooters.

"Come on, Sam!" Gerald cried. "She's getting—"

Gerald's foot slipped from the pedal as he looked back toward the bicycle rental station and he juddered to keep upright. Sam's bike lay abandoned on the footpath. And Sam was desperately trying to wrestle free from the two policemen who had him firmly by the arms.

CHAPTER 13

Gerald had to choose.

Help Sam? Or escape?

The policemen held Sam tight despite his kicks and struggles. One gendarme wrenched on a flailing arm till it was pinned between Sam's shoulder blades. Sam's face shone a belligerent red. He was being bundled into the back of a police car, still kicking and screaming.

Then Gerald saw the man in the front passenger seat staring right at him.

Inspector Jarvis.

And he had blood in his eyes.

He barked an order. The policemen shoved Sam inside and slammed the door. One gendarme jumped behind the driver's wheel and the other set off on foot, after Gerald.

The moment to choose had passed. Gerald turned and pressed down on the pedals, cycling like fury to catch up with Ruby.

Sam was on his own.

"Ruby!" Gerald urged the heavy bike onward, dodging through the clogged traffic. "Ruby!" He caught up with her half a block away.

"Where's Sam?" she asked, the thrill of the ride glowing on her face.

"Police." Gerald tried to catch his breath. "Jarvis got him. The bike stand."

"What?" She slammed the brakes and threw her head around to look back down the street. In the distance, they could see the flashing light bar on top of the police car. It was stuck in the late afternoon traffic. But the lone policeman on foot was gaining on them. Gerald could see him talking into his police radio as he ran.

"We've got to get away!" Gerald yelled.

"But what about Sam?" Ruby's eyes were fixed on the car that held her brother prisoner. "We can't leave him."

The policeman was only a few feet away, edging between the stalled lanes of cars and trucks. Gerald shook Ruby by the shoulder. "We've got to go," he yelled at her. "Now!"

Ruby let her eyes linger a moment too long. The policeman had almost reached them. He was only a car length away. His face was bright red and Gerald watched in despair as he lunged toward Ruby. But just as he stretched out an arm, a young woman on a scooter appeared between two cars and straight into his path. Gerald shook Ruby even harder and screamed: "Go!"

Ruby snapped out of her trance and mounted her bike, driving the pedals hard. Gerald was on her tail, surging forward with each pump of his legs. He glanced over his shoulder to see the policeman still trying to untangle himself from the woman on the scooter. Jarvis was way behind, stuck in traffic. But so was Sam, and Gerald knew another difficult decision was looming.

He powered ahead, drawing up beside Ruby. "Quick, down here," he called, and they veered off the busy street into a narrow laneway. The lane ended a hundred feet ahead at a stairway to a lower terrace. Gerald spun his rear wheel around in a wide arc and skidded to a halt. Ruby pulled up and was off the bike in a second, letting it clatter to the ground. She ran up to Gerald, anger etched into her face.

"What happened?" she demanded. "How did you let them catch him?" Her eyes were red and she was breathing fast.

"I didn't let them do anything," Gerald said, taken aback by her ferocity. "They must have been waiting near the station and jumped Sam as we took off. Jarvis is with them—giving the orders."

Ruby wasn't listening. She pounded her fists on Gerald's

chest. "Why didn't you help him?" She was furious. "You could have done something."

Gerald, still straddling his bike, almost fell to the cobbles as he jumped to avoid the barrage of punches.

"Stop it, will you?" he shouted. "There was nothing I could do. There were too many of them. They would have got me too."

Ruby dropped her fists and bit her bottom lip. "This really slows us down," she muttered, almost to herself.

"What do you mean?" Gerald said.

"We can't miss that train to Rome," Ruby said, pacing up and down the cobblestones. "Any delay and we risk Charlotte getting there first." Gerald could see she was weighing a dozen options that were bouncing about in her brain. Then she stopped. A decision had been made.

"We have to leave Sam," she said.

"What?"

"There's no other choice. How can we possibly steal him away from the police? It can't be done. We have to go on without him."

Gerald was gobsmacked. "But we can't just leave him," he said.

"Why not? They'll take him back to London and our parents will collect him. It's not like he's done anything really wrong. It's you that Jarvis wants, not us."

Gerald didn't know what to say. Ruby seemed determined

to abandon her brother and keep on with the hunt.

"He'll even put in a good word for you, Gerald," Ruby said. "You know, with the police."

"But he's your brother," Gerald said.

Ruby didn't seem to hear him. She nodded, her mind made up. "It's the best thing to do. We can still make that train if we hurry."

Gerald stared at Ruby in disbelief. It was like he'd never met her before. Ruby had always had a determined streak, but this was something else. Abandoning her own brother?

But deep down, Gerald knew she was right. There was nothing they could do to help Sam now.

He picked up his bike and threw his leg over the crossbar. "Okay," he said, "where's the station?"

Ruby jumped on her bike and headed back toward the main street. She had gone only a few yards when two gendarmes drifted across the opening to the laneway. And stopped.

Gerald didn't wait. He called to Ruby to follow him and spun his rear wheel around, and they bolted back along the lane, with the policemen chasing after them.

Gerald was standing on the pedals, driving the bike toward the narrow set of stairs. He looked back to Ruby. She was pumping the pedals with everything she had. But the gendarmes were keeping up, even gaining on them. They were wearing Rollerblades, and were sprinting like speed skaters at the Winter Olympics.

Gerald doubled his efforts, driving himself forward, straight at the stairway.

"Get ready to jump!" he yelled back to Ruby. Then he launched himself over the lip of the top step. The bike soared out into the void. Gerald lifted himself off the seat and braced for the impact of the landing. He seemed to float in air for ages. Then his rear tire clipped a step about two thirds of the way down. The jolt rattled through the heavy frame and shook every bone in his body. The front wheel touched down and Gerald pulled back to stop himself flipping over the handlebars. A teeth-jarring second later he was on the lower level. He shot like a bullet down a rifle barrel between two parked cars that were squeezed onto the gutters on either side.

Gerald glanced back over his shoulder just as Ruby took off from the top step. He couldn't tell whether the scream was one of delight or terror, but she landed her bike, with a crunch of metal and buckling spokes, and sped along the lane toward him.

"That was awesome!" Ruby screamed as she skidded to a halt. "I so want to do that again."

"Maybe some other time," Gerald said. "But at least those guys on skates won't get down here so fast."

Gerald almost choked on the words. Behind them the two police officers appeared at the top of the stairs and didn't hesitate. They leaped into the air, slammed their skates onto the metal handrails, and grinded to the bottom in a blur of blue uniforms.

"Let's go!" Ruby yelled, and peeled around a tight corner into a winding backstreet. Gerald was on her rear wheel, coursing in her wake. They sped past a string of street cafés, the coffee drinkers' heads turning to watch them fly by, followed seconds later by the two policemen on skates. Ruby led the way, bouncing over the cobbles, riding like a jockey on a Thoroughbred with the finish line in sight. But with the two policemen in close pursuit, there seemed no end to this race.

Gerald caught up with her, driving hard. "Keep going," he called. "You're slowing down." The shouts from the pursuing policemen followed them around a tight corner.

Ruby hoisted herself onto the pedals and pushed harder, but she still drifted behind. Gerald looked back with alarm.

"You've got a puncture," he called. "Your back tire is flat."

Ruby looked urgently over her shoulder. The two policemen were only a few steps behind; Gerald could make out Ruby's reflection in their wraparound sunglasses.

"Jump onto my bike!" Gerald yelled. He stood up, leaving the saddle open for Ruby to make the leap.

"Are you nuts?" Ruby yelled back. She struggled to keep pace, her rear tire dragging in the ruts and grooves of the roadway.

"There's no time to stop. Jump for it."

Gerald eased back until the two bikes were level. Ruby glanced over her shoulder; one of the gendarmes had sprinted ahead. He was barely two steps behind them.

"Now, Ruby!" Gerald yelled. "Do it now!"

Ruby stared at Gerald, dread on her face. The gendarme had closed the gap to a foot or two, the clatter of his skates against the cobbles a staccato drumming in the air. Ruby gave a frantic burst of pedaling, inching ahead of Gerald as they reached a downhill stretch. She then stood on one pedal and spun her other leg over the seat so she was standing on one side of the bike as it coasted along.

"Get ready, Gerald," Ruby called, "here I come!" Using all her strength and gymnastic agility, Ruby threw her trailing leg around and she spun across the gap to the seat on Gerald's bike. She landed with a grunt, facing back toward the pursuing policemen. One stretched out a hand, but just as he touched her shirt the abandoned bike slid under his skates.

The crash sent the gendarme skidding across the cobbles, wiping out a flimsy wooden table outside a café. Ruby's eyes widened at the scene as diners flooded out of the building to find a policeman buried in a pile of tables and chairs.

"Oh my," Ruby said.

Gerald leaned forward and struggled to keep up the pace with the added weight on board.

"The other policeman's still coming!" Ruby yelled over her shoulder. "Hurry up!"

Gerald tried to blink away the sweat running into his eyes. "Hurry up? I'm cycling for two up here."

"Lucky you're such a big strong man then, isn't it? Now shut up and pedal."

Gerald dipped his head and powered on. He knew his thighs couldn't take much more of this—they felt like they would explode at any moment.

"Come on, Gerald! He's catching up."

Gerald glanced back. He was horrified to see how close the policeman was. They emerged from the winding street onto a broad junction. Across the busy intersection Gerald spied a possible way out.

"Hold on," he said to Ruby. "This could get rough."

He plowed through the crossing without missing a beat. Cars and vans skidded to avoid them—the junction filled with the squeal of brakes and the smell of burning tire rubber. Gerald surged on, jumping the gutter with the front wheel but hitting it hard with the rear, sending Ruby jolting into the air before she landed back in the saddle with a squeal.

"Steady on," she cried. "I haven't got much to hold on to here."

They shot across a broad footpath and through a large set of iron gates into an enormous park. The gendarme stuck to them like chewing gum in hair.

Gerald bolted along a crushed stone path, past wooden

benches and a line of statues toward a lake. Children playing with wooden sailboats were snatched out of the way by
their parents as Gerald tore by, closely pursued by the flying
gendarme.

Then Gerald saw a team of workmen on a path leading
deeper into the gardens. They were leaning on their shovels
by a barrow of gravel.

"This better work," he called back to Ruby. "Think
light thoughts."

He turned the handlebars and steered right at the cluster of workmen. The gendarme was seconds behind. Gerald
sucked in a huge breath and gave it his all, streaming his
energy into the pedals. They hit the freshly dumped layer
of gravel, tires biting deep. The workmen jumped clear.
Rock chips sprayed out behind as the wheels sunk into the
path. The bike slowed, sending Ruby flying forward into
Gerald's backside, her feet spread wide in the air. The shunt
from behind urged Gerald onward and he kept the bike
moving. But the fresh gravel was too deep for the pursuing
policeman. His skates hit the path and he came to a crashing halt, face first onto the loose stones.

Ruby broke out into an enormous grin. "Oh my gosh,
Gerald. You did it."

Gerald didn't look back. The angry cries from the workers told him to keep moving. He gave one last surge and the
bike broke free from the path's clutches. They passed some

playground equipment crawling with children and cruised through a set of gates on the far side of the park and onto a narrow street outside.

Gerald was spent.

"Let's never do that again," he said to Ruby. "My legs are killing me." He wiped the sweat from his forehead on his sleeve and started a slow pedal through the deserted backstreets.

"Are we still taking the train to Rome?" he said.

Ruby tapped Gerald on his side. "Stop here."

Gerald pulled over and rolled off the bike to collapse onto the gutter. He stretched his legs out in front of him and rubbed his burning thighs. Ruby stood over him, clearly considering her next words carefully.

"Sam would want us to go on," she said. "To find the Tower of the Winds."

"But he's your brother," Gerald said. "I thought twins were super close."

Ruby rubbed her fingers against her temples and screwed her eyes shut.

"What is it?" Gerald said.

"I'm getting a message," she said.

"A message?"

"Yes. A message from my stupid twin brother, who was too slow to avoid the police."

Gerald frowned at her. "Yes, very funny. But seriously.

You want to go on without him?"

"It's not what I want to do," Ruby said. "It's what we have to do. I know it. You know it. And Sam knows it too."

Gerald dropped his head. He just hoped that Sam would forgive him one day.

This time, Ruby sat facing forward on the bike and they eventually found their way to a main road.

"I think there's a bridge up here. That'll take us across the river," Ruby said. "It can't be much farther."

Gerald slammed on the brakes. Ruby shot off the seat and buried her face in Gerald's backpack. "What'd you do that for?" she shouted.

Gerald stabbed a finger toward the middle of the snarl of traffic ahead of them. "That's Sam," he said. "In the back of that police car."

Ruby shoved the pack out of the way and looked to where Gerald was pointing. The car was crawling ahead at a snail's pace in the center lane, hemmed in on both sides by traffic. They could see the blond hair on the back of Sam's head through the rear window and what looked very much like the shape of Constable Lethbridge sitting beside him.

"What do you think?" Gerald said.

Ruby swung off the bike seat. "I think you better go wait beside that laneway up there and get ready to ride like you're in the Tour de France." Then she ducked low and scouted ahead, keeping below the tops of the cars. Gerald pedaled along the sidewalk, holding back, until the police car had passed the laneway. He stopped and watched Ruby shadow the car that was carrying her brother. He could make out Inspector Jarvis in the front, next to the driver. Ruby was a car length behind them, and one car to the right.

The flow of traffic came to a halt.

Then Ruby made her move.

She calmly walked between the lanes of cars to the back door of the police car, and tapped on the window. There was a pause, then a flurry of activity inside the vehicle. Both front doors shot open as Jarvis and the driver tried to get out. But because the lanes of traffic were so tight, the doors couldn't open more than a few centimeters. Again and again, Jarvis and the driver banged at the doors. But they were stuck. The muffled sound of shouting came from inside.

Ruby tapped at the window again. In the backseat, Lethbridge raised his hands to Jarvis in a gesture of "what do I do?" There was more shouting. Then the window wound down. Lethbridge peered out at Ruby with a sheepish grin on his face.

"Hello," he said.

But that was all he had the chance to say. The moment the window was open far enough, Ruby shoved Lethbridge aside and dived headfirst through the opening. She grabbed Sam by the front of his shirt and, with a single heave, pulled him right out the window. To Gerald, it was like watching a baby giraffe being born.

Sam landed on the road in a shambolic heap. His hands were bound behind his back with cable ties. He writhed around on the ground before Ruby took him by the collar and lifted him to his feet.

Jarvis was screaming from inside the police car: screaming at the driver, at Lethbridge, and finally at the gods. There was another barrage of door banging, which was answered by shouts of protest and the blaring of horns from the drivers of the vehicles that were hit.

Ruby and Sam appeared at Gerald's side. Sam had a huge grin on his face. "I knew you'd come and find me," he said. Ruby ignored Gerald's pointed look while she shunted Sam onto the bike seat.

"Come on, Gerald," she said, lifting herself into the basket on the handlebars. "We've got a train to catch."

Gerald launched the bike down the narrow laneway toward the river. With three on board, it was especially hard going—and it wasn't made any easier by Ruby singing "Raindrops Keep Falling on My Head" at the top of her voice as they bounced along the cobblestones.

CHAPTER 14

Ruby turned the lock and tested the compartment door. It held firm. She flopped back onto a lower bunk and propped her feet against the window. Outside, the suburbs of Paris were gliding by, bathed in the pale yellow light of the dying day.

On the opposite bunk, Gerald laid out a small feast. Baguettes, cheese, ham, olives, a box of chocolates. He twisted the top from a bottle of cola and took a long swig before passing it to Sam. Sam was rubbing his wrists, trying to get the blood flowing again after being released from the tight cable ties. He took the bottle with a nod of thanks and drank deep.

"That Inspector Jarvis has it in for you, Gerald," Sam said, passing the bottle to Ruby. "He was furious that the French police let you get away. He's convinced that you killed Green. I don't think he's going to give up the chase anytime soon."

Gerald sliced open a baguette with his pocket knife and layered in some ham and cheese. "How about Lethbridge? Wasn't he putting in a good word?"

"He tried," Sam said. "But Jarvis wasn't listening. He's obsessed."

"Did Jarvis ask you anything?" Ruby said. She accepted a baguette from Gerald and took a bite.

"Ask me anything? He didn't stop. 'Where are you going? Who are you meeting? Are you armed?'"

"Armed!" Gerald said, spraying breadcrumbs across the train carriage. "As if we'd be carrying guns."

"Like I said"—Sam bit into his roll—"he's obsessed."

"So what did you tell him?" Ruby asked.

Sam finished his mouthful and swallowed. "That Gerald was on a quest to return a magical monkey's fist to a curio shop in the grand bazaar of Cairo before the next full moon or all humanity was doomed."

Gerald and Ruby looked at him in disbelief.

Sam took another bite. "I don't think he believed me, though."

Ruby's eyes rose to the carriage ceiling. "At least he doesn't know where we're actually going," she said. And then, "You idiot," for good measure.

Gerald smiled to himself. It was good to have everyone back together again. Sam polished off the last of his roll and broke off a chunk of cheese. "So what's the plan from here?"

"Well, the train gets into Rome tomorrow around ten," Ruby said. "I guess we head to the Vatican Museum and find the Tower of the Winds."

Gerald cocked his head. "The Vatican Museum—doesn't Professor McElderry have a friend who works at the library there? He mentioned him when he was first researching my family seal."

"You're right," Ruby said. "Maybe it's time to give the professor a phone call?"

"Weren't you worried that the police might be listening in to his calls?" Gerald said.

"Maybe it's time to start taking a few risks."

Sam popped an olive into his mouth. "Yeah, we haven't done near enough of that so far."

Gerald pulled his wallet from his pocket and went through the contents. "I've got enough to buy a phone card and not much else. Those train tickets have wiped us out."

Sam eyed the black American Express card inside the wallet. "You couldn't use that?"

"One risk at a time," Gerald said. "We can't let Jarvis know where we are." He folded the wallet shut and slid it back into his pocket. "I'm not sure what we're going to do for cash now."

Ruby lay flat on her bunk and fluffed up a cushion for a pillow. "I can go busking in Rome," she said.

Sam laughed. "I don't think freak shows bring in much

money." He ducked as Ruby's pillow hurtled across the compartment.

"I meant I can sing," Ruby said.

Sam clambered up to a top bunk. "I don't think freak musicals do much better."

Gerald wrapped up the dinner leftovers and shoved them into his pack. They'd have to be breakfast as well. Then he kicked off his boots and sank into his bunk. His legs ached from the bike ride, but a sense of calm washed through him. He took a pen from his pack and tried to re-create the illustration from the book on the back of a train menu. But he couldn't concentrate. He reached into his pack and retrieved the ruby. The gem seemed to vibrate in his hand. He wrapped his fingers around it and closed his eyes. Soon the roll of the train, the clickety-clack of the wheels, and to a lesser extent, the sound of Ruby's singing lulled him to sleep.

That night, for the first time in a long time, Gerald dreamed about Sir Mason Green.

It wasn't like the dreams that had dogged him in India, where Green had somehow infiltrated his subconscious using one of the golden rods. Those events were painful, distressing—like someone had attached a vacuum hose to his forehead and tried to suck out his brain.

This dream was actually relaxing. Gerald and Mason Green were enjoying a quiet lunch together in one of the private dining rooms at the Rattigan Club in London.

"Some bread, Gerald?" Green held out a silver plate laden with rolls.

"Thank you, Sir Mason," Gerald said, selecting a sour-dough roll. "Very kind of you."

"Not at all, old chap. Now, tell me, how is the hunt going?"

"That's the strangest thing," Gerald said. He placed a pat of butter on the side of his plate. "I'm really not that clear on what it is I'm looking for. We're always running and chasing and hurtling along. But we never get closer to anything. It's very frustrating."

Green topped up his glass from the bottle of wine chilling in an ice bucket. "The first rule of any hunt, Gerald, is know your quarry. That's where you're going wrong. From the start, I knew exactly what I was after. You have never had a clue. And yet, what you seek is very close by. You just need to look within yourself, Gerald. It's all there."

A slender woman, her dark hair pulled back in an efficient bun, appeared at the table, and laid a bowl of soup in front of each of them. Gerald couldn't remember ever smelling anything quite so delicious.

"Ah, this looks good," Green said, laying his napkin on his lap. "You've met my niece, haven't you, Gerald? She's a dab hand in the kitchen."

Gerald looked up to find Charlotte beaming down at

him. She produced a pepper grinder from behind her back.

"Cracked pepper?"

Her uncle declined.

"And you, Gerald?" Charlotte said, holding the grinder above his steaming bowl. "Cracked poison for you?"

"Poison?"

"Slip of the tongue," Charlotte said with the faintest of smiles. "Pepper, naturally."

"Uh, no thanks," Gerald said. He wasn't sure he wanted to taste the soup after all.

"Do dig in, Gerald," Green said. He held a spoonful to his lips. "It's very good."

Gerald could feel Green and Charlotte staring at him, waiting, while he dipped his spoon into his bowl.

The soup smelled so good. Gerald brought the spoon to his mouth and closed his lips around it. The liquid warmed his throat. Green and Charlotte watched with satisfaction. Then Gerald's throat started constricting, as if someone was clenching his hands around his neck. His head jolted back and forth, and panic welled in his eyes. His airway was cut off—he couldn't breathe.

Just as he thought he was going to pass out, he sat up and banged his head, prompting a snort from Sam in the upper bunk.

Gerald rubbed his forehead and stared into the blank darkness of the train carriage. It was an hour before he could rid his thoughts of Sir Mason Green and finally fall asleep again.

Gerald, Ruby, and Sam crammed into the phone booth inside the main entrance to Rome's Termini train station. The concourse was an ants' nest of activity, with commuters dashing to trains that were heading out across Italy and all over Europe.

Gerald held the phone to his ear and motioned for Sam and Ruby to stop arguing. "It's ringing," he said. Then the call to London was answered. "Professor McElderry? Hello? It's Gerald."

There was a pause at the other end of the line. Then the reply came back, "Oh, hello . . . Mother."

Gerald cupped his hand over the mouthpiece. "He just called me Mother."

"There must be somebody with him," Ruby said. "The police, maybe?"

Gerald took his hand away and held out the phone so they could hear. "Is there somebody else there?" he asked the professor.

"Oh, about half past ten," McElderry's voice crackled through the tiny speaker.

Gerald shot a concerned look to Sam and Ruby. "Professor, we need to see your friend at the Vatican library—do you think you can arrange it?"

"Um, half a dozen eggs and a pickled herring will do nicely."

Gerald screwed up his face. "Is that a yes?"

"Just ask for Dr. Serafini, Mother. He'll see you right."

Gerald motioned for Ruby to write down the name. "Dr. Serafini? Is he your friend at the library?"

The professor's reply was sharp and to the point. "Yes, that's right, Mother. Is your dementia acting up again?"

"We found another ring, Professor," Gerald said. "And there's a third gold rod, but Green's niece stole it from us. She wanted to know about the Tower of the Winds. Do you know it?"

"The Tower of—" McElderry checked himself. "I'll call the doctor myself and make an appointment for you. He sounds exactly the right person to help you with your . . . condition. Turn up this afternoon and I'm sure he'll see you straightaway."

Ruby and Sam gave Gerald a thumbs-up. Gerald took a long breath before speaking again. "Are we in big trouble?" he asked the professor.

McElderry's voice sounded through the phone speaker. "Put it this way, Mother, unless you find the cure to your condition very soon, I don't like your chances."

The queue outside the main entrance to the Vatican Museum snaked and baked its way for hundreds of yards along the sidewalk, with no respite from the fierce summer sun. Gerald, Sam, and Ruby were happy to bypass the thousands of tourists outside and take a side entrance into the air-conditioned comfort of the main building. They were ushered into an office overlooking a vast grassy courtyard. A young woman asked them to wait, and went to fetch Dr. Serafini.

Gerald and Sam wandered over to the tall windows that looked down on the courtyard. Tourists gathered in whatever shade they could find.

"Do you think this guy is going to let us see the tower?" Sam said.

Gerald shrugged. "This is a dead end if he doesn't."

"It's all pretty fancy," Ruby said, as she studied the collection of baroque paintings that lined the high walls. "Oh my gosh, is this a Caravaggio?"

A deep voice rumbled across the room. "Not a particularly good one, I'm afraid, Miss Valentine. But they have to hang them somewhere."

Gerald looked up to see a bear of a man filling the doorway. He stood over six feet tall. His cheekbones formed an overhang as treacherous as anything in Gerald's school climbing gym, and he wore a dark beard like a burglar might wear a balaclava. He could have stepped from any one of the paintings on the walls. He looked at Gerald and smiled.

"Ah, you are admiring the Cortile della Pigna—my little garden plot. It is quite a view, yes?"

"Mr. Serafini?" Gerald said.

"I prefer Dr. Serafini, please. Doctor of Religious Antiquities. Our mutual friend McElderry speaks highly of you, Gerald, and you, Miss Valentine." His eyes settled on Sam, who had picked up a small statue from the desk in the middle of the room. "And this must be Mr. Valentine," Dr. Serafini said. "Knox has spoken of you as well." His eyes moved to the statue in Sam's hands. "Perhaps you might place that back where you found it. It survived the sacking of the Serapeum in Alexandria in 391 AD; it would be a shame for it not to survive you."

Sam replaced the statue, which wobbled for a second on its fragile base but then settled into place. "There."

Dr. Serafini said, "All is as it should be. I'm sure Knox was mistaken when he said you were the stupidest boy in the world."

"Huh?" Sam said.

"You are twins? Always interesting things, twins."

"Things?" said Ruby.

"Rome was founded by twins, of course," Dr. Serafini continued. "Romulus and Remus, descendants of a prince and raised by wolves, so the story goes. Now there's a childhood! And of course there's the legend of Castor and Pollux, the Dioscuri."

"Dios—?"

"Dioscuri—twin brothers from Greece. You may have heard of their Latin name—Gemini. A very interesting pair. When Castor died, Pollux was so upset that he asked the gods to let him share the death."

"How do you share a death?" Ruby asked.

"Pollux would spend one day enjoying life on Olympus while his brother was in the underworld. Then they'd swap places the next day. A fairly good arrangement, given the circumstances."

Sam looked confused. "How do you mean, underworld?"

"He means dead, Sam," Ruby said. "He means you'd spend every other day dead and buried."

Sam thought for a few seconds. "Well, that doesn't sound much fun at all."

Dr. Serafini studied Sam with a wary eye. "Knox may have been on to something after all," he said. He turned to Gerald. "I am so glad you have come to visit, young Wilkins. Come, I have something to show you."

Dr. Serafini crossed to the desk. In the center of the polished wooden surface sat a shallow rectangular box, about a foot long. A piece of soft leather covered the top.

"What is it?" Gerald asked.

Dr. Serafini pulled back the cover. "I was hoping you would tell me," he said.

It was a wooden display case. Under the glass top was a piece of yellowed parchment covered in writing of the faintest ink. A black leather lace was threaded through two holes at the bottom of the paper, and tied in the middle was a gold disk, about the size of a hockey puck.

"I think you might recognize this," Dr. Serafini said to Gerald.

Pressed into the gold disk was the clear impression of three forearms clamped at the elbows forming a triangle around a blazing sun.

"Your family seal, I believe," Dr. Serafini said, watching Gerald's reaction. "Professor McElderry was asking about it some weeks back. When he told me you were coming, I thought you might like to see it."

Gerald looked carefully at the disk. The detail in the metal was exquisite.

"What does the writing say?" Ruby asked.

"This, Miss Valentine, is a letter written in 394 AD by one Quintus Antonius to Theodosius the Great, emperor of Rome."

Gerald took in a sharp breath.

Quintus Antonius.

His ancestor.

"Professor McElderry told us the emperor sent Quintus and his three sons on some secret mission," Gerald said, scarcely able to believe what he was seeing.

"As ever, Knox has done his research," Dr. Serafini said. "This letter is a report of that very mission."

"Does it say anything about golden rods?" Sam asked.

Gerald winced, and he saw Ruby screw her eyes shut.

Dr. Serafini glanced sideways at Sam. "Nothing as interesting as that," he said. "My Latin is a little rusty, and this letter is written in the vernacular, the common language of the day. It is possible to translate it many ways."

"That's okay," Sam said. "Just give it your best shot."

Dr. Serafini looked at Sam again. "My best shot, eh?" He pulled a pair of glasses from his pocket and adjusted them on his nose. He then read the letter written to the emperor more than sixteen hundred years ago.

Our group is a day's ride from Brundisium. We meet with a company of your legionnaires in a week. All is unfolding as planned. I will take the young men into my confidence once we are at sea. My sons serve Rome well. Your eternal reign is secure.

Your servant,
Quintus Antonius, Consul of Rome

Gerald's eyebrows were arched high. "Wow. Do you have any idea what they were doing?"

Dr. Serafini peered at him over his glasses. "I thought you might know something about that."

Gerald felt Dr. Serafini's eyes drilling into him. "There was a map in London," Gerald said. "With three paths coming out of Rome. We thought it might have shown the routes taken by Quintus's sons when they smuggled the . . ."

His voice trailed off. He suddenly felt very uncomfortable with the direction the conversation was taking.

Dr. Serafini tilted his head a little. "Smuggled?"

"Three golden rods," Sam chimed in. Ruby landed a sharp kick to her brother's right ankle, sending him to the floor with a yelp of pain.

"Aren't you clumsy?" Ruby said to her brother. She helped him to his feet. "You ought to take more care." She turned to Dr. Serafini. "Three olden roads," she said. "What my clumsy brother was trying to say was they must have taken three olden-day roads on their trip to wherever." She gave a light laugh.

Dr. Serafini stroked his beard. Gerald could tell he didn't believe a word Ruby said.

"Brundisium is the ancient name for Brindisi," Dr. Serafini said. "It was the main port for all Roman shipping to Greece. Ferries still ply the route today."

"So Quintus was traveling to Greece?" Gerald said.

Dr. Serafini folded the leather cover back over the display case. "Possibly. But wherever they went, it's ancient history now," he said. "However, I digress. Knox tells me you are interested in the Tower of the Winds."

"That's right," Gerald said, happy to move the conversation on. "I hear there's some interesting paintings in there. Sam is really interested in art."

Dr. Serafini raised an eyebrow.

"He is?"

"Sure," said Sam. "Why not?"

"You don't strike me as the sit-down-for-a-long-period-of-time type of boy. But yes, there are some extraordinary frescoes in there. Come. It will be my pleasure to show you."

Sam shuffled next to Gerald as Dr. Serafini led them out of the room and down a long corridor. He whispered into Gerald's ear, "What's a fresco?"

Ruby was about to take another shot at Sam's ankle, but Dr. Serafini turned around to face them. "The Tower of the Winds is not open to the public. It would be too difficult to manage crowds in such a tight space; few have seen its treasures."

"Is it true the tower was first used as an observatory?" Sam asked.

Dr. Serafini gave him a surprised look. "That's right. The meridian hall still has the marble line across the floor where they marked their observations of the positions of the sun hundreds of years ago."

They stopped in front of a door. Brown paint was peeling from its surface. Dr. Serafini opened it and they went inside.

"Take a seat," he said. "I'll be back in a minute."

"Where are you going?" Ruby asked.

"To fetch a key," he said, smiling. "I won't be long."

Dr. Serafini pulled the door closed. And then came the

sound of a lock turning.

Gerald moved to the door and rattled the handle. It wouldn't budge.

"I don't like the look of this," he said. He crossed to the windows on the opposite wall.

"Why would he lock us in?" Ruby said, and she tried the door again.

"I don't want to hang around to find out," Gerald said. "There's a ledge out here. It runs the length of the building. I reckon we could climb down to the courtyard."

Ruby joined him by the window and looked at the twenty-foot drop to the ground below. "You're not serious?"

Gerald tugged on a metal bolt that secured one of the windows. "Dr. Serafini seemed awfully interested in the golden rods," he said. The bolt worked free and Gerald pushed the window open. "He may not be as friendly as he makes out."

But before Gerald could climb onto the sill, the door behind them opened.

Dr. Serafini stepped into the room, followed by Constable Lethbridge and the stern-faced figure of Walter. And in the corridor beyond, it seemed, was half the Vatican security service.

CHAPTER 15

A broad white bandage was wrapped around the top of Walter's head. He greeted Gerald through gritted teeth. Gerald looked from Walter to the open window.

Ruby stared at him in alarm. "Gerald, don't . . ."

Then Walter stepped forward. "Let me speak to the boy. I'm trained in child psychology," he said to Dr. Serafini, who nodded and left the room, closing the door behind him.

"Don't be mad with Dr. Serafini," Walter said to Gerald. "He contacted us after hearing from Professor McElderry this morning. He was concerned about your safety." Walter gave Gerald a look of practiced pity. "As we all are, Gerry."

"Rubbish!" Sam said. "You're just worried about Gerald's money."

Walter smiled. "Such negative energy in one so young."

"Is that right? How's the head?" Sam replied.

Walter's smile vanished. He placed a hand on the bandage and pressed his lips together. "I am willing to forgive the assault by your sister," he said. "Don't push it."

Walter faced Gerald and forced another smile. "You are a child. A simple boy. Your brain isn't developed enough to be making important decisions. That's why you're in such trouble. I bet you find yourself in trouble at school all the time. Am I right? You need to let an adult decide for you. I know what's best."

Gerald couldn't believe what he was hearing. "Is that how you see my mother? You know what's best for her, too?"

Walter took a pace toward Gerald with his hands extended. "Come home, Gerry. Face up to what you've done. Confession will shore up your foundations—give you a firm footing from which to construct a new and better tower of you. Now, you will have to start your new life in the basement. Or prison, more like. And it may delay access to your inheritance for a few years. But what are years at your age? And your mother, with my guidance, will manage the estate for you."

Ruby snorted. "How considerate," she said.

Walter lowered his hands. "It's the best offer you're going to get today, son," he said. "The constable and I are ready to take you home."

Gerald turned to Lethbridge, who was standing just

inside the closed door. "You know there's no way I killed Mason Green. It had to be Charlotte."

The policeman was gazing out the window with a lost look on his face.

"When you saw her," Lethbridge said, "did she mention me?"

Gerald was surprised by the question. "Um, I think she said something about meeting you."

Lethbridge sighed deeply. "She was very beautiful. Her lips . . . they were like a big jam doughnut . . ."

"I'm not sure I'd put it quite like that, but yeah, I guess she had nice lips."

Lethbridge's gaze was stuck on the window. "All I ever wanted was a friend," he said. "And my pigeons." Clouds drifted over the sun, drawing a gray curtain across the sky.

"Constable Lethbridge?" Ruby said. "Are you all right?"

Lethbridge's eyes misted over. "You really think you can catch her?" he asked.

"I really think we have to try," Gerald said.

Walter had heard enough. "Listen, you." He walked over and prodded Lethbridge in the chest. "Your job is to bring this kid back to England to face justice. No one cares about your love life. Cuff him and let's get out of this dump."

Lethbridge reached for the handcuffs on his belt.

The door banged open and Gerald was bundled into the corridor, his hands behind his back and a scowl set on his face. Lethbridge had a heavy paw on his shoulder and was shoving him forward.

"Stop struggling!" he barked. Gerald muttered a curse under his breath. The constable turned to the group of security guards who were still waiting in the hallway. Somehow they all had cups of coffee. "Thank you for your assistance," Lethbridge said. "*Molte grazie*. We have a car waiting to take us to the airport."

Lethbridge was followed out of the room by Sam and then Ruby, who pulled the door closed behind her.

Dr. Serafini stepped from an adjoining office, a puzzled expression on his face. He called after Lethbridge as they barreled down the corridor. "What about the American?"

Lethbridge looked back over his shoulder, still pushing Gerald ahead of him. "He's on the phone to the embassy," he said. "He won't be a moment."

Lethbridge shoved Gerald harder. By the time they reached the end of the corridor they were almost running. They burst around the corner and set off.

"How long do you think we've got?" Sam asked, his feet skating across the tiled floor.

"As long as it takes for Walter to free himself," Gerald said.

"Those handcuffs aren't coming off without a key," Lethbridge said. "And that radiator pipe will take some moving. He won't be going anywhere for a while."

"Nice touch with the sock, by the way," Sam said to Gerald. Gerald felt his bare right foot squelching inside his boot.

"I wouldn't fancy having it stuffed into my mouth," Gerald said. "I haven't changed it in three days. But it should keep Walter quiet for a bit."

Ruby laughed. "It couldn't have happened to a nicer person."

They reached a flight of stairs and took them two at a time. Gerald stepped over a velvet rope strung across the top and into a gallery full of tour groups.

Lethbridge, Ruby, and Sam clustered around him. "Which way now?" Ruby asked.

"Dr. Serafini said the Tower of the Winds isn't open to the public, and I don't fancy asking a security guard for directions," Gerald said.

"Maybe we should join the tourists and keep an eye out for a sign?" Ruby said.

"I guess that's as good a plan as any," Gerald said. He turned to Constable Lethbridge. "Thanks for helping us get away, but it's probably best if we go it alone from here. You tend to stick out a bit."

Lethbridge nodded and wiped his palm down the front of his trousers. "The least I could do," he said, shaking Gerald's hand. "I was getting sick of being bossed around by that fellow anyway."

"Won't you be in trouble?" Ruby asked. "Will Inspector Jarvis be angry?"

Lethbridge snuffled a laugh. "Inspector Jarvis was born angry. I'll say you forced me to do it."

"What!" said Gerald. "Won't that get me into trouble?"

Lethbridge turned to the exit. "No more trouble than you're already in, sunshine," he said. And with a wave, he was lost in the crowd.

"He's not as silly as he looks," Gerald said.

They tagged on to the end of a school group and tried to blend in. They passed through gallery after gallery with walls and ceilings covered in murals.

"Look," Ruby said to Sam, "I think we're coming up to the Sistine Chapel." Before Sam could open his mouth, Ruby said, "Don't ask. Just look and appreciate."

The torrent of tourists swept through a doorway and emptied into a large chamber. The first thing Gerald noticed was that everyone was looking up with their mouths flopped open.

His eyes were drawn up too.

And he joined the slack-jawed masses.

"Oh my," Ruby whispered. "It's . . . magnificent."

The ceiling of the Sistine Chapel stared back at the crowd below. The entire surface, including the walls, was covered in the most extraordinary frescoes. Light poured in from tall windows, lifting the colors on the walls to even greater brilliance.

"Look," said Ruby. "*The Last Judgment. The Creation of Adam*. It's astounding."

Even Sam seemed impressed. Gerald scanned the walls. The artist had divided them into a jigsaw of shapes, all filled with re-creations of the stories of antiquity. Hundreds of figures were depicted across the ceiling and walls, their clothes a rainbow of oranges, yellows, and blues. Cherubs and angels vied for attention with mortals and prophets. Around the perimeter were a dozen giant portraits, each with its name inscribed underneath.

An Irish priest guiding a party of nuns around the chapel stopped beside Gerald. "Look, sisters," he said. "The twelve seers. There's Daniel. And Ezekiel. Over there is Jonah. And right in front of us is the sibyl of Delphi." Gerald followed their gaze to a painting of a young woman holding a scroll in one hand. She was one of the most beautiful women he had ever seen. She had a purple cape over her shoulders and her head was wrapped in a plain scarf. She looked off to the side, as if distracted by someone entering the room. What was she thinking? What could she see?

It took the blast of a police whistle to snap Gerald back to reality.

His head darted around, searching for the guards. The whistle seemed to come from all directions at once. But another blast pinned the origin. By the chapel entrance stood three security guards.

And they were all pointing at Gerald.

Ruby dashed up to him, dragging Sam by the arm. "The exit's this way," she said, and dived into the crowd.

The guards moved as one, making their way through the crush of tourists. Gerald didn't falter—he flew after Ruby and Sam, and they elbowed their way to the exit.

"Quick!" Ruby said. "Through here."

She hurdled a velvet rope strung across a narrow entryway and they bolted up a tight stairwell to a small alcove facing a closed wooden door.

Gerald turned the handle and they bustled into a gallery that seemed to stretch on forever—the high vaulted ceilings accentuated the narrowness of the room. The walls were hung with enormous paintings of maps, which gave the gallery a blue hue of water.

All the tourist traffic was coming toward them. Gerald could see they would have to battle the tide.

"We can't go that way," he said with a jab of his thumb. "That'll take us back to the Sistine Chapel."

Ruby prodded him between the shoulder blades. "Then lead on, MacGerald," she said. Sam gave her a confused look and she raised her eyes to the ceiling. "I'll explain later."

Sam fell in behind Gerald as he plowed through the various groups of school students and retired Americans. They finally reached a set of glazed double doors and heaved their way into another long gallery. This one was hung with enormous tapestries.

Gerald ducked into a corner next to the doorway. On the ground was a map of the museum that someone must have dropped. He unfolded it and Sam and Ruby crowded around to see.

"We must be here," Gerald said, pointing to a long gallery on the western side. "But I can't see 'Tower of the Winds' marked anywhere."

Ruby took the map and studied it closely. She shook her head. "Nothing," she said. "What do we do?"

Sam had taken a step back and was staring vacantly down the gallery. "What do you think *Torre dei Venti* means?" he asked.

Ruby and Gerald looked up from the map. "What was that?" Ruby said.

"*Torre dei Venti*," Sam said. "It's on a signpost up there." They followed the direction of his outstretched finger to a slender wooden pole with a number of cross boards showing the way to various galleries. "*Torre* sounds like tower. And *Venti* could be winds. It sounds right. What do you think?"

Ruby stared at her brother for a second—then hugged him. "You continue to surprise me," she said, giving him an extra squeeze.

Sticking close to the side of the gallery, they managed to avoid the main flow of tourists and were almost at the signpost when Ruby grabbed Gerald.

"Guard," she said in his ear. "Over by the stairs."

They shrank back and pretended to admire one of the tapestries. Gerald sneaked a look over his shoulder. The guard had a finger to his ear and seemed to be focused on listening to something through an earpiece.

"Is he getting an update on us?" Sam said.

"Well, I don't think he's listening to football," Gerald said.

Ruby looked further up the gallery. "Those stairs at the end must lead to the tower," she said. "There's nowhere else the sign can possibly be pointing to."

"How do we get past laughing boy?" Gerald said, nodding toward the guard. "Dr. Serafini knows we're looking for the tower. There's no way it's going to be left unwatched."

Sam patted Gerald on the shoulder. "Have you seen this?" He pointed to the tapestry in front of them. It was a particularly graphic depiction of the assassination of Julius Caesar in the Roman Senate, complete with thrusting daggers and tormented faces.

"That's great, Sam," Ruby said. "But now's not the time to discover a love of art."

"Don't be daft," Sam said. "This." Sewn into the tapestry in golden thread, at the bottom of a pillar, was a triangle of forearms, linked at the elbows, around a blazing sun.

Gerald shook his head. He was beyond being surprised by his family crest turning up in strange places. He resisted the urge to bend down and touch it. It couldn't be there simply for decoration—it had to signify something. An idea popped into his head.

"Gerald?" Ruby asked. He put a finger to his lips and glanced at the guard by the stairs, then ducked into the narrow gap between the tapestry and the wall.

"What are you doing?" Ruby said. Gerald could tell his feet were clearly visible beneath the tapestry. "There's no point hiding there."

Gerald popped back out with a huge grin on his face. "I wasn't hiding," he said. "I've found something."

He beckoned Ruby and Sam to follow him. But before they could take a step a shrill whistle cut through the crowd's murmuring.

Everyone in the gallery froze. The guard by the stairs to the tower had his finger to his ear again. The doors at the end of the gallery were open, and the three guards from the chapel stood in the entryway.

"Stop where you are!" The tallest of the guards at the door pointed a baton at Gerald.

Gerald's eyes darted about. It was a long shot. But it was the only shot they had. "On my signal," he said to Sam and Ruby, "drop to the floor and roll behind the tapestry."

Ruby nodded. "Okay. What's the sig—"

"FIRE! FIRE!"

Gerald's shout rang along the gallery. In a second, there

was a screaming stampede for the exits.

Gerald, Sam, and Ruby hit the tiles and barrel-rolled behind the tapestry. Gerald pushed Ruby through a tight manhole in the wall. Sam was through a second later. The feet of panicking tourists pounded by just centimeters away. The whistle kept up a constant screech, but it wasn't getting any closer. The guards couldn't make headway against the rolling crush of the crowds funneling through the doors. Gerald scrambled after Sam. He glanced back to see four sets of black boots on the other side of the tapestry. He fitted the manhole cover back in place and wished he could see the guards' faces when they realized that the three runaways had vanished.

A dim light from high above illuminated the tight crawlspace behind the wall. It was as if they were sitting in a fireplace and staring straight up the chimney. A series of iron rungs fixed into the brickwork led to the top. Gerald squeezed into place and started to climb.

Hand over hand, he hauled himself up. His backpack scraped against the bricks behind him and he strained to make as little noise as possible. Finally, he emerged in a cramped alcove at the start of a passage; the ceiling was so low he had to sit on the floor. He shunted along to make space for Ruby and then Sam as they climbed out of the shaft.

"I wish we'd got new batteries for the headlamps," Ruby whispered. "I can't see a thing."

"It's all right," Gerald whispered back. "Looks like the only way out is along here and it seems lighter up that way."

He started along the passage on his hands and knees. As far as he could tell, they were angling back across to the other side of the tapestry gallery. Up ahead, light filtered through a cluster of holes in the center of a panel in the wall.

Sam and Ruby bunched up behind Gerald as he put an eye to one of the holes.

"Can you see anything?" Sam whispered. For a few seconds, there was no response. "Gerald?"

Gerald looked back over his shoulder, his eyes bright. "I think we might be close," he said.

"What is it?" Ruby asked.

Gerald put a finger to his lips and turned back to the panel. He ran his fingers around its edges and found what he was looking for. He twisted two wooden latches, took hold of the anchor points on either side, and shoved it. Light flooded into their escape tunnel, blinding them for a second. Gerald tumbled through the opening, rolling onto a cold floor of brown paving stones. Ruby and Sam followed.

"Wow," said Sam.

And that seemed to sum it up for Gerald and Ruby as well.

They were standing in the heart of a chamber that seemed to climb to the heavens. Every wall was covered in brightly colored frescoes. One depicted a shipwreck, its survivors struggling onto a rocky shore. High above, the ceiling was painted an intense blue. Angels and cherubs danced around its perimeter. In the center, directly above Gerald's head, was what appeared to be an enormous clock face, its hands pointed together.

"This must be the Tower of the Winds," Ruby whispered. "It's just like the picture on the book."

Gerald turned a full circle to take in the kaleidoscope of colors and images. It was almost too much to digest. Then he looked down to the floor and saw the white line that split the room in two, just as Dr. Serafini had described it. It ran from the tunnel opening they'd fallen through across to the opposite wall. In the center of the room, where Gerald was standing, the line bisected an octagonal design set into the tiles. Each of the eight points in the octagon was connected by thin lines to every other point.

"What do you make of this?" Gerald asked, pointing to the pattern at their feet.

"Looks like a compass to me," Sam said. "North, south, east, west, and the points in between."

"But what's any of this got to do with the three golden rods?" Ruby asked.

Gerald was following the white line to the far side of the room when Ruby called out, "Gerald, there's something on the back of your head."

A ghostly spot had appeared right in the middle of

Gerald's mop of dark hair. He smacked his hands over his crown, but the spot remained.

"It's a light," Sam said. "Coming from up there." He pointed to high up the wall behind them. A beam of light was shining through from a painted sun in a fresco depicting a boat on pitching seas.

"There's a hole in the wall," Gerald said, the light now shining on the middle of his forehead like a laser. "The clouds must have cleared."

"Get out of the way, Gerald," Ruby said. "I want to see where it's pointing."

Gerald stepped aside. The light fell on a painting at the bottom of the opposite wall. "Now, why has this one been singled out from all the others in the room?" Ruby said.

It was a rather plain painting in reddish browns of a man in a traveling cloak sheltering from winds blowing in from the puff-cheeked gods in the clouds.

"He's copping some weather," Gerald said. "What does that tell us?"

"Not much," Ruby said. "But maybe this writing does."

Sam nudged in next to her shoulder. "What's it say?"

The spot of light fell on faded lettering in the scrollwork beneath the painting.

"*Skiron di Atene*," she said. "I guess it's Italian."

"Athens," Sam said.

Ruby looked at him. "I beg your pardon?"

"*Atene*. It's Italian for Athens. Capital of Greece."

"You are on fire!" Gerald said, clapping Sam on the shoulder. "How about the first bit? Skiron. Is that a place in Athens?"

"I haven't heard of it," Sam said. "But it could be."

"Greece," Ruby said. "That's where Quintus and his sons were going. Dr. Serafini said so, from that letter to the emperor. This must be the clue that the monks left on Gerald's book. The Tower of the Winds shows us the next step—Athens."

"The clue that Charlotte was looking for," Gerald said. He sat back on his heels. "Skiron must be where Quintus was heading on his secret mission. So that's where we need to go too."

Their exit from the Tower of the Winds was a lot easier than their entry. They followed a corridor from the fresco chamber and found themselves at the top of the stairwell that led down to the tapestry gallery. There was no sign of the guard. The crowds had returned after Gerald's impromptu fire drill, and within minutes Gerald, Sam, and Ruby were through the nearest exit and back on the street.

"How are we getting to Athens?" Ruby asked as they retraced their steps of earlier that day. "The airport will be on alert. Probably the train station as well."

"And we don't have much cash left," Sam said.

They reached the piazza in front of St. Peter's Basilica.

Banks of seating stood vacant under the rain-threatening sky. A few pilgrims made their way to the last of the day's tour buses parked around the perimeter. All across the piazza pigeons scavenged for stray seed in the cracks between the paving stones. At the far end, in front of the steps leading up to the basilica, a choir was rehearsing; snatches of a hymn floated on the breeze.

Gerald was about to set off toward the closest metro station when Ruby stopped him.

"Look. Isn't that Constable Lethbridge?" She pointed to a lone figure seated by a tall column in the center of the piazza. His elbows were on his knees and he was staring at the police cap in his hands. He didn't look up when Ruby tapped him on the shoulder.

"Are you okay, Constable?"

Lethbridge gazed up at them through tired eyes. "My name's David," he said. "I don't think I'll need the *constable* bit anymore."

"You're going to quit the force?" Gerald said. "Don't do that. I'll tell Inspector Jarvis it was all my fault."

Lethbridge studied the badge on the front of his cap. "I was always rubbish at being a policeman," he said. "All I ever wanted was to breed pigeons. Run a little loft somewhere in the country. Meet a nice girl . . ." His voice trailed off.

Ruby gave Gerald and Sam an uncertain look. None of them knew what to say.

The clouds scudded across the sky. The choirmaster urged his choristers to greater heights.

Lethbridge turned to Gerald. "Your mother is here," he said.

"She is?" Gerald was surprised. "Why?"

"Her only child has run away from home accused of murder. I'd say she's worried about you. She and that Walter fellow are staying at the St. Regis."

Gerald was surprised to find a lump in his throat. He tried to swallow it down. "Thanks," he said. "Thanks, David."

"What will you do now?" Ruby asked Lethbridge.

The constable folded his cap into a tight bundle and shoved it into his pocket. "Start planning the next bit of my life, I guess."

"You've got to chase your dreams," Ruby said.

Lethbridge gazed across the piazza and nodded. The choir was building, voices soaring like birds. A fresh gust of wind parted the clouds and a shaft of sunlight fell onto the paving stones twenty paces away—right onto the figure of a young woman feeding breadcrumbs to the flock of pigeons and doves that was descending around her.

As if in slow motion, she tossed back her head, throwing out a mane of auburn hair.

Lethbridge looked like he'd just seen an angel. He stood, reached out, and shook Gerald, Sam, and Ruby by the hand.

"Best of luck," he said. "And thank you. Now, excuse I."

Before any of them could respond, Lethbridge was marching toward the woman. He paused, bent down, and scooped one of the birds up in a meaty paw.

"Will you look at that," Ruby said.

Lethbridge was talking to the woman. And she was talking back. There was lots of gesticulating and finger pointing. Nodding of heads. Then the woman laughed.

"Do you think he speaks any Italian?" Gerald said.

"He doesn't need to," Ruby said. "He speaks pigeon. And so does she."

"I hate to admit it," Sam said, "but that's sweet."

"What's the matter, Sam? Are you going all soft?" Gerald said. They wandered out of the piazza toward the station.

"No, it's not that," Sam said. "Old Lethbridge wasn't that bad. It's nice to see good things happen to good people."

Ruby threw her arms around Gerald and Sam's shoulders as they descended the stairs into the subway.

"Then let's hope we count as good people," she said.

Chapter 16

Gerald stared at the number on the door. It was painted a brooding shade of red and matched the flamingo of the corridor walls and the maroon of the carpet. His finger hovered a centimeter from the doorbell. He'd assured Sam and Ruby that he was okay with this, that they didn't need to worry about him. Gerald had left them in a piazza to find a phone box while he set off on this task alone.

But now he was having second thoughts.

What if she wasn't pleased to see him? What if Inspector Jarvis was inside waiting?

What if?

What if?

Gerald swallowed. And pressed the doorbell.

The door flung open almost immediately—as if someone inside had been waiting for him.

A woman launched herself across the threshold and threw her arms around his neck.

Gerald gave in to the embrace, instinctively closing his eyes and breathing in the familiar scent of Chanel No. 5 and cold tea. Vi Wilkins pulled her son into the hotel suite and spun him around, making his boots skiffle across the top of the plush carpet.

"My darling boy," she trilled, a little too shrilly, in Gerald's right ear. "I've been worried sick."

Gerald's face was pressed into his mother's bosom and for a second he struggled to breathe.

"Mum!" His muffled cry searched for an exit from the folds of the silk blouse. "Mum! Lemmego!"

With a shove, Gerald managed to extract himself from his mother's bear hug. He stumbled backward and his foot caught the corner of a coffee table, sending him to the floor.

He stared up at his mother—and was shocked at what he saw.

Tears.

Genuine tears.

His mother was crying.

"Mum, what's the matter?"

Vi let the tears track channels through her makeup. She dropped to her knees and took Gerald's hands.

"We've been so worried," she sniffed, her eyes ringed in red. "We had no idea where you were, if you were safe. Your father's in London in case you turned up back there. He's in a state and all. Why did you run, Gerald? You know we'll always support you, no matter what you've done."

Gerald pulled his hands from his mother's grasp. "But I haven't done anything!"

"Of course you haven't. That's what I meant to say. Your father and I just need to know that you're safe."

Gerald wasn't sure what to make of his mother's performance. "But Mum, all you seem to care about is the money," he said.

Vi was fiddling with an enormous diamond ring on her right hand. "Oh, Gerald, that's not true. I won't deny I've enjoyed your new wealth. But anything I've done has been with your long-term interests in mind, my darling boy. When you were born, your great-aunt Geraldine paid for all of us—your father, me, and you—to move to Australia. She insisted it would be better for your health. I wasn't keen at first. I thought she was trying to hide us away on the far end of the world. But I always tried to keep in Geraldine's good books. You know. Just in case. So I put up with the heat and the flies and the isolation and that appalling accent. And it's paid off, my darling boy. Look at us now!"

"Mum, I'm on the run accused of murder."

"Yes. Well. Apart from that, everything else has gone swimmingly."

Gerald tugged on his mother's hand and she sat on the rug next to him.

"Mum, when we were in India, Mr. Hoskins told me

that Geraldine sent us to Australia because she thought I was special somehow. She wanted to protect me."

Vi spun the ring on her finger. "I suppose there must be some reason she left you all that money."

Gerald pulled out the photograph of Great-Aunt Geraldine from his wallet. It was damaged at the edges after the drenching in the grotto. He peeled open the billfold. It was empty. He laughed to himself. "Walking-around money," he murmured.

"What's that, dear?"

"When Geraldine left me her estate, she also left me this wallet. It was full of cash—walking-around money, she called it." He laughed again, then sat upright, electrified by a jolt of realization. "It's all walking-around money!"

"It's all what, dear?"

"Her whole fortune—all the money, the houses, helicopters, and yachts. It's all one huge wad of walking-around money, to give me the freedom to find the secret."

"Secret? What secret?"

"Behind the hidden caskets, Mum. Why our ancestors defied an emperor and paid for it with their lives. Why Mason Green was so desperate to get hold of the golden rods. And why Charlotte has taken over where he left off."

"Charlotte?" Vi was having trouble keeping up.

"Geraldine wanted me to solve this puzzle and she left me the means to do it. If only I had those letters she left for me too." Gerald felt a surge of determination reignite his insides. The path forward was clear. He pulled himself up from the floor.

"Gerald?" Vi looked at her son with uncertainty. "What are you going to do?"

Gerald leaned down and kissed her on the cheek. "What Great-Aunt Geraldine wanted me to do."

He crossed to the door but paused before opening it. He turned back to face his mother. "Mum, about Walter . . ."

Vi wafted a hand through the air. "Oh, I've sacked him," she said.

"Sacked Walter!"

"Yes. He turned up here an hour ago spouting some nonsense about being assaulted by your little friend Ruby and being manacled by that nice Constable Lethbridge. And some rubbish about your sock, Gerald! I could hardly trust my emotional and physical future to someone as unstable as that."

Gerald smiled wider than he had in ages. "I love you, Mum."

Vi looked surprised. "Why, I love you too, my darling boy."

Sam and Ruby were waiting, just as they'd arranged, by a fountain in a piazza. Children splashed in the shallow water, shrieking with delight. The square was teeming with tourists and locals taking in the warm evening air.

"Here you go," Gerald said. He handed Sam and Ruby

a thousand euros in cash each.

Sam's eyes bulged. "Where did you get that?"

"Billionaire," Gerald said. "Remember?"

"I'm hardly going to forget," Sam said as he folded the money into his pocket. "But I thought you weren't going to use your credit card."

"I wasn't going to. But then I passed an American Express office and thought, why not? Jarvis knows we're in Rome, so there's no harm using it here. And I told the teller I needed the money for a trip to Portugal. That should buy us some time. So, did you guys make your phone call?"

Ruby screwed up her face. "Yeah. Mum was pretty upset—glad to hear from us and everything. But worried."

"Did you tell her what we agreed?"

"She left that to me," Sam said.

"I can't lie to my own mother," Ruby said. "Even for you, Gerald." Her cheeks flushed and she turned away to look at the children playing in the fountain.

"Lucky for us I have no such issues," Sam said. "They're convinced we're on our way to Russia."

"Great," Gerald said. "Between that and Portugal, Jarvis should have no idea where to look. Now we just have to get to Brindisi."

Ruby let out a light sob.

"What is it?" Gerald asked.

Ruby's chin was on her chest and her eyes were closed.

"This better be important, Gerald. I'm letting down a lot of people here."

Gerald put a hand on Ruby's shoulder. "You don't have to come," he said. "You can be on a plane home tonight if you want."

Ruby wiped her eyes with the back of her hand and sniffed.

"Nah. Can't bail out now and leave you behind, can I? Besides"—she sniffed again—"I've never been on a ferry."

Chapter 17

By the time the battered Kombi van rattled into the Athens bus station, Gerald had lost all feeling in his buttocks.

The side door opened and he rolled out onto the buckled concrete driveway.

"Numb bum," he said, jumping on the spot to get the blood flowing again. "Numb bum."

Ruby insisted on giving the three Swedish backpackers they'd hitched a ride with a one-hundred-euro note.

"Please take it," she said. "You've been so helpful."

Sofia accepted the money with a summer-tanned smile. She hugged Ruby and they all waved farewell as the van coughed and pulled into the choking Athens traffic.

It had been three days since Gerald, Ruby, and Sam

had left Rome, and they were living the backpacker dream. They'd taken a bus to Brindisi, and there had been no sign of Inspector Jarvis or any incidents with the Italian police. From Brindisi they'd caught a ferry to Greece, retracing the route taken by Quintus and his sons more than sixteen hundred years before.

On the ferry they'd met Sofia, Anna, and Malena.

"I reckon Sofia was keen on me," Sam said, still waving as the van disappeared from view.

Ruby shook her head. "There's no delusion like self-delusion," she said. She pulled her backpack onto her shoulders. "Come along. Let's see if anyone can help us get to Skiron."

The bus terminal bore the effects of years in the Athens sun. Traffic grime caked the outside walls, and weeds endured stubbornly in the cracks in the paving. A dozen stray cats of all colors and patterns lay spread-eagled in whatever shade they could find.

Ruby pushed on the glass door and they walked into the squat terminal building. It was almost deserted. A couple sat at a round table, their suitcases nearby, and sipped on small cups of coffee. An elderly man dozed, propped in a chair in the corner. Another man, alert to the newcomers, wandered up and offered to sell them lottery tickets. When Ruby declined, he shrugged and went back to his seat by the window.

Sam eyed a café at the far end of the room, and a glass case stuffed with pastries. "Why don't you go ask at the information desk while I find us some lunch," he said.

Gerald watched his friend saunter over to the café. "Does he ever not think of food?"

Ruby looked across at her brother and gave a shrug. "Only when he's eating," she said.

The information desk had a few faded posters of islands and beaches stapled to the front, and some curled postcards tacked to the wall. Ruby picked up a tourist map from a stack on the counter. It was coated in a thin film of dust. A woman sat behind the desk, chewing gum. She was engrossed in a novel and didn't look up.

"Hello," Ruby began, "we're trying to find a town called Skiron. Can you help?"

The woman snapped her gum. The expression on her face didn't need translating. She glanced over at a group of men who were clustered around a table at the far end of the depot.

She shouted out to them in Greek. One of the men yelled something back. She responded with another shout.

"What's going on?" Gerald asked Ruby.

"Not sure," she said. The verbal volleys grew in intensity.

"They must be related." It was Sam, back from the café. His cheeks were covered in pastry flakes. "Want some?" He held out a bag of triangle-shaped delicacies. Gerald and Ruby munched in silence while the shouting continued.

Finally, the woman picked up her novel and jerked her head in the direction of her opponent. "He will take you," she said, returning to her book. "Taxi."

"Is Skiron close by?" Gerald said.

"Quite close—maybe thirty minutes from here." The voice belonged to a tall man who had ventured across from the group in the corner. He extended a hand toward the door. "My taxi is out the front."

In the forecourt stood a car that looked like a refrigerator box on wheels. Its front bumper was held in place with duct tape. The hubcaps were missing and the hood was almost rusted through. The taxi was parked under a scraggly tree and the mottled shadows made it look even more like the subject of a machine-gun attack.

"We're seriously getting in that thing?" Sam said.

Ruby studied the vehicle from under an arched eyebrow. "It does look a bit rattley."

Gerald grabbed a door handle and pulled. He nearly jerked his shoulder from its socket. The door didn't budge.

"You need to use your hip," the driver said. He thumped into the side of the car and lifted the handle at the same time, jolting the door free.

Gerald peered inside. A faded blanket was spread across the backseat; a corner was scrunched up to reveal torn vinyl and disintegrating padding underneath. Asleep in the middle of the blanket was a large ginger cat.

"Um," Gerald said, looking back at the driver.

The man frowned at the backseat and clicked his tongue. He reached in and grabbed a handful of ginger fur at the back of the cat's neck and hauled it out. The cat was dumped under the tree. It took two steps, then flopped onto its side in the shade.

"It's times like this that I miss Mr. Fry," Sam said. They piled into the back of the taxi.

The driver dropped behind the wheel and the car lurched to the side, the springs groaning under the shift of weight. "You want to see Skiron, yes?"

The taxi engine fired into life and they edged away from the bus station into the packed Athens traffic. The driver introduced himself as Christos and kept up a steady travelogue as they wound through the center of town.

Under the relentless summer sun, the inside of the car was stifling. "Do you have air conditioning?" Sam asked. "It's roasting back here."

"You have a choice," Christos said, glancing at Sam in the rearview mirror. "If the air is on, the car is off. This way is better, I think." He wound down his window and a hot gust blasted the back of the taxi. "Nice breeze."

Sam flopped back into the seat. "What are we going to do when we get to Skiron?" he said. "It's not like we have any idea what we're looking for."

Ruby leaned her arms on the top of the front seat. "Is Skiron very big?" she asked the driver.

"Big?" Christos said, sounding surprised. "No. Not very big. The same as the others."

"The others?" Gerald said, but Christos didn't reply.

Twenty minutes later they pulled off the main road and entered a twisting maze of narrow laneways, bordered on each side by whitewashed buildings with front doors opening right onto the street.

Christos drove into a small square and pulled over to the side of the road. An imposing hill, rocky and sparsely treed, towered above them. An ancient building was perched on top.

"What do you make of that?" Gerald asked Sam.

Sam blinked up at the building's white columns, stark against the brilliant blue of the sky.

"Isn't that the Acropolis?" Sam asked.

"That's right," Christos said. "The birthplace of democracy."

"But," Sam said, "isn't the Acropolis in Athens?"

There was an awkward silence.

"We're in Athens," Christos said. "Where did you think we were?"

"You were meant to take us to Skiron," Sam said.

The taxi driver turned in his seat and stared at Sam, Ruby, and Gerald.

"Skiron isn't a place," he said. "Skiron is a person."

"A person?"

"Yes," Christos said. He twisted in his seat to point out

the window. "He's over there."

Gerald led the exit from the back of the car. His eyes followed the direction of Christos's pointed finger toward a large block of land that was overgrown with weeds and wildflowers and strewn with the remnants of ancient buildings. At one end—the target of Christos's finger—stood an eight-sided building.

"What? Does he live in there?" Sam said.

Christos regarded him evenly. "You're not the smartest boy alive, are you? That's the Tower of the Winds."

Gerald's jaw dropped. Had he heard right?

"There's a Tower of the Winds in Athens?"

"Of course," Christos said. "It's been here for two thousand years. Go and have a look."

Gerald looked to Ruby. "Why not?" she said. "We've come this far."

Gerald paid the fare and Christos turned the taxi in a tight circle. "Say hello to Skiron for me," he called out the window as he motored out of the square.

A spiked iron fence ran around the outside of an area about the size of a soccer field. It was littered with broken columns and chunks of castoff marble. Stray cats poked their heads above the clumps of grass and weed, playing tigers in the grass. Gerald walked up to a ticket booth and bought three passes from the elderly woman sitting inside. "Uh, Skiron?" he asked.

The woman poked a thumb toward the white marble tower at the end of the block.

"This must be it," Gerald said. He increased his pace across the stony ground. "This must be what the clues have been leading us to."

Sam and Ruby rushed to keep up with him.

"I wish I shared your confidence," Sam said.

"What do you mean?"

"The taxi driver said Skiron was a person, right?"

"Yeah."

"And we found out about him from a painting in the Tower of the Winds in the Vatican, right?"

"Yeah," said Gerald, this time with less certainty.

"A painting done four or maybe five hundred years ago."

"Um . . ."

"And you're thinking this Skiron bloke has been hanging around here since then, on the off chance that you might pop by for a chat?"

"Sam?" Gerald said.

"Yeah?"

"Shut up, will you?"

They reached the tower and gazed up at its smooth marble walls. The eight sides rose twelve meters or so and were capped by a conical roof. A man in dusty blue overalls was sweeping a path that ran around the base of the tower.

"What do you think?" Ruby said. "Could it be him?"

Sam snorted. "He must be the oldest cleaner in Athens, then."

"Weren't you shutting up?" Ruby said.

Gerald gave a determined nod and walked up to the man. "Excuse me?" he said.

The man stopped sweeping and looked at Gerald. He did seem incredibly old. "Yes?"

"Skiron?" Gerald asked, his eyes widening.

The man looked at Gerald as if he hadn't heard him quite right. Then a smile spread across his face. "Skiron," the man said with a slow nod.

Gerald was astounded. Could this possibly be the man mentioned in a five-hundred-year-old painting?

"You . . ." Gerald started. "You're Skiron?"

The man nodded again. "Skiron." Then he pointed to the top of the tower behind them. "Skiron."

Gerald looked closely at the upper portion of the building. Each of the eight walls was topped with a carving, a frieze, showing a man in the midst of some activity.

Gerald had a sinking feeling in his gut. "One of those guys is Skiron?" he asked.

The man took Gerald to a corner of the tower and pointed to a carving of a bearded man flying through the sky and carrying a pot with smoke wafting from it.

"Skiron," the cleaner said. He pointed in the direction the bearded man faced. "Hot winds. Yes?"

Gerald nodded slowly. "The hot winds come in from this way?" he said. "And Skiron is some god or other who blows them in?"

The cleaner smiled and gave Gerald the thumbs-up. "Skiron," he nodded. "Hot air."

"You got that much right," Ruby said. The man smiled again and went back to his sweeping.

Gerald flopped down onto a block of marble and stared up at the bearded figure on the wall. A mythical figure who blew in the summer winds. Terrific. Was this where his search had been leading? A dusty corner of some Athens tourist attraction, among the weeds and stray cats?

Ruby sat next to Gerald. "Maybe there's something hidden around here," she said. "Some other clue."

Gerald kicked out at the stones at his feet, sending a spray across the path and startling a kitten that had been stalking something in the grass.

"I give up," he said, almost to himself.

Ruby didn't look up from her shoes. "You don't mean that."

"All this running about on some stupid thousand-year-old treasure hunt. We don't even know what we're looking for. It's ridiculous."

"But what about Charlotte and the murder of Mason Green?" Ruby said. "The police still think you did it."

"Maybe. But they have to prove their case. What evidence have they got?"

"Your DNA on the murder weapon, for a start!" Ruby was almost shouting at him. "Or had you forgotten that?"

Gerald opened his mouth but, before he could say a word, a sharp shove on his chest sent him sprawling backward off the marble block into the weeds. Startled, he looked up to find Sam standing over him, and the face of Skiron staring down over Sam's shoulder.

"What did you do that for?" Gerald said.

Sam glowered at him, his face beet red in the heat. "Because I'm sick of you changing your mind all the time. You're all over the shop. One minute you're gung-ho and all guns blazing. Then it's some sook-fest: 'Oh, it's all too hard. I just want to crawl under a rock and have a good cry.' Well, boo-hoo, mate. Make your mind up."

Gerald raised himself on his elbows from among the weeds. "You're not so relaxed today, then," he said.

"Give us a break," Sam said. "You're like that guy in the Shakespeare play, the one who's got murders going on all around him and can't decide what to do."

"Hamlet," Ruby said.

"Who?" Sam asked.

Ruby looked at her brother and shook her head. "You really did come out of the oven a half hour too early," she said. "So what's it going to be, Gerald? Do we keep looking or are you going home to face the music?"

Gerald felt the twins' eyes boring into him. What was he supposed to say? His only way out of a murder trial was to find Charlotte. But what hope did he have of doing that? And besides, wasn't that a job for the police? Or private detectives? Couldn't he just throw some money at it and make the problem go away? Wasn't that the billionaire thing to do?

"Let's go home," he mumbled. "I'll sort everything out from there."

Sam threw up his hands in disgust and stalked off.

Ruby leaned over and squeezed Gerald's arm. "Are you sure?" She gave him a soft smile. "Because I'm happy to keep searching with you."

Gerald screwed up his eyes. He was so tired.

"Let's find our way home," he said. "Do you still have that map?" Ruby seemed about to protest but bit her lip. She dug into her backpack and found the map she'd picked up at the bus station. As she handed it over, Gerald noticed an ornate compass face on the cover.

His hand froze in midair. The design looked awfully familiar.

"Hey, Sam," he called out.

Sam was kicking around in the grass at the base of the tower. "Yeah, whaddyawant?" he grumbled back.

"You remember that compass design—the one on the

floor of the tower at the Vatican?"

"Yeah. What about it?"

"How many sides did it have?"

Sam thought for a second. "Eight."

"And each point corresponded to a direction on the compass, right?"

"Right."

"How many sides does the tower here have?"

"Um . . . eight?"

"So, geography boy, what direction do you think our mate Skiron is facing?"

Sam craned his neck. "Judging by where the sun is now, I'd say that he's looking to the northwest. What are you thinking?"

Gerald took the map from Ruby and flattened it on the ground. "I don't know," he said. "But let's have a look."

Ruby and Sam crouched opposite him. "Okay," Gerald stabbed at a point on the map with his index finger, "here we are in Athens. If we go northwest, the way Skiron's looking, what do we find?" His finger traced a line out from the city.

Ruby and Sam saw it at the same instant. They chorused a cry of recognition.

"What is it?" Gerald asked.

"Can't you see it?" Ruby said. "Right there!" She pointed to a place name, spelled out in Greek letters.

Gerald shook his head. "What do you mean?"

Ruby clicked her tongue, then spun the map around so that it was upside down for Gerald. "There," she said. "Now do you see?"

Gerald stared at the map. The Greek place name had transformed into a series of shapes. A ten, a circle with a line through it, a Y, an arrow, and a triangle.

"Look at that," Gerald whispered. "The symbols on the envelope that Geraldine left for me. The ones Lucius carved in the cave under the abbey."

He spun the map right side round again.

"Greek letters. They're Greek letters, not some stupid code. And we've been looking at them upside down."

Not ΙΟΦ∀ƎⱯ.

But ΔΕΛΦΟΙ.

"But why would Lucius carve them upside down?" Ruby said.

"He didn't," Gerald said, getting excited now. "He was lying on his back. So when he scratched them onto the rock it was right-side up to him. We were the ones looking at it the wrong way around. He was leaving us directions."

"To where?" Ruby said.

Gerald looked again at the map, his hands shaking. There was an English translation under the Greek name. "To Delphi. It's Delphi in Greek."

Ruby looked at the point on the map. "To the northwest

of Athens," she said. "Skiron points the way."

"I'll bet you anything that's where Quintus and his sons were going all those years ago, on that mission for the emperor," Gerald said. "And where Charlotte is going now."

Gerald looked at his two friends. The fire was back in his eyes.

"So we're not going home now?" Sam asked.

Gerald grinned like a madman. "Are you kidding?" He slapped Sam hard across the shoulders. "Going home is for wimps."

CHAPTER 18

Ruby flicked on the reading light above her head. She settled into her seat on the coach and opened the travel guide that she had bought at the bus station in Athens.

"Right," she said. "Let's see where we're going."

The suffocating urban jungle of Athens had quickly opened up to an expanse of farmland and parched fields. The bus sped north across the plains toward a mountain range just visible in the hazy distance.

Inside the air-conditioned coach, Sam gave his sister a dubious look. "You don't seriously think you're going to find the answer to this mystery in there," he said.

Ruby didn't look up from the book. "I find all information is useful," she said. "It's called having a clue. Maybe you should try it."

Gerald could sense a Sam-and-Ruby blowup brewing.

He had no desire to see one erupt in the close confines of the bus. There were only a few people on board, but it was probably wise to keep a low profile.

"It can't hurt knowing something about the place," Gerald said. "It's not like we know what to look for when we get there."

Sam ignored the peep of triumph that came from behind Ruby's book. "I would have thought you'd be interested to know that Greece is the most seismically active country in Europe," she said.

"Really?" Sam said.

"Yes. And that Delphi was once the spiritual capital of the ancient world. For over a thousand years it was considered the most powerful city on earth."

"Never heard of it," Sam said.

Ruby continued to flick through the pages. "A temple to the sun god Apollo was the centerpiece of the ancient city, and over its history Delphi became home to— Oh my gosh!"

"What?" Gerald said.

Ruby's eyed were fixed to the page. "Delphi became home to one of the richest treasures ever assembled on earth. Gold, diamonds, jewelry . . ." Ruby lifted her head and stared at Gerald. "That's what Mason Green was after."

Sam screwed up his face. "What? Some buried treasure? He was already a billionaire. Why would he want any more?"

"Not just any treasure," Ruby said. "It says that around the main temple different countries set up buildings to house all the money they sent there."

"Like banks, you mean?" Gerald said.

"Exactly. Dozens of them. All stacked to the ceiling. In all the digging the archeologists have done there, no trace has ever been found of any of the treasure."

"So what are you saying?" Sam said.

"Think about it. That amount of gold and diamonds. It would be worth more than a fortune today. It would have made Green the richest man alive."

Gerald rocked back in his seat. He had a vivid memory of a conversation with Sir Mason Green, outside the Rattigan Club in London.

Greed is a dangerous master, Gerald. If it takes hold, it can make people do shocking things . . .

"That's got to be it," he said. "Green wanted to be the wealthiest man in the world. His niece found out about it and greed got to her. She killed him and now she's after the treasure for herself."

Ruby snapped the book shut. "Good. If she's after the lost gold of Delphi, then that's where we'll find her."

Gerald's ears popped as the bus pulled to a stop. It had taken three hours to get to Delphi and the contrast between this place and the jumble of Athens couldn't have been greater.

They had driven along a narrow ridge for the last six miles. On the high side were the rocky slopes of Mount Parnassus. Beneath them, the slope fell away to a valley shrouded in the gray-green haze of olive groves. Beyond the valley the distant waters of the Gulf of Corinth shimmered in the early evening sun.

Gerald, Sam, and Ruby jumped down from the bus onto a narrow road that wound back through the center of town. Gerald looked up at the barren cliff face that seemed to lean over them. "The most seismically active country in Europe, you say."

Ruby followed his gaze to the boulder-strewn landscape above them. "That's what the book said."

"I'll try to keep the earthquakes to a minimum," Sam said as he shouldered his pack. "What are we doing? Looking for a hotel?"

They started the slow walk into town. Cars were parked up on the footpaths on both sides of the road, leaving only a narrow gap for the occasional vehicle to squeeze through.

"After what happened on Mont Saint-Michel, I'm not sure a hotel is a great idea," Gerald said.

"Wherever we go, it needs to have a laundry," Ruby said. "You two are foul."

Sam looked at Ruby in surprise. "It's only been a few days." He stuck his nose into his armpit. "I can't smell a thing."

Ruby recoiled in disgust. "Then your nose must have packed it in. I've smelled sweeter roadkill."

Gerald felt a tug at his elbow. A young boy was looking up at him.

"Do you need a place to stay?" the boy asked in perfect

English. His manner was businesslike. "I have a good place for you."

The top of the boy's head barely reached Gerald's chest but he stood on the path as if he was the mayor of Delphi. His jet-black hair swept across his forehead in an elaborate wave, framing a pair of dark eyes that seemed a half size too big for his head. He couldn't have been more than ten years old.

"What's so good about your place, then?" Sam said. "You got a swimming pool filled with ice?"

The boy stared blankly at Sam. "It is clean, it is cheap, and it is close by." He frowned. "We do not have a swimming pool."

Sam grinned and looked to the others. "Sounds good to me," he said. Gerald and Ruby nodded—close by was good.

"Show us the way, boss," Sam said.

The boy gave Sam another curious look, then set off up the road. Gerald and Ruby followed as Sam chatted with the boy. He led them past lines of gift shops with dusty window displays stacked with reproduction busts of various Greek deities. Restaurants were opening their doors for the first of the early diners. Gerald peered through the door of one to see a dining room overlooking a spectacular view of the valley and the waters of the gulf.

"You really feel like you're clinging to the side of a cliff here," Ruby said.

Gerald looked up to the mountain on the opposite side of the road. The twilight had painted the rocks in yellows and ochres. "I wouldn't mind having a climb up there," he said.

"You might have to yet," Ruby said.

"How do you mean?"

"I've been thinking. That lost treasure could be anywhere—in the valley, in the town, even up in those hills. And if that vile Charlotte woman is here, she's bound to have some idea where to look. Mason Green was always two steps ahead of us."

"You think Green would have told her where it's hidden?"

"Or she extracted it from him with one of her potions, the witch."

A few paces ahead, Sam was still trying to strike up a conversation with their guide.

"What's your name?" Sam asked.

"Nicolas," the boy answered.

"Yeah? I've got a joke for you. You'll like this one."

The boy didn't look like he was into jokes.

"Okay?" Sam said, trying to stop himself from laughing. "Knock knock."

Nicolas blinked at Sam. "What do you mean, knock knock?"

"It's a joke. I say: 'Knock knock,' then you say: 'Who's there?'"

"But you are there," the boy said.

"I know I am. But I'm not the one knocking at the door."

"But you just said 'knock knock.'"

"I know I did . . . Look, just say 'Who's there?' okay?"

The boy blinked again. "Okay."

"Right. Knock knock."

"Who's there?"

"Nicolas."

There was a pause. "But I'm Nicolas."

"Yes, I know you're Nicolas. That's the point."

"So why would I answer the door if I am the one knocking on it?"

"Don't worry about that."

"It would be pointless. If I am already inside the house, why should I knock on the door? Am I an idiot?"

"Just say 'Nicolas who?'"

"What?"

"When I say 'Nicolas,' just say 'Nicolas who?'"

"Have I forgotten who I am?"

"Just say it, okay?"

The boy shrugged. "Okay."

"Right. Knock knock."

"Who's there?"

"Nicolas."

"Nicolas who?"

Sam could barely contain himself. "Nicolas girls shouldn't climb trees!"

The boy stared blankly at Sam. "Now what do I do?"

Sam stopped laughing. "You laugh."

"At what?" Nicolas said. He looked around, surprised by the sound of Ruby and Gerald in fits of giggles.

"You can call me Nico," the boy said to Sam.

Ruby wiped the tears from her eyes and tapped Nico on the shoulder. "Don't worry about him," she said, tapping her head and indicating Sam with a nod. "It's the heat. Is your place far?"

They had come to a set of stone steps that ran up between two shops. Nico nodded toward the stairs. "Not far," he said, and started to climb.

Sam bounded after him. "Hold on," he called. "I've got another one."

Gerald nudged Ruby with an elbow as they made their way up the stairs. "Sam seems to get on well with little kids," he said.

"He always has," Ruby said. "It's a very sweet part of his nature. I don't have the patience. But Sam really enjoys talking with them. Though this kid's sharper than most."

The stairs seemed to go on forever. Gerald's thighs were still suffering from the Paris bike ride and he was relieved when they reached a shaded doorway. They followed Nico inside. Gerald dropped his backpack from his shoulders and let his eyes adjust to the dark interior of what appeared to be a neat but modest bed and breakfast. An older woman dressed entirely in black sat at a table in a corner of a living room. She was shelling peas into a metal bowl. A small television on a bench flickered in the dark—some afternoon game show was on.

Nico spoke to the woman in Greek and she gave the newcomers the once-over. Then she spoke back to Nico. "My aunt says it costs thirty euros per night," he said. "For each of you. Breakfast included."

Gerald took his wallet from his pocket and pulled out some notes. "I guess we'll be here for a few nights," he said, and handed the money to the woman. She counted it, twice, and slid it under the bowl on the table. She nodded at Nico and he led them down a hallway to a large bedroom at the far end.

"You are the only ones staying here," Nico said. He pushed the door open.

Sam elbowed Gerald and Ruby out of the way to be first inside. "Cool!" he said. "Bunk beds. I've got the top one." He clambered up a ladder and launched himself across the mattress.

Nico gave Sam one last curious look, then left them alone.

Gerald dropped onto the lower bunk and Ruby kicked off her boots and flopped onto a single bed against the opposite wall.

"Aaah," she sighed. "This is the first proper bed I've been in for days." She crooked a foot onto her knee and massaged her toes. "So we've got a place to sleep. Now what do we do?"

"Sleep," mumbled Sam from the top bunk.

Gerald sat up and emptied his pack onto the end of

his bunk. Out tumbled his headlamp, Ruby's guide book, some pencils, scraps of paper, and a lot of lolly wrappers. The last thing to tumble out was the ruby. He looked down at the sorry pile.

"Not much to go on, is it?"

"We should get new batteries for those lights," Ruby said. "You never know."

Gerald picked up a scrunched piece of paper. After the dunking in the grotto in France it had dried into a tight ball. He tried to flatten it out but it disintegrated in his hands.

"Was that the drawing of Mont Saint-Michel?" Ruby asked.

Gerald nodded. "Yep, the thing that got us started on this chase."

Sam spoke up from the top bunk. "You should try drawing something, Gerald. See if we can't jolt a clue out of you."

"I had the three gemstones last time we did it, in India," Gerald said. "But I guess we could give it a try with one."

Sam jumped down from his bunk and the three of them faced each other in the middle of the room. Gerald put his pencil on top of a notebook on a side table. He picked up the gemstone in his left hand.

"Are we ready?" he said.

Sam and Ruby nodded. Then the three of them held out their right arms and formed a triangle. Gerald looked down at the ruby in his palm. Its dark heart remained dull.

He raised his eyes to Sam and Ruby.

Both stared back.

Nothing happened.

"Well?" said Ruby. "Anything?"

Gerald shook his head. "Not even a tingle. Nothing at—hey!"

Sam had suddenly clamped down hard on Gerald's elbow, his hand shaking uncontrollably.

Sam's eyes rolled back, the whites exposed. His mouth dropped open and an otherworldly voice rolled out like a chariot through the gates of hell. "I am the messenger . . ."

The voice was inhuman. Demonic.

Ruby gasped. "Sam?"

"I have a message . . ."

"Sam?"

"The one you call Sam," the voice rasped. "The good-looking one . . . he is extremely hungry . . ."

Ruby dropped her grip and shoved her brother hard in the chest. Sam collapsed onto the bottom bunk, convulsing with laughter.

"You idiot," Ruby muttered.

Tears welled in Sam's eyes. "The look on your face," he said. "That was priceless."

Ruby's eyes narrowed to slits. "Are you quite finished?"

Sam rolled upright and gasped for breath. "You've got to have a good laugh," he said. "Now, let's eat."

Walking down the stone stairway from Nico's house was far easier than going up. They stepped onto the main street.

"What do you feel like eating?" Gerald asked.

Ruby pointed up the street. "Let's try this way." And she set off.

She breezed straight past half a dozen cafés and restaurants, each with enticing aromas wafting through the doors.

"What's wrong with these places?" Sam asked, struggling to keep up.

"Just a bit farther," Ruby said over her shoulder. "You and your inner food demon are going to have to be patient."

Gerald jogged along to catch up with Ruby. "Are you looking for anything specific?"

"No," she replied, maintaining her determined march forward. "Just teaching hollow legs back there a lesson."

She increased her pace. Every shout of complaint from Sam as he trailed farther behind seemed to generate a fresh spurt of energy.

In quick time they passed right through the village and onto a walkway that ran along the ridge. The valley was laid out beneath them to the right; barren cliffs soared above them to the left.

"Where are you going?" Sam shouted out, now a good twenty yards behind Ruby and Gerald.

"I think there's a good place a bit farther on," Ruby

called back. "Not far to go."

Gerald smirked. "You're evil, you know that?"

"Only when I'm pushed," Ruby said evenly.

They rounded a bend and the valley opened up, revealing a sight that stopped them in their tracks. Sam finally caught up with them.

"What's with the route march?" he puffed. "Where are—" He stopped midsentence.

They stared down at an ancient ruin on a broad terrace beneath the ridge, before the valley swept away.

It was a rotunda set on a platform with three steps encircling it. Three of the building's towering columns were intact; the rest were broken stubs that marked out the perimeter, like a mouthful of busted teeth.

Gerald couldn't believe his eyes.

"It's exactly the same," he breathed. "Exactly the same as the burial chamber under Beaconsfield."

CHAPTER 19

T hey scrambled down the path toward the rotunda, boots skidding over loose stones.

Chunks of white marble were strewn across the grass like discarded toy blocks from the gods. Gerald jogged down a broad path of crushed stone, with the eerie sensation that it was a trail trodden hard by the feet of millions of pilgrims before him.

Finally, they were at the base of the rotunda, staring up at the columns.

"Just like Beaconsfield," Gerald said. "It's in ruins, sure, but it's exactly the same."

"Can't you just see the major and Mr. Chesterfield walking up there," Ruby said, her voice a library hush. "Just before they . . ." She didn't finish the sentence. The vision of the two men being cut down in a volley of arrows was still fresh in her mind.

"How can there be one of these buried under Beaconsfield and another one perched on a Greek mountainside?" Sam said. "I mean, it's not like they come flat-packed with an Allen wrench. What's the connection?"

Gerald sat on a broken plinth and gazed up at the ruins. "I think when we can answer that, we can answer everything."

A dragonfly droned past Gerald's ear and he took a distracted swipe at it. Ruby settled onto a boulder next to him. "So let's go over what we know," she said. "Your great-aunt left you a bunch of letters."

"Which the thin man stole from my bedroom in London and gave to Mason Green before I could read them," Gerald said.

"Right. Now we know that one of the envelopes had the word *Delphi* written on the front."

"Yep."

"What was on the other ones?"

"Um, *Family Tree* . . ."

"Which Mason Green used to connect you with Quintus and his sons," Sam said.

" . . . and *Fraternity*."

"Which was the brotherhood in India that swore to protect the emerald casket," Ruby said. "Both your family tree and the Fraternity are central to this mystery. So Delphi must be really important as well. Otherwise, why would Geraldine single it out? And why would Lucius carve it in stone as his dying act? This must be the place. Gerald, give me your backpack."

Ruby fished out the guidebook and flipped to a dog-eared page.

"Look, here's a map of Delphi," she said, holding the book up for Gerald. "This must be the road we followed out of town. We came around this bend, so down here must be—"

"The Sanctuary of Athena," Sam said.

Ruby and Gerald both looked up at him.

"How did you know that?" Ruby asked.

Sam pointed to a block of stone by their feet. "It's carved into the side of that thing," he said.

Ruby exhaled and turned back to the guidebook. "Thank you, geography boy. Invaluable, as ever. Now, it says that this building was called the Tholos. It dates back to the fourth century BC."

"Wow," Gerald said. "Old."

"No one knows exactly what it was used for, but it could have been a meeting place, or a burial chamber," Ruby said.

"That makes sense," Gerald said. "Gaius was buried under the one at Beaconsfield. That's where the professor found this ring." He held out his right hand and studied the gold band. Then he held out his other hand. "And this one was with Lucius in France."

Sam picked up a handful of pebbles and started tossing them into the undergrowth. "So the ring that Charlotte has around her neck must be from Marcus," he said. "From India."

"Of course," Gerald said. "It was Viridian, Mason Green's ancestor, who killed Marcus, trying to find the emerald casket. He must have stolen it, and it's been passed down through the family." Gerald closed his eyes and thought hard. "Three brothers. Three rings. Three caskets."

"And three golden rods," Sam said. "Do the rods somehow unlock the treasure of Delphi?"

Gerald tilted his head back and took in the view. It was so tranquil. From nearby came the sound of water tumbling over rocks—a spring or underground stream perhaps? Stray cats warmed themselves on sun-baked stones. Wildflowers added sprays of purple and red to the marble white and blue sky. Gerald could see how Delphi had been the ancient world's spiritual capital. It was a place ripe for contemplation.

"Okay, how's this for a theory," Gerald said. Sam and Ruby turned to him. "My ancestors were sent here on a secret mission by the emperor of Rome. That mission was to steal the greatest fortune ever amassed in the ancient world: the treasures of Delphi. But when Quintus and his sons got here they saw just how vast the treasure is."

"What? And they decided to take it for themselves?" Ruby said.

"Do you remember what Green said to us outside the Rattigan Club? Greed can make people do strange things. And what did you say before, Ruby? The main street of Delphi was lined with banks brimming with gold and diamonds? That would tempt the strongest man. I think Sam's right. Somehow, the three golden rods unlock the vault where the treasure is hidden."

"So if they had the golden rods, why didn't they steal the loot and take off?" Sam said.

"Maybe it was just too much to haul away," Gerald said. "And maybe they didn't trust each other."

"I bet that's it," Ruby said. "They put the rods into three different caskets, and then gave each other a different key: a diamond, a ruby, and an emerald. That way no one of them could open the vault, or whatever it is, without the other two being there. Then they split up."

"But why split up?" Sam said. "That's what I don't understand."

"Maybe they'd agreed to meet back here at a set date and bring horse carts or whatever to haul the money away," Gerald said.

"But wouldn't they already have carts with them if they were going to steal it all for the emperor anyway?" Sam said.

Gerald rubbed his chin. "That's a good point," he said. "I can't answer that. But that's the best theory I can come up with. And when the emperor learned that his loyal servants had decided to take the treasure for themselves, he sent an assassin after them."

"But what about the map in Green's room at the Rattigan Club?" Ruby said. "It showed three paths leaving from Rome."

"I think Green's map was wrong. The brothers did take three separate journeys, but they went their separate ways from Delphi. Not from Rome. That letter from Quintus that Dr. Serafini had at the Vatican showed they were all together when they left Rome for Brindisi. They were coming here."

Ruby picked up a stick and traced a pattern in the dirt. "I like it," she said. "It answers all the questions."

"So you're descended from a bunch of thieves?" Sam said to Gerald. Then he shrugged. "I suppose you did grow up in Australia."

Gerald smiled. "You know what they say: You can choose your friends but you can't choose your relatives."

He stood up and dusted off his backside. "The three golden rods are the key. And for the first time since when— 394 AD?—they're all together again. Charlotte has them and if she's not here somewhere already, she can't be far away."

"Wherever she is," Sam said, throwing the last of the

pebbles into the bush, "I don't plan on meeting her with an empty stomach. Let's find something to eat."

Gerald pulled Ruby to her feet and they took a last look at the Sanctuary of Athena, then set off to the village to the sound of birdsong, cascading water, and Sam's rumbling stomach.

Chapter 20

"Would it kill you to wash?"

A look of disgust spread across Ruby's face like an oil slick as Sam and Gerald pulled on the same shirts they'd been wearing all week.

"What's the problem?" Sam said, running his hands down his chest to flatten out the creases. "This looks fine."

"It's not the look I'm concerned about," Ruby said, wrinkling her nose. "You two really smell."

Sam stuck his nose under his armpit and sniffed. "Only to other people," he said.

Ruby was dressed in a clean blue T-shirt and dark shorts that she had bought the night before. She had tied back her freshly washed hair and was stuffing dirty clothes into a laundry bag. "Nico's aunt said she'd wash our clothes if we wanted. Last chance."

Gerald and Sam looked at each other and shrugged. Ruby let out a weary sigh. "I'm living with pigs."

"Don't worry about it," Sam said. "It's not like we can smell any worse."

Over a breakfast of olives, feta, and bread they decided that a trip to the town's museum might be useful.

"A bit of local history could fill in some gaps," Ruby said.

Gerald rocked back in his chair. This whole adventure had started in a history lesson back in Sydney two months earlier. He shook his head at the memory of the daydream in Mr. Atkinson's class—of fighting a shaggy giant who kept bellowing, "Nothing is certain!"

Gerald stifled a laugh. He'd got that much right—nothing over the past two months had been even close to certain.

They stepped out into the morning sun. The day was promising to be a scorcher. Before they got down half a dozen steps, Nico had scampered to join them.

"I can show you the museum," he said. "I know all the old stories."

"I bet you do," Ruby said. "You're quite the tour guide."

Nico gave an earnest nod. "Yes," he said. "I am."

Sam tapped the boy on the shoulder. "Hey, Nico," he said. "Here's another one for you: What's a Grecian urn?"

"I beg your pardon?" Nico said.

"What's a Grecian urn?" Sam asked again, his eyes sparkling.

Nico raised and lowered a shoulder. "It is a large—"

"About twenty pounds an hour!" Sam slapped Nico across the shoulders and laughed.

Nico didn't miss a beat. "Agreed. That is what you will pay me for today's tour."

Sam stopped laughing. "What? No, I didn't mean—"

"It is agreed," Nico said with a note of finality. "Twenty pounds an hour." He then strode ahead, toward the Sanctuary of Athena.

"Looks like it's your shout today, Sam." Gerald threw an arm over his friend's shoulders. "Very good of you."

Sam's confused expression stayed with him until they reached the museum. It was a modern structure on the high side of the road, built into the rocky cliff. The occupants of half a dozen tour coaches milled around the forecourt waiting for the museum to open.

"There are many visitors today," Nico said. "It would be better to visit the ancient city first, then the museum."

"There's an ancient city?" Gerald said. "Not just the sanctuary that we saw yesterday?"

"Of course," Nico said. "That is why the tourists are here." He paused for a second, studying Gerald closely. "Isn't that why you are here?"

Nico stared into Gerald's eyes. Gerald could feel the

gaze piercing his soul. He had to look away.

"Of course," Gerald said. "Like you said—why else would we be here?"

Nico looked at Gerald for a second longer, then he turned and led the way along a broad footpath beneath shady trees.

"Does this kid ever smile?" Gerald whispered to Ruby. He held back a few steps to let Sam catch up with Nico for his latest attempt at a joke.

"He's a curious one, all right," Ruby said. "Why? You're not suspicious of him, are you?"

"No, I guess not," Gerald said. "He's just a bit strange."

Ruby looked ahead at Nico and Sam. She grunted. "No stranger than most."

They stopped in a small clearing just inside the entrance gates and bought their tickets. Nico cleared his throat and pointed to a path leading up a steady slope. "The Sacred Way," he said. "This is where the pilgrims would walk to get to the Temple of Apollo."

"Who's this Apollo, then?" Sam said.

Nico stared blankly at him. "Delphi is dedicated to Apollo. It was he who killed the giant python that lived in these rocks at the beginning of time. He was a god of many things: music, art, medicine. But mostly he was a sun god. He is usually shown with a bow and arrow. What is the word? Archer."

Gerald's brain skipped a gear. "Did you say archer?"

"Of course," Nico said. He pulled his ticket from his pocket and held it up. A color illustration on the back showed an archer with his bow at full stretch against a blazing sun.

Ruby yelped. "The Archer Corporation logo!"

Gerald stared at the ticket in Nico's hand. His great-aunt had chosen a company logo with some history in mind.

"Nico, was there some huge treasure here?" Gerald asked. "Maybe hidden in the temple?"

"Oh, there was a very big fortune here," he said. "But it wasn't hidden."

"What do you mean, it wasn't hidden?" Ruby said.

"Come. I'll show you." Nico started the climb up the Sacred Way. "Do you see the remains of all these buildings?" Both sides of the path were lined with the foundations of ancient stone structures. "All of these were treasuries. Each from a different kingdom or region. They were filled with gold, jewels, pearls—untold wealth."

"Why would people send all that stuff here?" Sam asked.

"To thank Apollo. This is where kings and princes would come to have their questions answered. Should I invade this country? When should I plant my crops? They would send riches as a show of gratitude. And they wanted their gratitude to be known by all, so it was displayed in these treasuries for the pilgrims to see."

"So it was a status thing," Ruby said. "I'm richer and more powerful than you, and here's my mountain of diamonds to prove it."

"But what stopped people from stealing it all?" Gerald said.

Nico's face grew dark. "No one would risk the wrath of Apollo," he said. "No matter how great the temptation."

"How does a Greek god respond to a question?" Sam asked.

"He does it with a helper," Nico said. "And he does it here."

They had reached a broad terrace halfway up the slope. High above them stood the remains of a vast amphitheater. Rows of seating stepped up the hillside and looked back over the valley and the waters of the gulf. In front of them was a rectangular expanse of stonework, the foundations of a once-large building.

"This was the Temple of Apollo," Nico said. "At one time, it was the most important place in the known world. This is where Apollo spoke to the mortals."

Sam stared at the broken columns and paving stones that marked out the boundary of the temple. "So was there a flash of lightning and a voice booming down from the clouds?"

Nico frowned at Sam. "Have you not heard of the Pythia? Of the Oracle of Delphi?"

Sam blinked back at him. "Should I have?"

Nico's frown deepened. "Apollo was the god of prophecy. He knew everything that would ever happen." He pointed to the far end of the temple. "The Oracle would bathe in the waters of the Castalian Spring before going into a chamber beneath the temple. There, she would burn laurel leaves and breathe in the smoke. Pilgrims would ask her questions and she would commune with Apollo, then pass on the answers."

"She?" Ruby said. "The Oracle was a woman?"

"Only women could be the Oracle," Nico said. "An unbroken chain of women for over a thousand years."

"So was she any good?" Gerald asked.

Nico shrugged. "The pilgrims heard what they wanted to hear." He jerked his thumb toward the boulevard of treasuries they had climbed past. "All of those were filled with gold and jewels. You don't get that for disappointing people."

Gerald's eyes traced the trail of buildings up to the temple steps. "She obviously knew how to play to the audience."

"It was one of the richest places on earth," Nico said.

"But what happened to it all?" Gerald asked. "What happened to Delphi?"

"No one knows for sure, but they say the emperor in Rome was jealous of the Oracle's influence. So around 400

AD he sent out a squad of assassins to kill her and destroy the temple. The gold probably ended up back in Rome."

Gerald's voice caught in his throat. "The emperor sent killers here?"

Ruby put a hand on Gerald's arm. "Quintus and his sons?"

"My ancestors were a Roman hit squad?" Gerald dropped down onto a boulder in the grass. "Nothing surprises me anymore."

Nico surveyed their faces and his brow furrowed. "Do you want to visit the museum now?"

Gerald could barely muster the strength to stand. If the day's heat wasn't draining enough, the news that he was descended from killers wasn't exactly putting a spring in his step. And not just ordinary killers—the Antonius boys had managed to end a thousand-year-old culture and tradition. The weight Gerald had felt wrapped around his shoulders since he'd inherited his great-aunt's fortune seemed to double as he plodded down the rocky path.

He and Ruby walked in silence, following Sam and Nico toward the museum. Gerald scuffed his boots through the leaves that littered the way.

"Know what I think?" Ruby said at last. Gerald didn't respond, stuck in his fog of despair. "I think it doesn't matter. Whatever happened here was a long time ago. You can't be blamed for stuff that your ancestors did."

"But you're the chaos theory queen," Gerald said. "If they hadn't come here and killed the Oracle I would never have been born."

"Gerald, you'll do your head in thinking like that. Let's concentrate on finding Charlotte and getting you off your own murder charge."

Gerald knew Ruby was right—she had a knack for keeping him on course.

The crush of tourists at the museum entrance had thinned, but inside the building was crowded. Nico elbowed through a clutch of older Americans who were all wearing identical sneakers, fanny packs, and baseball caps. Gerald, Sam, and Ruby followed him.

"So what are we going to find in here?" Sam asked. They were in a large gallery filled with statues.

"Nico?" Ruby said. "Has any of that treasury gold been found around here? Some random coins, or something?"

The boy shook his head. "Not a coin, not a gem. It was all stolen by the Roman assassins."

Gerald stared down at his boots. He didn't want to catch anyone's eye.

The tour group poured into the gallery and surrounded two large marble statues in the center of the room. Their guide, a short woman with a severe haircut, plopped down a three-legged stool and stepped onto it.

"Here are two of the greatest finds from the ancient

city," the woman began. "The twin brothers, Castor and Pollux . . ."

"We're not going to find anything here," Gerald said. "We might as well go."

". . . archeologists had almost given up hope of finding any examples of the art of the region—the site had been quite picked over . . ."

"Are you sure?" Ruby said to Gerald. "Shouldn't we find out more about the treasure? Ask an attendant or something?"

". . . but these two beautiful specimens remind us just how popular the cult of the twins was at the time . . ."

Gerald shook his head. "Maybe, on the way out," he said. He didn't wait for the others; he turned and squeezed through the crush of bodies between him and the exit. Before he could make it to the door, his path was blocked by a tall figure in dark clothes.

"Excuse me," Gerald said, not looking up, "could I get past, please?"

The sound of the reply froze his blood.

"Aren't you going to say hello, Gerald?"

Gerald looked up and found himself staring into the venomous face of Charlotte Green.

Chapter 21

The gallery was packed. Bodies pressed against bodies. The air conditioning strained to fend off the heat. But the buzz of conversation, the flash of holiday photos being taken, and the ebb and flow of the crowd were all invisible to Gerald. The only other person in the room was the woman who had twice tried to kill him.

The smile painted on her face was a pancake of malice and lies. Charlotte raised her hand and casually removed an ivory hairpin from a scroll at the back of her head. She tossed her chin and shook her tresses loose to cascade over her shoulders. Gerald watched as she eased a silver stopper from the end of the hairpin, revealing a gray-blue point.

"I have dipped this in poison," Charlotte said, as calmly as if she were inviting Gerald for a pot of tea. "It is a concoction of my own making. There is no antidote. No cure. A simple scratch on your skin and you will die the most excruciating death."

Gerald focused on the tip of the hairpin just centimeters from his cheek.

"A thing of beauty, isn't it?" Charlotte said. "It's carved from the tusk of an African bull elephant." She paused for a second. "I killed it." The statement had the desired effect on Gerald. His face turned white. "I was on safari in Kenya," Charlotte said. "I brought it down with a single dart to the neck." She spoke as if it were her proudest moment.

Before Gerald could respond, a jolt of surprise flickered in Charlotte's eyes. Nico was standing beside her, the top of his head barely up to her waist. He held a switchblade in his right hand and was pressing the point hard into Charlotte's ribs. His grim stare showed he wasn't fooling around.

Charlotte shot a venomous glance at Gerald. "You couldn't afford a full-size bodyguard?"

Gerald took a pace back, getting some distance between him and the hairpin. Sam appeared behind Nico and pulled him out of range.

"And the gang's all here," Charlotte said, as Ruby emerged from the crowd. "So nice to see you again, Miss Valentine. And don't you look beautiful, even in this heat. Isn't it frightful?"

Ruby scowled. "What are you doing here?"

"The same as you, I expect, my dear."

Gerald found his voice. "You think the Oracle's treasure is still here?"

Charlotte cocked an eyebrow. "You have come up to speed," she said. "And there was my uncle thinking you didn't know anything about your family secret. Naturally, the treasure, as you so quaintly put it, is still here. But, unlike you, I have the means to unlock it."

"The three golden rods," Gerald said.

"Isn't this a lovely irony, then," Charlotte said, looking at Gerald, Sam, and Ruby. "Three against one."

"Four!" Nico piped up.

Charlotte peered at the boy. "Three and a half," she said. "Now, before you get any wild ideas of calling for help, you should know there is enough poison on this pin to kill a dozen people." She narrowed her eyes and stared at Gerald. "You wouldn't want that on your conscience, would you?"

"You are a vile human being," Ruby said.

Charlotte swung her gaze onto Ruby and Sam, then to the tip of the hairpin, as deadly as a scorpion's tail.

"I should have killed you in France when I had the chance," she said. She whipped the hairpin in front of her. Ruby recoiled, her eyes wide. A mirthless laugh fell from Charlotte's lips, then she slipped the silver stopper back into place.

"I don't know what you're hoping to achieve here," she

said. "You can't possibly go to the police—there's an international warrant for your arrest. You have no clue where to find your so-called treasure, and I hold the only key." She slid the hairpin back into place. "I suggest you leave Delphi. The next time we meet, it may not be so crowded."

Charlotte turned toward the exit, but before she could take a step Nico jumped high and lashed out with his hand. Charlotte swayed her head back, but not fast enough. Nico's fist closed around a gold ring suspended on a leather strap around her neck. With a sharp tug, he broke the leather and was halfway to the exit before Charlotte realized what had happened. Gerald, Sam, and Ruby stood rooted to the spot.

Charlotte glared at them. "It appears your bodyguard is also a thief," she said, struggling to contain her fury. And she stalked out of the museum.

Gerald let out a long breath. "We better go find Nico," he said. "Just in case she's going after him."

"I don't think she'll bother," Ruby said. "She's after bigger things than one of your family signet rings."

Gerald stared back into the gallery. The tour group was taking turns to be photographed next to the ill-fated twins Castor and Pollux.

Gerald had the uneasy feeling that his own quest was heading for an ill-fated conclusion as well.

CHAPTER 22

By the time Gerald, Sam, and Ruby had made it back to Nico's house, Ruby was worried.

"What if Charlotte caught him?" she said. "What if she's done something to him?"

Gerald did his best to reassure her, but every minute that went past with no sign of Nico only added to her fears. Nico's aunt didn't understand their attempts at mime and she didn't seem worried that Nico wasn't about.

Ruby had almost convinced Gerald and Sam that they'd have to go to the police when Nico popped his head around their bedroom door.

"Nico!" Ruby said, dragging him into the room. "Are you all right?"

He gave Ruby one of his earnest looks, unsure what the fuss was about.

"Why would I not be all right?" he asked. "I'm not a child."

Nico pulled his hand from his pocket. Resting in the palm was the ring that he had snatched from Charlotte's neck. He gave it to Gerald.

"What made you grab this from Charlotte?" Gerald asked. Nico shrugged and pointed to the pair of identical rings that Gerald was wearing.

Gerald nodded, then he worked the rings off his right hand. He gave one to Sam and one to Ruby.

"Does this mean we're engaged?" Sam said.

"Don't be stupid," Ruby said. She slipped on the ring and stared down at the gold band on her little finger. "Thank you, Gerald. This means a lot."

Gerald raised and lowered a shoulder. "It's probably time the brotherhood was reformed," he said. "Though with less murder this time around."

Sam twisted the ring into place. "Well, here's cheers to the three musketeers."

Nico leaned up against the doorway and looked first to Gerald, then to Ruby, and finally Sam. "Who is this woman from the museum? Why did she threaten you?"

Gerald knew he owed Nico some answers, but he was too exhausted to explain the whole story. "She's trying to find the lost treasure of Delphi and we're trying to stop her."

Nico stared at him blankly. "Why? What does it matter to you if she finds it?"

"I guess it doesn't really matter," Gerald said. "It's more the way that she's going about it."

"The way?"

"It's a long story. Let's just say that we need to find her so we can let the police know where she is."

Nico thought about this for a second. "I know where she is," he said.

There was a silence in the room.

"You know where Charlotte is?" Ruby said.

"Of course. I followed her after she left the museum."

"Why didn't you tell us?" Sam said.

Nico transferred his gaze to Sam. "You didn't ask me."

"Oh for . . . okay, I'm asking you now: Where is she?"

"I followed her to a house just north of the town. A big place overlooking the valley."

Gerald pulled his backpack from under the bed. "Can you show us where it is?"

"Of course."

Ruby fixed Gerald with a questioning look. "I thought you just wanted to find Charlotte and let the police do the rest."

"Yeah, that was the plan. But like Charlotte said, that's pretty hopeless now. It was probably always fairly hopeless. We need to give the police a reason to be interested in her."

"What do you mean?" Sam asked.

Gerald flipped open the top of his pack and sorted through the contents. "There's no point going through a replay of the Mason Green trial. We need more evidence that she's the killer than just our say-so."

Ruby nodded. "Gerald's right. We need some proof she at least had a motive to kill her uncle."

"How do we get that?" Sam said. "All the evidence points to Gerald being the killer." He glanced across at Gerald. "Sorry, but it does."

Gerald pressed his lips together. "Not all the evidence. The blowgun may have been found in my room, but where would a kid get that kind of poison? Maybe we can find something to tie Charlotte to the poison dart that killed Green."

"And take the suspicion off you," Ruby said. "Great idea."

"I hope so," Gerald said, "because I'm running out of them."

The late summer evening sky lost the last of its light shortly after ten o'clock. Four heads appeared on the ridge above the house, barely distinguishable from the boulder-strewn landscape around them. Nico led them to a nest of rocks that provided a vantage point overlooking a floodlit courtyard on the other side of a wire fence. Gerald dropped in beside Sam and surveyed the scene. Beyond the expanse of the courtyard was the top floor of a modern house, which stepped down over a number of levels following the slope of the hillside.

"How do we do this?" Sam asked. "Just climb over the fence?"

"I guess so," Gerald said. "It's only eight feet high. We should be able to get over easily enough. Nico, any idea where the front door is?"

Nico pointed to a corner of the house cast in shadow. "The woman went in over there," he said. "There is a path that leads to the other side of the house."

Gerald nodded. "Seems easy enough. Watch for my signal and come down."

Gerald made his way down the slope as quietly as he could, taking care not to dislodge any stones with his boots. He edged into the pool of light at the front gate and looked both ways. The fence was easily eight feet high and stretched along the boundary out of sight.

He peered into the courtyard. It was a good twenty paces to the front of the house. He looked back up the slope and could just make out the shape of three heads; he thought he saw Sam give him a thumbs-up.

Gerald was about to reach up and grab hold of the wire fence when he saw a small yellow sign attached to the gate— a sign with a red lightning bolt on it.

Are you kidding me? An electrified fence?

Gerald looked back to the silhouettes on the hillside, an expression of defeat on his face. All he got back was another thumbs-up from Sam.

"Oh, for crying out loud," Gerald mumbled. He kicked about the ground until he found what he was looking for: a stout stick, about three feet long.

This better work, or it's barbecued Gerald.

He edged the stick between the bottom two wires of the fence and ground the end of it into the dirt on the far side. Then he pushed up on the stick, levering the upper wire as high as he could. Gerald felt the pulse of the electricity conducted into the stick: a dull thump, thump, thump.

He put a rubber-soled boot onto the bottom wire and opened up the gap even further. Gerald looked at the two wires; each carried enough voltage to blow him back up the hill to Sam, Ruby, and Nico. He swallowed hard and squatted to duck through the gap.

Then he heard the breathing.

For a second he thought the short, tight breaths were his own. But with a sickening rupture in his stomach, Gerald knew he had company. He lifted his eyes to see the sharp end of a guard dog pointed right at him, barely five feet away.

A Doberman.

A very large Doberman. Black and tan and mean, with a metal-spiked collar around its neck.

The dog stood perfectly still. The only movement was the rapid-fire pumping of its chest. Its eyes were black beads. It stood close enough for Gerald to see the stippled surface of its nose, glistening wet in the floodlights.

Gerald was paralyzed. He could feel the stick in his hand, his only possible weapon. But he couldn't convince his arm to move. His brain was focused on the Doberman's head—the power of its jaws, the laser intensity of its stare.

The dog peeled back its top lip in a snarl, revealing perfect white fangs.

Its muscles were tightening, its shoulders tensing like a spring.

Then it leaped.

It sprang forward with impossible speed, launching its bared teeth at Gerald's throat. All four paws were off the ground; it was a flesh-and-bone missile.

Gerald fell back with a cry, driving with his legs as hard as he could. He lost his grip on the stick and the fence wires snapped back into place—right onto the dog's metal-spiked collar.

A white halo of sparks exploded around the dog's head. The shock jolted the beast through the air. It landed a few feet back inside the compound. The floodlights shorted and the area was plunged into darkness.

Gerald landed with a thud on his back. He lay there for a second, waiting for the Doberman to tear his throat out. But instead of the black eyes of the guard dog, Gerald was surprised to see Ruby, Sam, and Nico staring down at him.

"Nice job, Gerald," Sam said. "Dog problem and electric-fence problem solved in one simple step. Too easy."

Gerald sat up and rubbed his neck. "Yeah," he said. "Too easy."

They clambered through the fence and past the prone shape of the Doberman.

"It's breathing," Ruby said.

"I'd rather not be here when it wakes up," Gerald said. "Let's make this quick."

Nico led the way to the front door. He tried the handle. It was locked. They ducked down the side of the house, descending a steep line of steps cut into the hillside. There was a light in a window at the very bottom of the building. Gerald motioned for the others to follow. He moved close to the side of the house until the light from the window washed across his face.

He eased an eye around the corner and peered inside to see a large dining room with a long table running down its center. The end wall was made entirely from glass and provided an uninterrupted view of the valley and the distant harbor lights. A wooden chandelier suspended from the ceiling lit the room with at least two dozen flickering candles.

"The table's set for two," Ruby whispered. "Charlotte must have a guest."

The remains of a simple meal sat on the table, together with a half-drunk bottle of red wine.

There was no sign of anybody.

Gerald looked along the side of the house back toward the top of the slope. "Feel like having a look around? There's an open window up there."

Ruby tucked her fingers under the edge of the window and eased it open. With a light kick, she hauled herself up and slid inside. A second later she reached out a hand to pull Nico up; Sam and Gerald followed.

"Come on, Gerald," Ruby said as he landed on the carpeted floor. "Time for some mischief."

Gerald fumbled in his backpack and pulled out his headlamp. A shaft of light cut into the darkness, illuminating the inside of a large, empty walk-in wardrobe.

"How do you know Charlotte's not asleep on the other side of that door?" Ruby whispered.

Gerald put his hand on the door handle. "There's only one way to find out," he said. He extinguished his headlamp and waited a few seconds for their eyes to adjust to the darkness. Then he opened the door.

The bedroom was empty. Gerald tiptoed across the carpet and opened the door a crack. There was no movement in the hall. Slowly, he inched the door wider and slipped through. The glow from the candles in the dining room filtered up from the right. Gerald edged along the corridor like a curious moth.

He reached a mezzanine level; a spiral staircase led down to the dining room. He was about to set foot on the top step when Sam stopped him and whispered, "You've got to see this."

Gerald looked back. Ruby was beckoning from an open doorway. They ducked inside and closed the door behind them. Ruby flicked on her headlamp and set the beam wide. "Behold," she said, "the evil witch's lair."

The light played across a laboratory that would be the envy of any mad scientist. Racks of beakers lined the stainless steel benches. There were glass flasks and test tubes containing a rainbow array of liquids, Bunsen burners and clamp stands, titration tubes and distillation equipment, a stone mortar and pestle, and an entire wall given over to a wooden cabinet with at least a hundred square drawers, each one meticulously labeled.

"Cactus barbatus," Ruby read. "Cactus berteri, Cactus chlorocarpus . . ."

"Yeah, eye of newt, toe of frog," Sam said. "This must be where she brews up her poisoned apples."

Gerald shone his light around the room. A whiteboard was attached to the far wall. On it was a map held in place by a magnet at each corner. And beside the map was a long list. Six of the items were crossed out with a red line.

"What is this, Nico?" Gerald asked.

"It's a map of the area," he said. "And this is a list of place names."

"What about the red lines?" Sam said.

"If it's a bunch of place names, it could be Charlotte's checklist of where she thinks the treasure is hidden," Gerald said. "The crossed-out ones might be places she's already looked. What do you reckon, Nico? You're the local. Could any of these be a hiding place?"

Nico scratched his chin and thought for a second. "The Korykian caves, maybe? I climbed up there last year with my friend. If you go really deep inside, there could be a place."

Ruby pulled open one of the drawers in the wooden cabinet and peered inside. "Shouldn't we be concentrating on finding the poison that killed Mason Green? I say we take a bunch of this stuff and drop it off at the local police station with a note."

Gerald was jotting down the place names from the whiteboard onto a piece of paper. "I wouldn't touch any of that," he said. "Who knows what it could do to you."

Ruby withdrew her hand from the drawer and wiped it on the back of her shorts. "What do we do, then?"

Gerald folded the paper into his pocket. "There's enough material in this lab to keep a forensics team busy for a month. Let's get in touch with Inspector Parrott and tell him what we've found. They're bound to find a trace of the poison."

They gathered beside the door and switched off their headlamps. "Okay, back to the window and back to Nico's house," Gerald said. He eased the door open and slid into the hallway. They crept back up the corridor. Gerald had his hand on the bedroom door handle when the house lights came on. The sudden brightness caught them by surprise—as did the sight of Charlotte standing a bare ten feet away from them. She was dressed in her commando chic and was aiming a handgun at Gerald's head.

"Do not move," she said, cool as a winter's dawn.

Gerald didn't hear the shot. He just felt a searing pain in his neck.

And blackness.

Chapter 23

Gerald's vision was slow to clear. It was as if a set of worn wipers were smearing road grime across a windscreen. He could sense the room around him—the light and the shadows—but nothing gelled. It was as if he were waking from surgery and had no recollection of whether the doctors were supposed to be taking something out or putting something in.

Finally, his eyes cleared and he could lift his head. He went to touch a hand to the pain throbbing from his neck but his arms wouldn't move. Gerald looked down and discovered he was sitting in a high-backed chair. His wrists were bound to the armrests with gaffer tape.

He was at the end of a long wooden table. Somehow, it looked familiar. It was the dining room that he had seen earlier that night. In Charlotte's house.

Charlotte's house!

Gerald's mind snapped back into gear. It was still dark outside. He tugged at his arms but they were tied tight. Then he found his ankles were taped to the chair legs. He wasn't going anywhere.

"You've woken, have you?" Charlotte walked into the room, carrying a wooden tray. She laid it on the table. Gerald was surprised to see a bowl of soup. Steam was winding up from its dark green surface.

"I thought you might be hungry," Charlotte continued. "One of the side effects of the drug I used on you, I'm afraid." She put the bowl on a placemat in front of him, and a spoon to one side. On the left she put a basket of crusty bread.

Gerald looked at the bowl and felt a twinge in his belly. He was starving, but there was no way he was going to let Charlotte know that.

"I can't exactly pick up the spoon, can I?" he said. His eyes darted around the room. There was no sign of Sam or Ruby, or Nico. Just a cavernous dining room overlooking the valley and the lights of the harbor miles below.

Charlotte followed his gaze out the floor-to-ceiling window.

"It's like we're looking down on the world from the nest of the gods," she said. "I love it. My uncle used to bring me here on summer holidays to help him with his research.

There's a tremendous variety of succulents growing in these hills; they have the most interesting chemical properties. It's quite the botanist's treasure trove."

Gerald listened to her words but couldn't take his eyes from the soup in front of him. It smelled delicious.

"Where are the others?" he asked. He was starting to salivate.

Charlotte pulled out a chair and sat down next to him.

"Your little friends? They escaped. Scuttled into the night like cockroaches behind the kitchen fridge. They are of no interest to me." Charlotte's porcelain skin glowed in the candlelight from the wooden chandelier high above. She tilted her head to the side and smiled at Gerald. "Are you sure you won't try some soup? I prepared it myself from a very special recipe." She picked up the spoon and dipped it into the bowl, turning slow circles in the thick liquid. Gerald's eyes followed the furrows of creamy green that the spoon left in the surface. His mouth salivated anew. He couldn't remember ever being this hungry.

Charlotte took the spoon to her lips. She puckered, and blew a cooling breath over the contents. "There are all sorts of marvelous herbs in here." Her voice was as soft and warm to the ear as the soup promised to be to Gerald's ravenous stomach. "I picked them myself up in the hills." She paused and raised her eyes to Gerald. "Are you sure I can't tempt you?"

She held the spoon to Gerald's mouth, running its rim

297

along his bottom lip. "It's really very good."

Gerald knew he had to stop himself. There was no telling what nastiness was mixed into the witch's brew.

The muscles in his neck coiled and he clenched his mouth shut. He had to resist.

But his stomach was howling.

He craved to taste it.

He had to have it.

His lips parted a fraction—and Charlotte's eyes smiled.

She slid the spoon into Gerald's mouth and his teeth closed around it.

The warmth flooded through his body like an incoming tide, faster and more overwhelming than anything he'd experienced on the mud flats at Mont Saint-Michel.

"It's good, isn't it?" Charlotte said, tipping another spoonful into Gerald's now eager mouth. He swallowed and asked for more.

In minutes the bowl was clean. Gerald sat back in his chair, with his eyes closed and his body exultant. He felt incredibly drowsy.

"What was in that soup?" Gerald slurred. His mouth struggled to form the words.

Charlotte glowed with pride. "Split peas, parsley, mushrooms, and ham. And wild thyme and fennel. My mother's recipe. It's my favorite."

Gerald blinked. "It's not drugged?"

Charlotte laughed. "You offend me, Gerald. I take my cooking very seriously. I would never drug someone's food."

"Oh. Good."

"It would spoil the taste." Charlotte lifted a leather doctor's bag onto the table. She unclipped the top and popped it open. "I find it far more efficient to use a syringe." Gerald could see the bag's red velvet interior was lined with pockets, each one holding a stoppered vial.

"My little bag of tricks," she said with a smile. "Now let's see—no point in using a truth serum on you, Gerald. It's not like you're consciously hiding anything. What we really need to do is unlock your deepest memories." She selected a vial containing a pink liquid and laid it on the table. From a side pocket, she took out a fresh hypodermic syringe.

Gerald's eyes fixed on the needle in Charlotte's hand. "What are you going to do?" His voice was on the edge of panic.

"As you may have guessed, Gerald, I have quite a talent in the chemistry laboratory." She pierced the vial's seal and filled the syringe with its pink contents. "I am going to unlock your memories, Gerald. You may not realize it, but you have a strong link to Delphi. I need to know what you know."

"How can I know anything about Delphi? I hadn't even heard of it until two days ago."

Charlotte held up the syringe and tapped the barrel with her finger, working out any air bubbles. "Maybe so," she said. "But your family was intimately associated with the place. Who knows what your ancestral genes have locked away inside you."

Gerald thought about Quintus and the murderous rampage that he and his sons had led through Delphi. He struggled against his bonds. "You don't need to do this," he said. "It's not like you need anything more."

Charlotte pressed the plunger a millimeter; a drop of serum formed at the needle's tip and wound slowly down its length.

"I am not an evil person," Charlotte said. "I just want something really, really badly."

"Why can't you want the cure for cancer really badly? With your skills you could save thousands of lives."

"Ah, the answer to cancer," Charlotte said. "Gerald, with what I'm seeking, I'll have the answer to everything."

She smacked the inside of Gerald's elbow until a vein bulged. Then she moved the needle's tip to his skin. "Now, let's see what you really know . . ."

Gerald flinched. His eyes flickered between the needle hovering over his arm and Charlotte's face focused on the syringe.

Then he sensed a change in the light: The shadows shifted. And over Charlotte's shoulder came the figure of

Ruby hanging upside down by the knees. Her legs were hooked over the wooden chandelier, which was being lowered slowly from the ceiling. Gerald's eyes darted up. Sam and Nico were on the mezzanine level, easing out the chandelier's support rope. He looked back to Ruby. She raised a finger to her lips. And winked. Her spare hand dropped into Charlotte's bag on the table. A second later, she pulled out a handgun.

"This may sting a little," Charlotte said, as she brought the needle to Gerald's arm.

Gerald sucked in a breath.

And the chandelier dropped.

Ruby went sprawling across the tabletop.

Charlotte swung around, holding the syringe out like a weapon. Ruby was flat on her side, tangled in a mess of broken timber and candles. But before Charlotte could move from her chair, Ruby raised the gun toward her. The shot landed a dart in the hollow at the base of Charlotte's neck. A second later, Charlotte was unconscious on the floor, the hypodermic still in her hand.

Ruby rolled off the table and rushed to Gerald.

"Are you okay?" she asked. "Did she inject you with anything?"

Gerald didn't respond. He was staring at the livid red mark across his forearm. Charlotte's needle must have scratched him as she turned to face Ruby. A ribbon of blood began to seep from the wound.

"Gerald?"

Gerald could sense Ruby pulling at his bonds. But even that was lost to him as his eyes blurred and his mouth sagged. All he could see was a dank stone cavern. And all he could hear was a thunderous roar.

A roar that sounded like, *Nothing is certain.*

CHAPTER 24

Sam popped another olive into his mouth. He bit into the meaty flesh, chewed a few times, then took delight in spitting the pit as far as he could into the bushes.

"Do you have to do that?" Ruby said. She dipped a chunk of bread into a pot of tzatziki and took a bite.

"Bet you can't get as far as me," Sam said. He fired another pit deep into the undergrowth. A kitten pounced on it, throwing itself between two potted plants. Sam picked up a second kitten that had been curling itself between his legs and tickled it under the chin.

Ruby took another bite of bread and eyed her brother evenly. "You're on."

Nico's backyard rang to the sound of Sam and Ruby's claims of victory as olive pits sprayed across the grass and stones. Gerald sat in a threadbare wicker chair; its seat was pushed through and weeds wound up each leg. He was struggling to keep his eyes open as the afternoon sun drained away the last of his energy. He turned a lazy eye toward Nico, who was helping himself to the lunch platter that his aunt had brought out for them.

They had slept in following their midnight visit to Charlotte's house. Somehow, with Sam and Ruby's help, Gerald had been able to get back to Nico's place. He was still trying to make sense of the vision he'd had—it was the same dank dungeon that he'd daydreamed in his history class all those weeks before. It made no sense. And Gerald knew he couldn't relax. They'd left Charlotte drugged on her dining-room floor, but she would soon be on the move. Gerald had called Inspector Parrott in London but the line kept dropping out.

"Nico," Gerald said. The boy looked up from his lunch. "What were those caves called again?"

"The Korykian caves," Nico said. "They're about a two-hour walk from here."

"And what's there?"

"Some caves. There's a hole in the ground. Not much else."

"What about this Oracle woman?"

"The Pythia."

"Yeah, her. Would she ever visit the caves?"

Nico shook his head. "Once a woman became the Pythia, she never left the temple. She spent the rest of her life in the service of Apollo."

"Until she died?" Gerald said. "That's some commitment. What would she do all day?"

"Not much. The Oracle would only commune with Apollo once a month or so. She'd go into a chamber under the temple. Legend says it would fill with gas from a crack in the earth and the fumes would send her into a frenzy. She had to sit on a special three-legged chair so she wouldn't fall in."

"And when she was in this frenzy, she'd see the future and give people advice?" Gerald said.

"That's right. She was the most powerful person in the world."

Ruby dropped down beside Gerald and poured herself a cup of water from a large pitcher. "Good to see a woman at the top for a change," she said. "But I can't see how the treasure could still be here. Archeologists have been digging around that site like badgers."

The lazy afternoon peace was cut by the sound of a helicopter landing somewhere north of town.

Nico shielded his eyes with his hand. "We don't get helicopters at this time of year. Just for injured skiers in the winter."

Gerald lifted himself out of the broken chair and hoisted

his backpack onto his shoulder. "Charlotte won't be waiting around," he said. "And we shouldn't be either. I say we check out those caves."

Something had shifted. Even though Gerald wouldn't admit it, there was now a new objective. It came from deep within him, an unnamed desire, a slow-burning fuse. Whether it was a response to fate or a suppressed instinct that had been waiting to be triggered, he didn't know, but Gerald Wilkins was now sure of his path. They had to find the lost treasure of the Oracle of Delphi.

The narrow path zigzagged up the mountainside, cutting across the rocky cliff face. The going was steep, hot, and dusty. Gerald was surprised by how quickly they left the village behind.

They reached a flat spot and clambered onto a large boulder that gave a panoramic view of the valley. The four of them dangled their legs over the edge and passed around a water bottle. They could see right down to the ancient ruins of Delphi: the temple, the amphitheater, the Sacred Way.

"It's so beautiful here," Ruby said, taking in the scene below. "It's like we're sitting on the edge of the world."

Sam took a long drink of water. "If you like that sort of stuff, I guess."

Gerald laughed and took the water bottle from Sam. "There's not a lot of poetry in you, is there? Look, I've been thinking. Do you remember what Dr. Serafini said about twins in history?"

"About how special we are?" Sam said.

"Special. Freaklike. Whichever," Gerald said. "He mentioned those twin brothers, Castor and Pollux. They took turnabout at being dead."

"What about them?" Sam said.

"When we were in the museum, before we saw Charlotte, there were two statues of Castor and Pollux. The tour guide said something about there being a cult of the twins around here. Seeing those two statues, and how they were dug out of the ground, gave me an idea."

"And what's that, Howard Carter?" Ruby said.

"But his name is Gerald," Nico said. "Why do you call him Howard Carter?"

"Howard Carter was the archeologist who discovered the tomb of King Tut in Egypt," Ruby said. "It was a joke."

Nico frowned up at her. "You are this boy's twin sister?" he asked, jerking a thumb toward Sam.

"That's right," Ruby said.

Nico nodded. "Your jokes aren't funny either."

Before Gerald could continue, a bright glint of light flashed across Ruby's face. The afternoon sun was reflecting off something, from down near Nico's house. "What's that?" Ruby said, shielding her eyes from the glare.

Then, carried on the still summer air, came a voice on a

megaphone. "STAY RIGHT WHERE YOU ARE!"

Gerald looked at Ruby. "That sounds like—"

"THIS IS DETECTIVE INSPECTOR JARVIS OF THE LONDON METROPOLITAN POLICE. STAY WHERE YOU ARE!"

"How did he get here?" Sam said.

"Helicopter," Ruby said. "That vile woman must have woken up."

Gerald scrambled to his feet and shouldered his pack. "I'm not hanging around to find out." He set off up the path at a jog, scrabbling over the loose scree. Sam, Ruby, and Nico followed close behind.

"Nico," Sam panted. "You don't have to come."

The boy set his jaw and soldiered on. "Twenty dollars an hour," he said.

They reached the brow of the hill before they heard the megaphone again.

"STOP!"

Gerald looked back but couldn't see any sign of the pursuing police.

"STOP. THERE ARE POLICE MARKSMEN WITH ME AND WE WILL SHOOT."

Ruby looked to Gerald. "Surely they wouldn't shoot."

A rock above Sam's head exploded out of the cliff face, showering him with shrapnel. A sharp crack echoed up the hillside.

Everyone ducked. "Or maybe they would," Ruby said.

"Quick!" Gerald led a crouching retreat over a boulder. They landed in the dust on the other side just as another shot cracked overhead.

"What are they shooting for?" Ruby said. "We haven't done anything."

Nico sat wide-eyed in the dirt. "It's the local police," he said. "They excite easily."

"What do we do now?" Ruby asked, her back flat against the boulder.

"Nico, how far are the caves?" Gerald asked.

Nico thought for a second. "Two miles," he said. "Maybe three."

"That's a hike," Sam said. "But it's got to be better than sitting here."

"We've got a good half hour's head start," Gerald said. "Let's not waste it."

A long, gentle slope ran ahead of them, boxed on either side by rocky cliffs. After the climb up the mountain they made good ground. The country was barren and supported only the scrappy trees and scrub that lined their way. They raced around a cairn of rocks and past a low-set concrete bunker with a steel manhole cover on top. They could hear rushing water bubbling deep underground.

After running for a solid thirty minutes without any more megaphone warnings or gunshots, they scurried up a dry creek bed and tumbled through a cleft in a rock face into an open expanse. The grass was littered with boulders

and cowpats. Hills rose on either side. The trail continued along a gully for another fifty yards before turning
to the left.

Ruby made for the shade of a gnarled olive tree by a
rock wall. "Time for a break," she said. "Jarvis didn't look
that fit. They'll be well behind." She dropped into the grass
under the tree and fished in her pack for the water bottle.
She drank deep and long.

"It's a shame Lethbridge wasn't leading the charge," Sam
said. "We could have taken all day."

Gerald's face burned red. His cheeks were streaked with
sweat salt. "How much farther, Nico?" he asked. His hands
were on his knees and he was sucking in deep breaths.

Nico looked around, getting his bearings. "Another
hour, maybe."

Gerald took the bottle from Ruby and took a generous
swig. He went to hand it to Sam, but—

"Sam?"

They spotted him on the far side of the tree, near a pile
of rocks that must have slid down the cliff wall. He was on
his hands and knees, poking around the base with a stick.

"Sam?" Gerald said. "What are you doing?"

Sam poked his head up and beckoned them over. "Check
this out," he said. He prodded the stick into a gap between
two large rocks, then dropped to his stomach and shoved
his arm in, up to the shoulder.

"Careful," Ruby said. "There could be snakes."

Sam writhed around for a second, then, "Gotcha!"

He pulled his arm back and in his hand he held a tortoiseshell kitten, only a few weeks old. He bundled the mewling ball of fur into his lap.

"Trust you to find a cat in the middle of nowhere," Ruby said.

"What is it with you and cats?" Gerald said.

"Simple," Sam said. "Cats mean no rats."

"We really don't have time for this," Gerald said. Then, out of the gap between the rocks came a cat's head. The kitten's mother slinked into the open, boxed its child around the ears with a paw, then clamped her mouth around the scruff of the kitten's neck and dived back through the opening.

Sam laughed and set about loosening some of the rocks at the base of the pile.

"Come on, Sam," Ruby said. "We need to get going."

Sam widened the gap and squeezed his head and shoulders through. "Hold on a sec," his muffled voice came back.

"Stop being an idiot," Ruby said, pounding his back with her fists.

Sam pulled his head back into the daylight, blinked, then grabbed a headlamp from his pack and dived into the rock pile again.

The space around Sam's head glowed from the lamp, then his shoulders slid through the rocky opening. And then he disappeared altogether.

"Sam!" Ruby cried. "What are you—"

A single shout of surprise echoed out of the gap. It was followed seconds later by a colossal splash.

"What's the idiot done now?" Ruby moved toward the hole, but Nico beat her there. The boy threw himself into the gap between the rocks, kicking up a plume of dust as he wriggled through. Gerald watched speechless as his boots disappeared.

He stared at Ruby, unsure what to do. The sound of another splash came out of the hole.

Ruby didn't hesitate. She grabbed a light from her pack, strapped it to her head, and slithered through the opening.

"Ruby!" Gerald called into the hole. "Can you see anything?"

There was a pause, then Ruby's voice came back, "I can't see them. Hold on." There was another pause. Then a cry of surprise.

And an enormous splash.

Gerald was alone.

He had no choice.

He had his light out and on his head just as the first of the policemen charged into the clearing behind him.

CHAPTER 25

Gerald spun his head to see three more policemen stumble into the broad expanse of grass and rocks. A second later they were joined by a sweat-covered Inspector Jarvis.

Gerald froze where he was, crouched low to the ground. The gnarled olive tree gave him some cover, but he knew any movement would give his position away. The policemen were looking straight ahead, toward the far end of the gully, and hadn't looked his way . . . yet.

Gerald's eyes locked onto the sniper's rifle that was slung over the shoulder of one of the local police. Nico was right—this one looked particularly excitable.

Gerald held his breath. Jarvis was barking orders to keep moving. They were barely twenty yards away. If he kept completely still, didn't flutter an eyelid . . .

A furry head appeared between Gerald's knees.

The kitten looked around, its eyes darting left and right, in search of mischief. It spotted a beetle shuffling through the grass, and pounced.

Gerald stifled a gasp of panic. His eyes shot back to the policemen. They were advancing up the slope, eyes still straight ahead.

The kitten launched itself into a scrubby plant, rustling among the leaves. Gerald slid out a hand and scooped it up. It wrapped itself around his fingers, then sank a mouthful of tiny teeth into his thumb. Gerald clamped his lips together, swallowing the cry that he wanted to bellow out. The kitten meowed in protest at its game being cut short.

The policeman with the rifle was thirty paces away— almost at the turnout of the gully. He stopped, pulled a water bottle from his belt, and took a long drink. If one of his colleagues looked back at him, Gerald was sunk.

The policeman drank and drank.

The kitten released its bite on Gerald's thumb and started licking the wound. Gerald let out a silent sigh of relief. A second later ten needlelike claws dug in as well.

The policeman with the rifle holstered his water bottle and set off after his companions. Jarvis was the first to reach the turnout of the gully and take a step up the rocky culvert.

Gerald released his grip on the kitten; his shoulders relaxed.

Then a distant shout of "Gerald!" echoed up out of the gap in the rocks.

All of the policemen stopped in their tracks.

Jarvis spun around.

"Wilkins!" he bellowed. "Stay where you are!"

Gerald's brain stalled—but only long enough to notice the policeman swing the rifle from his shoulder and point the barrel right at him.

The Inspector's cry of "NO!" and the shot came at the same time. An explosion above Gerald's head showered rock splinters down on him. He didn't wait for the policeman to reload. Still clutching the kitten, he scrambled through the opening like a terrier into a rabbit hole, headfirst into darkness.

Whether it was Gerald's boot catching a boulder on the way through, or the policeman's second shot dislodging a keystone, something caused a rockslide. Gerald's eyes were peppered with grit as the opening behind him was swallowed up in tons of rubble. He curled into a ball and toppled to his side, trying to make as small a target as possible as stones rained down on him. He held the kitten to his chest and looked up just as an enormous boulder loosened and fell toward him. He held his breath, waiting for the impact. But the rock wedged into a cleft and stuck fast, just centimeters from his nose.

Finally, the crashing and banging stopped. An eerie stillness settled in the cave. Gerald was flat on his back, breathing hard. His shaking hand found its way to his headlamp and he switched it on. The beam barely cut through the dust, like a lighthouse in fog. Then a raspy little tongue started giving him sandpaper kisses on the cheek. The kitten crawled onto Gerald's shoulder and nuzzled his chin, purring with delight.

Gerald lifted it onto his chest and looked around. There was no way to tell where the opening had been. All about him were prison walls of impenetrable rock.

He shuffled backward to find space to sit up. But in the darkness he didn't see the sinkhole behind him.

He toppled in.

Gerald hit the water on his back. The air was knocked from his lungs. The kitten was jolted from his grasp, and it disappeared into the total darkness that consumed them both.

His light blinked out. The rushing flow of water whipped it from his head. He flailed his arms, trying to right himself and search for the kitten. He was being carried along at a frantic pace in an underground stream. All around was dark but he could sense the roof of the tunnel whipping past not far from his head. A low-hanging rock and he would be knocked senseless. He'd drown in seconds.

The stream twisted, buffeting him against the smooth rock walls as it tore along its subterranean path. Gerald was swallowing water with almost every breath as he was jostled and pounded from side to side.

Finally he was jettisoned over a low waterfall and he tumbled into a rock pool. He found his feet and stood up in the waist-deep water. The sound of rushing water filled the black void around him.

Then came a voice.

"Gerald!"

It was Sam. The cry seemed to come from below.

A soft light appeared, just enough for Gerald to see he was standing behind a natural weir; a rock ledge was holding back the stream. Water poured through a break in the rocks to Gerald's right, shooting out in a massive arc into the darkness.

Gerald waded up to the ledge and called out. "I'm up here," he cried.

"Jump!" It was Ruby's voice this time. "It's okay—there's a deep pool at the bottom."

Gerald squinted into the darkness. A single beam swept across the surface of an inky pool about twenty-five feet below.

"Just let the waterfall carry you over," Ruby called up.

Gerald had jumped from the high board at his local swimming pool only once. It hadn't ended well: a wedgie had almost split him up the middle, like an English muffin.

"Come on," Sam called. "You have to see what we've found."

Gerald took one more look over the edge, then pushed into the current that led to the break in the dam. He was swept up in an eddy that spun him in circles and spat him into the void. The flight into black air was as close as Gerald was ever likely to get to a space walk. Time seemed to stop. He had no sense of which way was up and no notion of when he might hit the water.

He landed bum-first and disappeared under the surface, thinking he'd sink forever. He kicked hard toward what he hoped was fresh air, and made for the dancing light at the edge of the pool.

Hands reached out and dragged him up a shallow rock shelf and onto a pebbly beach.

He coughed out a mouthful of spring water. "Sam? Ruby? Nico? Is everyone all right?"

The beam from Sam's headlamp lit up Ruby's and Nico's smiling faces and a bedraggled kitten in Sam's arms.

Gerald reached around and plucked at his pants. "Yep," he muttered. "Giant wedgie."

Ruby threw her arms around his neck. The embrace took him by surprise. For a moment, he stood there, mute and awkward. "Uh, so," he said, finally, "clothes clean enough for you now?"

Ruby eased her grip and let her hands slip down till she

held Gerald by his fingertips. "What took you so long?" she said.

"Jarvis turned up and started using me for target practice," Gerald said. "I only just got through the hole when there was a massive cave-in. We won't be getting out that way."

Sam adjusted the lamp on his head, widening the beam as far as it would go. "We're down to one light," he said. "But it should be enough to have a look around."

"A look around at what?" Gerald said.

"Well, if you can stop groping my sister for long enough," Sam said, spinning him around, "you'll probably want to see this."

It took a moment for Gerald's eyes to adjust as the light swept up a gentle slope from the rock pool. Then he almost swallowed his tongue.

"What?" Gerald managed to say. "This . . . this can't be true." His mind was whirring too fast to process the information his eyes were feeding it.

Gerald took an unsteady pace forward and stopped.

Stretched out before him, as far as the light could penetrate into the gloom, was the ancient city of Delphi—intact and untouched for the past sixteen hundred years.

CHAPTER 26

The spring bubbled and frothed and swirled past the stone wall at the lower reaches of the city, then disappeared into a shallow cave mouth at the far end of the rock pool. Sam's light provided only faint illumination, but it was enough to make out the lower section of an immense metropolis that stretched up a steep incline into the shadows.

Of all the wonders that Gerald had seen on his holiday—the buried chamber under Beaconsfield, the lost city of Mamallapuram in India, the abbey of Mont Saint-Michel—the sight before him topped them all.

"This is incredible." Gerald's voice was barely audible. "What do you think, Nico?" he asked. "You're the local." Gerald couldn't bring himself to ask the question: Is this the ancient city of Delphi? It was too insane to put into words.

Nico was keeping close to Sam as they stepped onto a broad expanse of flagstones that led to the city gates. His mouth hung open.

"The Sacred Way," he said. "We learned about it in school." He reached out a hand and grabbed the strap of Sam's backpack for support. "But the pictures in our books were never as beautiful as this."

They walked through a marketplace that was preserved as if snap frozen in time. Stone countertops were stacked with pots and cookware, displayed as if waiting for the doors to open for the summer sales. Awnings hung over some of the shops. Gerald reached up to a section of cloth and it turned to dust at his touch.

"Look over here," Ruby said, pulling Sam to a tiny shopfront. She grabbed the back of his head and directed the light onto a tray on a stone pedestal.

"They're silver pendants." Ruby picked up an oval-shaped piece with a tiny loop at the top for a chain to thread through. She rubbed her thumb across the surface, removing a millennium of grime. The trinket shone faintly in the light. Ruby squinted as she tried to make out the design engraved on the front. "An archer," she said. "Apollo, I guess."

They passed shop after shop. Everything was cloaked

in dust but laid out undisturbed as if all the owners had ducked out for a lunch that had lasted sixteen hundred years.

They clung together as they entered the main gates, and gazed along the boulevard that led into the city. Sam's headlamp brushed across scores of statues on pedestals lining the Sacred Way. The unblinking eyes of the bronze honor guard stared down at Gerald, Ruby, Sam, and Nico as they made their way forward.

The only sound was the plashing of the spring and the crunching of boots over the grit-dusted paving stones. Gerald's eyes followed the bobbing light from Sam's headlamp. The beam played on marble columns and towering figurines. What must have once been grassed terraces planted with olive trees now lay as dusty moonscapes, cut off from the sun for centuries. Gerald crept on, uncomfortably aware of the bronze faces on either side of them; they seemed to be glaring down with disapproval.

"Anyone else feeling a little creeped out just now?" Gerald said.

"It smells like Sam's shoe cupboard," Ruby said, wrinkling her nose. "What do you think happened here?"

No one had an answer.

They passed huge bronze castings of ancient generals on horseback, and one of a bull. Chariots and spear-wielding warriors heralded their arrival in haunting silence. The skin on the back of Gerald's neck crawled as if it were alive with centipedes. He couldn't shake the feeling that every one of the statues around them was about to burst into life.

They came to a single marble column in the middle of the road. Several tall earthenware pots circled its base.

Ruby craned her neck to look up to the top of the pillar, about ten feet in the air. "What do you think this is?" she said.

Nico ran a finger across the sealed top of one of the pots and rubbed it against his thumb. He whispered something to Sam.

"Hey, Gerald," Sam said. "Do you still have that flint you bought for the camping trip?"

Gerald put his right hand to his throat. After all they'd been through, he was surprised to find the black leather cord was still around his neck. He pulled it over his head and gave it to Sam.

"What are you going to do?" Gerald asked.

"Nico wants to test an idea."

Their young guide had his knife out and was running the blade around the rim of one of the pots, easing out a clay stopper the size of his fist. He pulled it free and, with Sam's help, tipped the pot and poured its contents into a shell-shaped cup on the side of the column.

"Oil," Sam said as they put the empty pot back on the ground. "Now let's see if this thing works." He pulled the striker from the flint and dashed it along the side of the box. A nest of sparks erupted into the cup and a second later light glowed from the top of the column.

"Brilliant!" Sam said. "Ancient street lighting."

The light peeled back the darkness and bathed the area in a sepia haze.

"Nice one, Nico," Ruby said. "Look, there's another lamppost up here. Come on, Gerald. Give us a hand."

Together, Ruby and Gerald hauled one of the oil pots to the next column. Soon another flower of light bloomed. The glow spread, and Sam let out a sharp gasp. "Will you look at that . . ."

The lamppost stood opposite a tall building with two stout columns supporting a small portico. Gerald looked through a square window in the front wall to see a chest piled high with gold coins.

"Oh my gosh," he breathed.

"That's right, billionaire boy," Sam said, making a dash for the door to the building. "It's our turn to be rich now."

Gerald, Ruby, and Nico joined Sam in the doorway. The walls were covered with frescoes of maidens bathing in tree-lined streams. The painted faces gazed into the room at rows of golden ornaments arranged on oriental rugs across the floor. Chests of coins sat beside piles of glittering gems the size of quails' eggs.

Ruby plunged a hand deep into a bowl of pearls; the spheres dropped through her fingers in a lustrous waterfall.

"Incredible," she whispered.

For the next hour they walked along the Sacred Way, lighting streetlamps and revealing more and more treasuries as they went.

"This is truly extraordinary," Ruby said. She was holding a solid gold statuette of an archer. They were inside the largest of the treasuries, a long building outside a walled-off section of the city. Every space inside was piled high with offerings to the Oracle of Delphi and to Apollo. "That this place has been buried here for—what?—sixteen hundred years. And look at all this stuff. It's exactly the way it was in ancient times."

"I guess there's no wind down here to blow the dust around, so anything inside a building is going to be preserved," Gerald said. He was looking at a carving of a white bull the size of a house brick. "What is this? Ivory, do you think?"

Ruby gazed out the doorway to the path of lights that led down to the spring; it looked like a string of charms on a giant bracelet. She sat back on her heels and a thoughtful expression settled on her face.

"I don't get it," she said. "If this is the ancient city of Delphi, what are the ruins back in town?"

Gerald settled into a pile of silk cushions, each as perfect as the day it was woven. "The ruins are a twin," he said.

"A twin?"

"Yep. Just like Castor and Pollux: one living above the

ground and the other in the underworld. That's what was going through my mind when Jarvis took a shot at us. Remember the tour guide in the museum saying the cult of the twins was really popular around here?"

"Do you think the locals buried the city to protect the treasure from the emperor?"

"Nope," Gerald said. "I think my thieving ancestors did that."

"What? Quintus and his sons buried the entire city of Delphi?"

"Sure. Think about it. I couldn't figure how my rotten relatives could move this much treasure away from here. It would take a thousand horse carts and forever to do it. The trick is, they didn't move it. They left it right here."

"And buried it?"

"It sits in a natural valley in the hillside. The Romans were good at engineering. Who's to say they couldn't devise some sort of structure held up by some props? Grow some grass across the top and you'd never know if was here. Then you build a fake Delphi further down the valley."

"And make it look like the city has been trashed and all the treasure stolen?" Ruby said.

"Exactly. It's not like you'd need to take much care. It's meant to look like a ruin. That way when Quintus and the boys don't return to Rome and the emperor sends out a search party, it looks like they've stolen the treasure, torched the town, and taken off."

"When all the time the treasure is right here, just waiting for the three brothers to come back and take it." Ruby tilted her head to the side. "Nice theory." Then her face turned dark. "But what happened to all the people who lived here?"

Gerald breathed out. "My guess is Quintus probably forced them to bury the city. Remember when Dr. Serafini read that letter to the emperor. Quintus and his sons were due to meet up with a company of soldiers. They enslave the locals, get them to bury the city, create a fake Delphi, then"—Gerald paused—"then kill the lot of them."

Ruby gasped. "But that would be thousands of people."

Gerald closed his eyes. "I know."

Ruby looked down at the statuette in her hands. "But how would Quintus and his sons fool an entire company of soldiers? And if all the treasure is just laid out like this, what are the golden rods for? What do they unlock?" Ruby put the statuette back on its pedestal. "Nice try, Gerald. But I think your theory needs some work."

Nico and Sam appeared in the doorway. They both held blazing iron torches. Sam had a gem-encrusted crown on his head. "Come on, you two," he said. "Nico's just had a brainwave."

Nico's face was beaming. "These are the treasuries," he said, indicating the line of buildings they had been exploring. "The real prize must be up this way."

"What?" Gerald said. "Even more of a prize than this?"

"Of course," Nico said. "The Temple of Apollo—and the inner sanctum of the Oracle herself."

Sam slid his crown to the back of his head. "Then lead the way, Nico. If it's more impressive than this lot, it's something I want to see."

They climbed a set of stairs onto a terrace cloaked in shadow. They stopped at another lamppost, this one taller than the others and with three lanterns at the top. Nico broke the seal on an oil pot at its base and he and Sam emptied the contents into a well in the center of the pillar. Nico squinted into the narrow opening.

"One more, perhaps?" he said to Sam, and they poured in a second pot for good measure.

"This should keep it going for a while," Nico said.

Sam struck the flint and the three lanterns—*pop, pop, pop*—flared into life. Then, a second later, a colossal burst of light erupted to their left. A string of three-headed lampposts ignited in a chain reaction across the terrace, pouring out a wave of light that rolled over them and the exterior of the Temple of Apollo.

The darkness fell away as if someone had opened a curtain onto a sunny day.

"Holy cow!" Sam said. "That is awesome."

Gerald could almost hear a choir burst into song.

It was the most breathtaking sight.

Marble columns lined the outside of the long rectangular temple. Gold inlay glistered in the lamplight and brightly painted friezes capped the roofline. Standing to their right, across the terrace, was a colossal bronze statue of a man at least fifty feet tall draped in silk. In one hand he held aloft a blazing lantern, the brightest point of light in the underworld. In the other hand was a bow and arrow.

"Apollo!" Nico said. "The archer."

A shiver ran the length of Gerald's spine, then turned around and scuttled back the other way. Things seemed to be getting very close to home.

Ruby appeared at his elbow, holding two blazing torches. "Come on," she said. "Let's see what's so special about this temple."

The four of them approached the temple steps in a line. Columns towered above them and Gerald had a flashback to walking into the British Museum for the first time just eight weeks ago.

They entered the portico. The doors to the temple—two enormous wooden portals—stood closed before them. Gerald was so transfixed by the majesty of everything around him that he didn't see the slab of white marble jutting up from the floor. He stubbed his toe, hard.

"Ow!" he cried, hopping on one foot and holding back the stream of swear words that flooded his brain. "Why would you leave that in the middle of the floor?"

He pointed his flaming torch to the ground. The slab of white stone was about a yard square and lay right in front of the temple doors.

"Look," Ruby said. "There's something carved into it."

She moved her torch in closer. The flickering light waved across letters chiseled into the polished surface.

It read, in clear English: *Gerald Wilkins, welcome.*

Chapter 27

Gerald stumbled backward, almost falling to the ground. Ruby stared at the slab in astonishment. "How did that get there?" she said.

Gerald gazed dumbly at the letters carved into the stone.

"How could anyone know you'd be coming here?" Ruby said. "This place has been deserted for more than a thousand years."

"It's fate," Gerald muttered. "Someone must have known."

"Rubbish!" Ruby said. "It's just a—"

"Coincidence?" Gerald interrupted. He took Ruby by the wrist and pulled her torch down until the flames licked across his name on the slab. "Even this must be too much for the coincidence queen to write off as just one of those things. Two turns around the table in London didn't stop me from seeing this, did it? So much for the chaos theory. So much for nothing is certain. This looks pretty certain to me."

Ruby dropped to her knees and ran her fingertips across the chiseled letters of Gerald's name. "But if this was carved all these years ago, how would they know how to speak English? Wouldn't it be Greek?"

"The Oracle," Nico said. "It must have been the Oracle."

"She could speak English?" Sam said.

Nico shook his head. "The Oracle would go into a trance and communicate directly with Apollo," he explained. "The temple priests would write down the responses, even if they didn't understand them."

Ruby snorted. "So Apollo was dictating? He told her to expect a visit from a Gerald Wilkins in about sixteen hundred years and she'd better put the kettle on? That's ridiculous."

Gerald tapped his boot against the marble slab. "Well, it's a ton of ridiculous, whatever it is."

"It's signed," Ruby said.

There was a dull silence.

"What did you say?" Gerald asked.

"I said, it's signed. The Oracle's name is at the bottom."

"Well, that'll come in handy if I happen to bump into her down here. What's her name?"

Ruby swallowed. "It's . . . Clea."

"Clea!" Gerald said. "The same name as my dad's cousin? The captain of the parlor game goon squad?" He raised his head to the ceiling. "So that's just another coincidence, is it, Ruby?"

Ruby took in a sharp breath. "Oh my gosh, Gerald."

"What now?" Gerald asked.

"Your family tree from Mason Green's room in the Rattigan Club."

Gerald furrowed his brow, remembering the diagram of his family tree scrawled across the wall in Green's private rooms. It seemed so long ago.

"What about it?"

"Ever since we met your dad's cousin that night of the party, something has been bugging me. Don't you remember? The family tree showed your mother's family, all the way back to Quintus Antonius and his three sons."

"Yeah—that's why we're here," Gerald said.

"We've been concentrating on them all this time: the secret mission for the emperor, the three caskets, the assassin sent to hunt them down."

"So?"

"But what about your father's side of the family? Think about what was on the wall at the Rattigan Club. Your dad's family traced back to one woman."

Gerald focused his mind. He saw his father's name written on the wall, then lines and names branching back through the generations, and finally honing in on a single name.

"Clea!"

Gerald stared with saucer eyes at the writing on the marble slab.

Clea.

Was he a direct descendant of the last Oracle of Delphi—the same woman that his mother's ancestors had been sent to destroy?

"You are the progeny!" Ruby jumped up and grabbed Gerald by the arm, her excitement flowing through her touch. "That's what the fortune-teller in India told you. He saw it in you. After sixteen hundred years, the two sides of this puzzle have come together. Your blood flows from the Oracle of Delphi, and from the emperor's right-hand man."

Gerald tried to keep the curdling feeling in his belly from erupting into his throat. "Professor McElderry said something about the progeny at the fancy dress party," Gerald mumbled. "Something about a family legend."

"Of course!" Ruby said. "The big family secret that Mason Green kept banging on about. I bet that's why you had those visions—in the museum, and in Mr. Hoskins's bookshop in Glastonbury. Somewhere deep inside you, Gerald, lies the power of the Oracle."

Gerald stared again at his name in the white marble. A name carved in antiquity. He thought back to the golden rods, and the gems that had kept them locked away in the caskets. Of the visions he had experienced when under their spell. The sensation of being everywhere, of seeing everything.

Of having the power to see all that would be.

The power of the Oracle.

"What am I supposed to do?" Gerald looked Ruby square in the eyes. His voice quavered. "What am I supposed to do?"

Ruby reached out to Gerald's shaking hands.

"The door's open." It was Sam. He and Nico were standing at the temple entrance. One of the enormous portals stood ajar.

"How did you manage that?" Ruby asked.

"Um, I just sort of leaned against it and it moved," Sam said. "Want to take a peek inside?"

Gerald looked to Ruby. She gave him a reassuring nod. "Let's do it," she said.

Two torches flamed above the entrance, on either side of a large block of marble. Some script in Greek lettering was carved into the stonework. Ruby nodded toward it. "Nico, can you read that?"

Nico gazed at the lettering. "Of course. It says *gnothi seauton*—"

Gerald came to an abrupt halt.

"Did you just say 'nothing is certain'?"

Nico looked at him, confused.

Gerald advanced on him. "Did you just say 'nothing is certain'?" He was almost shouting at Nico.

Nico stared up at Gerald.

"Answer me!" Gerald's face was flushed and the torch-light cast deep shadows under his eyes.

"Steady on, Gerald." Sam moved to Nico's side. "He's just reading what's there."

"Then he can tell me if it says 'nothing is certain.'" Gerald's voice verged close to hysterical. "That phrase has been dogging me since the last day of school and I want to know if somebody carved it here two thousand years ago."

Nico cleared his throat. "It says *gnothi seauton.* It is a Greek saying."

Gerald was breathing hard, his temper bubbling under his skin.

"It means 'know thyself,'" Nico said calmly. "It is the most famous of the seven maxims that were said to be carved in the temple walls."

Ruby grabbed Gerald and pulled him away. "What's the matter with you?" she said. "Why are you yelling at Nico?"

Gerald clenched a fist against his forehead, punching himself. "It sounded like he said 'nothing is certain.' You don't understand. It was in a daydream I had at school. Then the fortune-teller in Delhi said it. Maybe I heard it wrong. But it's doing my head in. This whole Oracle thing . . . it feels like my brain is about to explode."

Ruby squeezed Gerald's arm. "We've come a long way, Gerald," she said. "You know I'm with you on this. No matter what."

Gerald's eyes were closed. He breathed deep, and nodded.

"We can't be far from whatever's at the center of all this," Ruby said, her voice a balm. "Let's just keep going."

Gerald opened his eyes to find Ruby staring at him. The corners of her mouth tweaked upward.

Gerald apologized to Nico and the four of them crossed the threshold into the Temple of Apollo.

The interior was lit by a string of oil lamps that ran the length of the ceiling high above.

"That's one impressive lighting system," Sam said. "It must all be connected to that lamp out the front. You Greeks were pretty clever, Nico."

"We still are," Nico said.

The temple was one enormous chamber filled with shrines and offerings to Apollo. Rich tapestries hung from the ceiling, gold and silver statues stood atop marble plinths, and murals of Apollo's heroic deeds covered the walls.

The only sound was the soft landing of four sets of boots on the polished stone floor.

"It's untouched," Ruby said. "This must have been exactly how it was in ancient times."

They reached the far end of the temple and a stairwell that descended into darkness.

"This must be the entrance to the inner sanctum," Nico

said. "The holiest place in the temple. Where Apollo talked to the Oracle."

"Are you feeling anything, Gerald?" Sam asked. "You know—vision things."

Gerald tried to concentrate, to conjure something out of his brain. But all he could sense was a head stuffed with cotton wool.

"Nothing," he said. He shone his torch down the stairwell. "May as well take a look." He led the way down.

"So, Nico, this Apollo," Sam said, "was he a good god or a nasty god?"

"He was the god of music, of the sun, and of prophecy," Nico said. "But all the gods had their failings. He would go into insane rages if women rejected him—Apollo could do terrible things."

"Terrific," Sam said. "At home with the nutty god of jealous fits."

Gerald reached the bottom of the stairs to find a blank stone wall. He moved his torch over the surface; the flames licked across a featureless lump of solid granite.

"No markings, no handle, no nothing," he said.

Ruby squeezed in beside him on the bottom step and wedged her shoulder against the rock.

"That's not moving for anyone," she grunted. "It must weigh a ton."

"Now what do we do?" Gerald said.

"Hey, Gerald," Sam said. "What's that on the wall by your elbow?"

Gerald looked down to his left. Set into the side wall was a bronze plate, about a foot square.

"It's flat metal," Gerald said. He squatted to his haunches to look closer. "There are three circles close together in the middle. There's something pressed into them. Hold on." He moved his torch in.

"Far out," Gerald breathed. He closed his eyes and leaned his forehead against the metal plate.

"What is it?" Ruby asked.

"My family seal," Gerald said. "Again."

The yellow light flickered across three clear indentations in the metal plate, each imprinted with the triangle of arms and the blazing sun of the Archer family seal.

Gerald plugged the three holes with the tips of his fingers. Then his eyes sprang open.

"The rings!"

"What?"

"The three signet rings," Gerald said. "Sam, come down here."

Sam shuffled down the stairs to stand behind Gerald and Ruby.

"The three rings are a key," Gerald said. "This must be the way into the Oracle's chamber. Gaius, Marcus, and Lucius must have locked it so that the only way to open it was for all three of them to be here." He pressed the seal on his ring into one of the holes. It fitted perfectly.

"Come on, you two," Gerald said.

Ruby placed her ring into position. It was a seamless match too. Sam leaned over Gerald's shoulder and stretched out to reach the bronze plate.

The moment the third ring slotted into place there was a low rumbling beneath their feet, as if a giant clockwork mechanism had been summoned to life. Ruby shot a glance at Gerald. "There better not be any booby traps," she said. The rumbling vibrated up their legs, then the massive granite block at the bottom of the stairs swung inward.

Gerald looked at the others. "Let's see what my relatives were keeping locked up in here."

They walked into a square room with a low stone ceiling.

In contrast to the extravagance of the temple above, the room was quite bare. Along one wall was a line of about twenty stone busts, all women, blank eyes staring into the center of the chamber. Two golden eagles, wings spread wide, perched on narrow stands on either side of a square section of the floor that was sunk about ten inches into the ground, forming a shallow pit. A single oil lamp was suspended from the ceiling above the sunken floor.

"It's a bit plain, isn't it?" Ruby said. "If you're going to commune with the gods, I mean."

Gerald surveyed the chamber. He hadn't known what

to expect, but this certainly wasn't it. He placed his torch into a metal bracket on one side of the door, and Ruby found another one on the other side.

"So this is where Apollo hung out," Sam said. "Bit of a dump."

Gerald crossed the floor, stepping over a white line of marble that split the room in two, and down into the shallow pit to look at the eagle statues. "Maybe he was impressive enough in person that he didn't need to decorate," Gerald said, running his fingers over the sculpted feathers on the eagle's chest.

"Or maybe it was all a load of rubbish," Ruby said. "A show for the pilgrims, to keep the money rolling in."

"Are you still saying all this is coincidence?" Gerald said. "What about my name carved in stone out the front?"

He couldn't make out Ruby's mumbled reply.

"Is that lamp getting dimmer?" Sam asked, looking at the light above Gerald's head. "Come on, Nico. Let's go top up the oil. Won't be a minute."

Sam and Nico disappeared back up the stairs. Ruby crossed the room and sat on the floor, her feet in the pit.

"So now what?" she said, letting out an enormous yawn. "We've found the treasure of Delphi. But that doesn't get you off the hook with the police."

Gerald plopped down next to Ruby. His shoulder brushed against hers. "I know. We're still no closer to proving that

341

Charlotte killed her uncle and framed me for it."

Ruby slumped an elbow onto her knee and took a deep breath. "I'm so tired."

Gerald blinked. "Me too."

"How do we get out of here? Do we just wait for Jarvis to find us?"

"I guess so." Gerald leaned up against Ruby's shoulder. "My eyes are so heavy."

Gerald slipped sideward to the floor. He rested his head on his arm. The adventures of the summer had finally caught up with him; he couldn't remember feeling so drained. He closed his eyes. There were footsteps coming down the stairs. Gerald lifted his head and forced his eyelids open. The lamp above them had dimmed even further. He could make out the shape of two people entering the room.

"Nico?" The voice slurred from his lips. "Sam?"

Gerald's mind was a fog. But he could swear that one of the faces staring down at him was that of a silver-haired man. And was that a walking stick in his hand?

Sir Mason Green smiled at him.

Then a wave of fatigue swept Gerald away.

Chapter 28

"Nothing is certain."

Gerald knew he was dreaming. He knew he was asleep and in the middle of a nightmare. But no matter how hard he tried, he couldn't open his eyes. It was like he'd forgotten how.

Everything was awash—like he was wearing a leaky pair of swimming goggles.

He was in the dining room at Avonleigh, his country estate near Glastonbury. But for some reason, the room was filled with water.

And there were people in the room. Lots of people.

There was his mother; her face suddenly came into focus. "Nothing is certain, Gerald," Vi trilled, then swam out of view.

His father wafted by, his face shimmering like oil on

343

water. "Nothing is certain, my boy." He executed a neat tumble turn and frog-kicked away.

Gerald tried to make someone stop and talk with him, but everyone was too busy. "Nothing is certain," Mr. Fry said before dashing off after Miss Turner, like a dolphin after a fish.

Alisha Gupta and Kali drifted past hand in hand, giggling. "Nothing is certain, Gerald," they chorused, blowing him kisses.

Mr. Hoskins, the old family friend, was sitting in a wingback armchair, trying to light a cigar. He darted out of the chair to shove a small white ball into Gerald's mouth. "Nothing is certain," Hoskins said, "not even peppermints." He kicked and swam out a window.

Gerald gagged as the mint bit into his throat. He spied his housekeeper fussing over a table arrangement that was trying to float off. "Mrs. Rutherford," he called, trying to get to her. But the harder he swam, the further away she drifted. "Mrs. Rutherford!"

From nowhere, the face of Sir Mason Green flashed up, leering at him. The old man raised his hand and struck it hard against Gerald's cheek.

Once.

Twice.

And Gerald was awake.

His face burned from the assault. He sat up with a jerk to find Mason Green glaring down at him. Green was standing between the statues of the golden eagles in the Temple of Apollo, leaning on his cane. A cane, Gerald knew, that contained a lethal sword.

"Gerald," the man said with a smug grin. "Aren't you going to say hello to an old friend?"

Gerald's mind buzzed. How could Green possibly be there?

"Stay out of my dreams!" Gerald managed to say. "Stay away from me."

Green's smile lingered. "Oh, this is no dream, Gerald. You are well and truly stuck in harsh reality."

Gerald stared up at the man through narrow eyes. "I don't care what deal you've done with the devil," Gerald said. "Where are my friends?"

Green laughed—a polite gentleman's laugh. "Such a fertile imagination. No, Gerald. I haven't done any deals. I just planned ahead."

Gerald went to stand. But Green whipped the sword from the scabbard and motioned for Gerald to resume his seat. "You didn't seriously think I gave myself up to the authorities to go through the tiresome inconvenience of a trial? The law is for other people, Gerald. I have more important things to do."

"But I saw you die," Gerald said. "In the court."

"Ah, did you see me? Or someone very like me?"

"What? Your twin brother?"

Green was horrified. "How could you suggest such a

thing, Gerald? Family is very important to me. No, that was merely a lookalike. I got the idea from one of those tin-pot African dictators who used a double to stand in for him at public appearances just in case someone decided to take a shot at him. It's amazing what can be achieved with cosmetic surgery. I found someone who sounded a bit like me and looked a little like me, and then paid him to look a lot like me."

Gerald was appalled. "Who would take money to get killed? That's insane."

"Oh, the chap didn't know about that little detail. He thought he'd serve a few years in prison at worst, then come out to a fat Swiss bank account. And as I hear it, the way my barrister was going, he was probably going to walk free anyway."

"Then why kill him?"

"A calculated gamble, Gerald. The best way to stop the police from snooping on your affairs is to have them think you're dead. And the best way to stop someone from getting in the way is to frame him for the murder. And thanks to my niece's delightful skills in the chemistry lab, we achieved both. She got a first at Cambridge, you know. We're very proud of her."

Gerald focused on the tip of Green's sword, which was still pointed at his chest.

"You see, Gerald," Green continued, "you were always

the greatest threat to my little endeavor. But after you survived your scrape in India, it was just too difficult to have you killed. It would have raised much suspicion. I came up with the idea for a double a few years ago. He'd been living a comfortable life in one of my Swiss chalets, learning my mannerisms and imitating my voice. He served his purpose well. But I didn't count on you escaping from the police."

"You've got your treasure now—all the gold in Delphi," Gerald said. "Big deal. You're already a billionaire. But you're a dead billionaire as far as the world is concerned. You'll have to stay in hiding forever."

Green laughed again. "Gerald, have you listened to nothing I've told you? It's not about money. It's about what every man, if he's honest with himself, is thirsting for. Power. Absolute power. To be subservient to no one—to be above all."

"How does a mountain of gold get you that?" Gerald said.

"It doesn't. All that shiny metal? Keep it. It's yours. Give it to the poor if that helps you sleep at night. Don't you know your family secret yet, Gerald?"

Gerald fixed the man with a flintlike glare.

"I am the progeny," Gerald said. "I am the two strands of this place, entwined again, sixteen hundred years after it was buried."

"Bravo, Gerald! You have done well. I've had my eye on

your family for longer than you've been alive. As you know, I collect ancient documents. And the legend of Delphi has long intrigued me. That's how I learned of your family's unique status. So when you were born, the product of the descendants of the Oracle and its destroyer, I knew you were special. Your great-aunt tried to protect you, of course, sending you to Australia. But your destiny would always bring you here. Gerald, you are tied to this place. That is why you had such a strong reaction when you touched these." Green lifted a slender tube from the floor and eased a cover from one end.

"The golden rods," Gerald said.

Green smiled. "What did you call them in India, Gerald? Cheap old relics?" Green snorted with delight. "They gave you quite the jolt. So they should. They are the key to everything. They key to knowing everything."

Gerald had a sudden flash of understanding. "That's what you're after?" he said. "To see the future?"

"Of course," Green said. "Knowledge—the ambition of every cultured human."

Gerald stared at him, horrified. "But if you see into the future, you can influence what's going to happen—change destinies."

"Yes," Green said with a smirk. "I will be a god."

The power of the Oracle in Green's hands—a man who had killed without hesitation. It was unthinkable.

"That's why Emperor Theodosius sent Quintus and his

sons here in the first place," Green said. "To steal the secret of the Oracle."

"Yeah, and kill everybody in the town," Gerald said with disgust.

"I believe that was the plan. But my research shows that Quintus and his sons decided that the Oracle's power was too great to be trusted to anyone, particularly the emperor. So they made sure he would never get it."

"They weren't after the gold?" Gerald said.

"Gerald, you've got to stop thinking in such base terms. This is about ultimate power. The Oracle was expecting your ancestors, of course. She knew what was coming. And she was prepared. Clea convinced Quintus to help with her plan. Together with the townsfolk they created a fake town, designed to look like it had been sacked. They then buried the real city, leaving the Oracle's secret safely inside. To make sure it was secure, the three brothers each took a golden rod in a locked casket and set off, never to see each other again. When the emperor found he'd been crossed, he sent my ancestor Octavius Viridian after them. As you know, he found Marcus in India and killed him. That's how Marcus's ring came to be mine."

Gerald was astonished. His ancestors weren't murderers—they'd tried to protect the Oracle's secret.

Green slid one of the golden rods from the tube. "I will be the most powerful person in modern history. Presidents and kings will bow down to me, just as the mighty prostrated themselves to the Oracle in ancient times." A look of ultimate greed shone in Green's eyes. "I just need one last thing before I fulfill my destiny."

The lamplight played across the surface of the rod like fingers on a gilded flute.

"I've asked you before, Gerald, and I'll ask again. Tell me what you see, when I do this?" Green dropped his sword and grabbed Gerald by the hair. He held out the golden rod and laid it across Gerald's forehead.

Gerald's eyes shot wide. The cotton-wool fog inside his head ignited in an inferno. Gerald could see with absolute clarity. He tried not to tell Green what he saw, but he was compelled to speak.

"There's a person." Gerald could hear his own voice filling the room, as if it were someone else speaking. "Wearing a mask. The most powerful being on earth."

Green whipped the rod away. Gerald collapsed to the floor with a colossal headache.

"Perfect," Green said. "Truly perfect."

Gerald was on his hands and knees in the shallow pit, sucking in air. His head felt like it had been fried. "Where are Sam and Ruby?" he breathed. "And Nico?"

Green took the remaining rods from the tube and laid them at his feet. "They are with my niece, where they belong," he said.

Gerald didn't understand. "Belong?"

"Naturally. Charlotte and your friends have known each other for years. She used to babysit them."

Gerald jolted his head. What was Green saying?

"Gerald, you need to understand—neither fate nor coincidence brought you here. I did."

Green paused to let the enormity of his words soak in.

"I thought I could find this place by myself, Gerald. That's why I framed you for the murder—to get you out of the way. But your escape from the police forced a change in plan. And it worked in my favor. Have you ever tried fly-fishing, Gerald? You really should. Using wit and subterfuge to fool another creature is the most tremendous fun: to dangle something in front of its nose until it risks everything to take a bite. How do you think I found you so quickly in this place? How do you think I've been able to follow you all the way? In Glastonbury with the diamond casket? Then in India and France."

"What are you saying?"

"Young Sam and Ruby have played their parts brilliantly. But surely you must have suspected."

Again, Green paused, glaring down at the horror dawning on Gerald's face.

Then, as if he was thrusting his sword into Gerald's chest, Green rammed the point home. "Sam and Ruby have been working for me all along."

CHAPTER 29

Gerald stared down at the dusty floor. Green's words were clear enough, but Gerald could make no sense of them. Ruby and Sam . . . had betrayed him?

"They were bait, Gerald. To get you to use your special talents to lead me here. And you swallowed it whole," said Sir Mason Green.

Gerald couldn't accept what Green was saying. It was impossible. His head swam with memories of the past two months. "But you tried to kill Sam in the burial chamber under Beaconsfield," Gerald said.

"Convincing, wasn't it? And yet"—Green spread his arms wide—"here we are. Simple Sam, loyal Sam—leaving little messages along the way. Do you remember the pigeon post that you used in India? Sam slipped in an extra note for me. And Ruby . . . such a pretty girl, don't you agree? So resourceful. So convincing. I bet you thought she liked you. Maybe even a little more than just liked you."

"You're lying!" Gerald cried. "Ruby would never deceive me."

"Really? How many times have you been on the brink of giving up this chase? Of going home and enjoying your massive fortune? A dozen times? More? And who has been the voice in your ear, urging you on? Giving you little hugs and words of encouragement."

Gerald felt like Green was landing hammer blows to his temple. Could it be true? Could Ruby have been playing him for a fool from the very beginning? Gerald's mind shot back to when he'd first met Ruby and Sam. It was in the British Museum, when the thin man was dragging him away. Ruby had turned up out of nowhere, batting her eyelids and stealing him to safety. Then, time after time, when Gerald had been on the verge of giving up, Ruby was always there—with a smile, or a squeeze on the arm, or a peck on the cheek. A laugh and a kind word. There were times when she was the only reason he'd kept at it.

Green hovered over him. "Just last night at Charlotte's house, didn't you think it odd that you were the only one captured, that the others miraculously got away, only to come back just in time to rescue you?" Gerald screwed his eyes shut, not wanting to listen. "But not before Charlotte was able to give you a little taste of one of her marvelous medicines—just enough to help you find this place. Just enough for you to lead me here."

Green was eyeing Gerald closely, watching his expression. "They deceived you, Gerald. It's amazing what money will convince some people to do."

Gerald's mind was awash with memories, and with the pain of treachery. "It can't be true." A sob caught in his throat. A tear budded in the corner of an eye and rolled down his cheek. His head slumped. After everything he had experienced, this was the hardest blow.

"Come, Gerald, don't take it to heart. People can be cruel. The secret is not to grow too attached to them. I never do."

Gerald jumped to his feet, but Green had his sword in his hand. "Don't be foolish, Gerald." The tip of the blade was at Gerald's throat. "You're in denial. You're feeling shock. Anger. Rejection. It's all perfectly natural. Sam and Ruby betrayed you. Accept it. Then do something about it."

Gerald looked into Green's eyes. They were snake's eyes—cool, without emotion, calculating.

"What do you mean?"

"I have no further use for them," Green said. "Take your revenge, Gerald." Green's lips spread like he was part crocodile. "It's delicious."

A lump the size of a golf ball lodged in Gerald's throat.

The old man shouted up the stairwell. Seconds later Ruby and Sam appeared in the doorway. They were laughing.

Gerald couldn't believe it. They were actually laughing.

"Hi, Gerald," Ruby said brightly. "How have you been?" Sam sniggered behind her. It was as if they were drunk with victory.

Gerald couldn't look at them. His knees buckled. He thought he was going to be sick.

Charlotte followed Ruby and Sam into the chamber. She held her ivory hairpin in one hand. "You will behave, won't you, Gerald?" she said. She tapped Ruby and Sam on the shoulder. "Come, children. Sit by me."

Ruby smiled up at Charlotte and nodded like an obedient puppy. "Okay," she said. Charlotte sat between Ruby and Sam on the far side of the shallow pit. Sam whispered something to Ruby and she burst into giggles. Gerald had to look away.

Green sheathed his sword and crouched down. He picked up one of the three golden rods and carefully held it by its ends. Then he twisted his hands. Gerald watched in amazement as the rod telescoped outward, extending to about three feet in length. The intricate engraving on its surface transformed to reveal the image of a python twisted around it.

Green's eyes shone at the golden shaft balanced in his hands. "Did you know, Gerald," he said, "that a three-legged stool will never wobble?"

Gerald edged back to the lip of the pit and sat down. "What are you talking about?"

Green laid the extended rod on the floor, and Gerald noticed three notches in the stonework by his feet. They formed a large triangle.

"The mystery surrounding the Oracle of Delphi has confounded scholars for centuries," Green said. He extended the second rod with a turn of his wrists and placed it by the first. "You may have heard that the temple was situated over a fault in the earth and would fill with gas, sending the Oracle into a drugged frenzy." Green picked up the last rod and unlocked it with a twist. He placed it with the other two: three identical poles, each decorated with a twirled snake. "I think the gas was actually a trap for intruders. It's what sent you off to sleep, Gerald. If I hadn't opened a vent you would have quietly asphyxiated. No, the true power of the Oracle resides in these three legs."

"They're legs?" Gerald said. "Legs of what?"

Green fixed him with a steady stare. "The Oracle's chair, of course. The holy tripod of legend. The ultimate seat of power."

Green picked up the rods and slotted each of them in turn into the three notches in the floor. Their tops came together to create a tripod. The moment the third rod fell into place, a low rumble sounded from deep beneath the shallow pit. Three fine cracks appeared in the stone floor, connecting the base of the tripod. A triangular paving stone sank, revealing a hole in the ground.

Green reached into its depths and his face lit up with

the thrill of discovery. He pulled two objects from the fissure in the earth. "The Oracle would sit on this saddle atop the tripod," he said. He held up a jewel-encrusted seat, which he fitted onto the apex of the golden rods. "And she would wear this to see the secrets of the future." Green held a gilded mask, molded to fit above the nose and entirely cover the eyes.

Gerald couldn't believe the look of absolute desire on Green's face. Across the pit, Charlotte straightened. Her eyes were fixed on the object in Green's hand.

"The Oracle's mask," Green whispered, his eyes reflecting the dance of gold light from the mask cupped in his hands. "It would blind her to this room, but open her eyes to all eternity."

Green dragged his gaze away from the mask and locked onto Gerald.

"And now, it is mine."

He crossed to Gerald's side and hauled him up by the shirtfront. "This is where you get your revenge, Gerald. The power locked in this mask is unlike anything known to this world. Such power is dangerous. For over a thousand years only women held the role of Oracle. There must have been a reason for that, so I'm not taking any chances." Green looked to Charlotte and dropped his voice so that only Gerald could hear. "My niece has graciously volunteered to be the first Oracle of the modern day. Through her, I will see all. But I want to test it first. And that's where Miss Valentine comes into play."

Gerald's eyes paused for a second on Ruby's face. A knot of hate twisted in his gut.

Green nodded at his niece.

Charlotte stood and held out a hand to Ruby. "Come along," she said. "We've got a surprise for you."

Ruby rose unsteadily to her feet and grinned at Sam. "I love surprises," she said.

Gerald frowned at her. What was she on about?

"Put her on the tripod," Green instructed.

"You want me to sit up here?" Ruby said to Charlotte. "Okay. But you stay close in case I fall off!" She laughed, then climbed into the saddle on top of the three golden rods. Charlotte stood behind her with a steadying hand on one shoulder.

Green held the mask to Gerald. "Put this on Miss Valentine's face," Green said. "I want to see it at work."

Gerald looked down at the mask. It glowed.

He reached out and Green tipped the mask into his hand. As it touched his palm, it softened; it seemed to mold to Gerald's fingers. He swallowed a jagged ball of pain as a lightning bolt shot up his arm and into his chest, piercing his heart like a blade. It took all his strength to stay upright, to hide the torment he was suffering.

And the scales were blasted from his eyes.

The golden rods had given Gerald a clarity of sight. But it was nothing to the purity of vision that he experienced holding the Oracle's mask. A white surge cleared everything from his mind; a wave of light silenced the usual mental noise, leaving a perfect emptiness.

Nirvana.

Gerald felt he could control the power in his grasp; he could direct it to whatever ends he desired. And he saw a way forward.

"Isn't it funny, Gerald." Green's voice cut through the white silence. "The number of times I've tried to kill you, only for you to wriggle free. And then you lead me right to the object of my desire. It's as if you were destined to live for that purpose."

Gerald's focus was absolute. He took a step toward Ruby perched on the Oracle's tripod. She was smiling at him. "Hello, Gerald," she said. "What do you have there?"

Charlotte and Green leaned forward.

Gerald raised his hand, holding the golden mask between his fingertips.

"That's it, Gerald," Green said, his eyes wide. "Let's witness the birth of a new Oracle."

Gerald's course was set. He couldn't let this treachery stand.

Nothing is certain.

Gnothi seauton.

Know thyself.

Ruby smiled again, her eyes calm and relaxed.

Gerald moved closer. The mask was centimeters from Ruby's face.

"*Gnothi seauton!*" Gerald cried. "Know thyself!"

Then he thrust his hand forward, and drove the Oracle's mask hard onto Charlotte's face.

The moment the mask bridged Charlotte's nose it molded onto her, sealing itself against her skin with a burning hiss. She howled with pain, throwing her hands to her face to tear at the metal veil across her eyes. The poisoned hairpin flew into the air in a lethal arc.

Gerald pulled Ruby clear of the tripod just before the pin skewered the seat. He threw her across the pit, straight into Sir Mason Green. The impact knocked Green sideways and he fell, striking his head on the stone floor.

Green lay motionless. Sam sat on the side of the pit, his eyes wide.

"I can see!" Charlotte howled, her hands pressed to her temples. "I can see everything."

Gerald raced to Ruby lying on the floor. She blinked up at him as he rolled her over and inspected the skin near the inside of her elbow. "Just as I thought," he muttered. He was looking at a fresh puncture wound.

"All the future is mine!" Charlotte stepped out of the pit and was stumbling toward the doorway. "The future is mine!"

Then she stepped across the white marble line in the floor.

The moment her foot touched the stone on the other

side, her spine snapped straight. Her screams reached a new level. Her arms flung back and her chin tilted up. She was like a white swan in the moment before flight.

A blinding pulse of energy burst through the eyeholes in the mask. White light filled the room like an exploding star. Gerald threw himself over Ruby and shielded his face. He could sense the raw power against his back. The brightness was overwhelming. Then Charlotte's screams stopped, and the temple was silent.

For a few seconds, Gerald didn't move. Then he slowly righted himself.

Charlotte stood frozen in place near the door to the temple, the mask still on her face.

Gerald yanked the hairpin from the Oracle's chair and held it out like a dagger. He circled to the front of Charlotte and looked up at her.

Her skin was a chalky white and her head was still tilted up, as if she was staring into the furthest corners of eternity. Gerald reached out a hand and tapped Charlotte's arm. At his touch, the limb disintegrated into a fine powder.

Gerald jumped back. "Holy cow!" The tip of the hairpin brushed Charlotte's shirt, and the rest of her body caved in. Like an imploding building, Charlotte collapsed in a mound of crystalline sand. Feet, legs, torso, shoulders— they all went down like a house of cards. Last to go was her head, which landed intact on the pile of sand on the floor.

The mask fell free, revealing a pair of calcified eyes, sealed against all light.

Gerald stared in shock at the fossilized head that gazed sightless back at him.

He moved only when he heard the muffled groan coming from Ruby.

"What happened?" Ruby was gulping in air. She wiped a hand across her face. "I feel kind of woozy." She raised herself to her elbows and looked around the chamber. "What happened to Charlotte?"

"Never mind her," Gerald said. "Do you remember anything after we fell asleep in here?"

Ruby thought for a second, then she placed a hand on her forearm. "There was a needle," she said. "Oh my gosh! She injected us with something."

Sam's voice floated across from the far side of the pit. He was flat on his back on the floor. "Whatever it was, it made everything hilarious."

Gerald grinned. "I knew it," he said. "Green tried to convince me that you were working for him."

"Are you serious?" Sam said. He stumbled over to them. "Who would ever believe that?"

Gerald cleared his throat. "Yeah," he said. "Ridiculous."

Ruby gave him a curious look. "What happened to Charlotte?"

"She crossed the line," Gerald said.

"I saw that," Ruby said. "But what happened to her?

It was like she turned to salt."

"I think she was . . ." Gerald struggled to find the right word. "I think she was consumed. When I held that mask, it was like I could see what was going to happen down here. I could see Charlotte stepping over that line in the floor and then petrifying like that."

"But why did it happen?" Sam asked.

"I think it's the reason the Oracle did her thing locked up in this chamber. If you're going to see into the future, you can't actually exist in the present."

"In English, please."

"Ruby was right. It's like that walk around the table at the restaurant back in London," Gerald said. "Everything anyone does has an impact on future events. The future isn't some predetermined place that we're traveling to—it's something that we create with every decision we make. By crossing that line on the floor, Charlotte must have moved from a place where the Oracle could have no impact on the outside world, to one where she could."

"And every step she took further into the outside world was changing the future," Ruby said. "Every time she moved, the future she was seeing had to be recast in her mind."

"It was too much for her brain to take. She couldn't process it," Gerald said. "It ate her up."

Sam let out a grunt. "I guess she didn't see that coming, then."

Gerald looked down at the mask, pitched into the pile

of sand. "Each Oracle must have been condemned to stay in this room. If she crossed that line, she'd end up like that."

Ruby looked over at the tripod in the center of the shallow pit. "That was the only safe place for her to sit until the day she died," she said.

Gerald scanned the line of busts along the wall. "This must be all that's left of the Oracles of Delphi. What a sacrifice." He knelt and picked up Charlotte's head. It was surprisingly heavy. There was a vacant plinth at the end of the wall and Gerald lifted the head onto it. As he settled it in place, he saw there was a word neatly engraved in the base: *Charlotte*. He looked at the bust next to it.

"Clea," he said. "Looks like she knew how all this would end from the very start."

Sam nudged the mask with the toe of his boot. "What do we do with this thing?"

Gerald pulled his T-shirt over his head and wrapped it around his right hand. Gingerly he scooped up the mask and carried it back to the opening beneath the tripod. "It was locked up safe in here for sixteen hundred years," he said. "No reason it can't stay here for the next sixteen hundred."

Sam suddenly shouted, "Nico!" He made a dash for the door. "They tied him up back in the temple."

Gerald went to follow, but Ruby held him back.

She looked up at him. "You know Green was lying, don't you? About Sam and me."

Gerald raised and lowered a shoulder. "I know. He just wanted to use you as a test dummy and he wanted me to do the honors. He almost had me convinced, though. What he said was true—you're the only reason I kept pursuing this thing. You're the one who kept me going. He made it sound like you'd put on an act. I couldn't believe you'd be interested in . . ." His voice trailed off.

Ruby smiled. "In you?" she said, her face lighting up. "Oh, Gerald. I kept urging you on because I know how important it was for you to solve this mystery, to do what your great-aunt asked. I would never lie to you."

Gerald bit his bottom lip. "You're a good friend," he said.

Ruby hugged him. "So are you," she said.

And, for the first time, Gerald hugged back.

A low moan sounded from the floor. Sir Mason Green was starting to come to. Gerald pulled the laces from his boots and bound the old man's ankles and hands.

"There," Gerald said, beaming up at Ruby. "Best defense to a murder charge there is—the victim with a pulse."

EPILOGUE

"Eight hearts!"

Mrs. Rutherford studied Sam over the top of her glasses.

"A brave bid indeed, Master Sam," she said, rifling through her hand. "Are you sure?"

Sam grinned with supreme confidence. "No guts, no glory, Mrs. R."

The game of Five Hundred had been a battlefield for the best part of an hour. Sam and Mr. Fry were partnered against Ruby and Mrs. Rutherford, and the scores were even. The tension over the card table in the drawing room at Gerald's Chelsea townhouse was starting to build.

Gerald and his lawyer, Mr. Prisk, sat in armchairs by the fireplace, going over a sheaf of papers on a low coffee table.

A tray with a pitcher of iced lemon squash sat untouched on the table.

Gerald looked up from the pad where he was doodling while listening to Mr. Prisk. "Hey, guess what?"

"What?" Ruby said.

"Did you know that *cheap old relic* is an anagram for *Delphic Oracle?*"

"Is that right?" Ruby said. She laid the joker on Sam's lead. "My trick, dopey."

The housekeeper beamed with delight. "Oh, well played, Miss Ruby. The girls win again."

"Ha! Who would have thought that parlor games could be such fun?" Ruby said. She gathered the cards together and cut the pack. "Another hand?"

Mr. Fry stood from the table and straightened his jacket. "I'd better not. I have an appointment in an hour and I'd best be getting ready."

"Dinner with Miss Turner again, Mr. Fry?" Ruby said. "That's the third time this week, isn't it?"

Fry turned a russet red. "Miss Turner will be going down to Cheltenham next week to oversee Miss Gupta's return to school. I am merely keeping her company while she is in London."

"Ignore her, Mr. Fry," Gerald said. "She's teasing. Have a great night." Before Fry could reach the door, Gerald spoke up again. "And Mr. Fry?"

The butler turned in the doorway to face him.

"Yes, sir?"

"Thanks again for what you did in France. There aren't many people who'd risk arrest the way you did. I'd be locked up if it wasn't for you."

Fry's face grew wistful. "I know. I think about it every day." He closed the door behind him as he left.

Mr. Prisk pulled the papers together on the coffee table and signed the top one. "Now, Gerald, you will need to come to court this Thursday, just for the formality of having the charges against you withdrawn. And I believe Inspector Jarvis will be asked to apologize for his, ahem, enthusiastic pursuit of you."

"I should hope so," Mrs. Rutherford said. "Shooting at children, indeed."

"To be fair, that was one of the local Delphi police," Ruby said. "Like Nico said, some of the local police were a bit excitable."

"What will happen to Sir Mason now?" Mrs. Rutherford asked.

"At the moment he's in jail in Athens," Mr. Prisk said, pouring himself a glass of squash. "The Greek authorities are trying to satisfy themselves that he's alive. The records still show that he's dead. And because he's officially dead, he can't access any of his money to hire lawyers. So he'll be there for some time, even before he faces any of the hundred or so charges that will be laid against him."

"It'll do him good to see what life's like without great wads of cash," Ruby said.

There was a light knock on the door and a housemaid announced that Inspector Parrott from the London Metropolitan Police had arrived.

The inspector greeted them all warmly and handed a shoebox to Gerald.

"What's this?" Gerald asked as he peered inside.

"It's the last of the material we recovered from Sir Mason's rooms at the Rattigan Club," he said. "It appears to be the documents stolen from your house by Green's associate."

Gerald flicked through a pile of newspaper clippings, envelopes, a dry-cleaning ticket . . . and a letter, with "Delphi" written at the top in Greek.

"The letter from Great-Aunt Geraldine," he said. He skimmed the contents and groaned. "It says Delphi is the key to the mystery. This could have saved us a lot of stuffing around."

Sam shrugged and took a chocolate-chip biscuit from a plate on the card table. "Never mind," he said. "It helped fill in the time."

"Have you heard from Constable Lethbridge?" Ruby asked the inspector. "How is he?"

"He's running a pigeon hospital in Rome with his new girlfriend," Parrott said. "He seems to be very happy." The inspector fixed Gerald with a penetrating stare. "You three certainly led the police on a merry chase across Europe. I'm still curious as to exactly how you located Sir Mason Green. In a cave. In Greece."

Gerald glanced at Sam, who looked to Ruby, who closed the triangle with a look back to Gerald.

"Um, we had help from a boy in Delphi," Gerald said, as innocently as he could. "He'd heard some rumors about an old man hiding in a cave. We found him and brought him out in an underground stream." He turned back to doodling on his notepad. "There's not much else to tell."

"What about Charlotte Green?" Parrott said. "The local police found her chemistry laboratory and the poison she used to murder Green's double in the Old Bailey, but they haven't been able to find a trace of her. It's as if she's disappeared in a puff of smoke."

"Um . . ." Gerald said.

There was a long silence, which ended with Mr. Prisk and Mrs. Rutherford both jumping to their feet. "Can't keep you all day, Inspector," Mr. Prisk said, ushering him toward the door.

"That's right," chimed in Mrs. Rutherford. "You're a busy man, Inspector. Let me show you out." There was a bustle of bodies in the doorway and finally Gerald, Ruby, and Sam were alone.

Gerald checked that the door was properly closed before

collapsing back into his armchair.

"Are you sure we did the right thing?" Ruby asked. "Keeping the real city of Delphi a secret?"

"Completely," Gerald said. "My ancestors gave up their lives to keep the Oracle's secret safe. It'd be poor form for me to give it away now."

"It's funny when you think about it," Sam said. "The mask actually protects itself. You can't wear it outside the temple without turning into a human sandcastle. And if you do put it on inside the temple, you're condemned to stay there for the rest of your life." He picked up another biscuit. "We could have spent the summer at the beach."

"I guess Marcus, Lucius, and Gaius went that one step further to make sure it remained a secret," Ruby said.

Gerald was putting the finishing touches to a drawing of Ruby. "Do you still think everything that happened was coincidence?" he said.

Ruby shuffled the playing cards and started laying them out, one by one, on the table. The first card she turned up was the joker. "I think there's a perfectly logical explanation for everything."

"Really? How about my name being chiseled into a block of marble sixteen hundred years ago?"

Ruby straightened in her chair. The next card she turned up was the ace of spades. "Just because I can't explain it doesn't mean there's no explanation," she said.

Sam let out a loud laugh, and flicked a rubber band at his sister. "I wonder how Nico is doing," he said.

Ruby flipped over the nine of diamonds. "I'm glad he didn't see what happened to Charlotte in the temple." She shivered lightly. "It still gives me the creeps."

"Do you think Nico will try to find the real Delphi again?" Sam said. "All that treasure would be tempting. Just one of those gold statues and his aunt wouldn't need to take in lodgers anymore."

Gerald pulled a document from the pile of papers Mr. Prisk had left on the coffee table. "I think Nico might be too busy to worry about buried treasure. The Archer Corporation's tourism division has just invested in some holiday accommodation in Delphi."

Ruby smiled at Gerald. "Oh, really?"

"Yes. We've found some local experts to run the place for us on an extended minimum loan repayment agreement."

"Just how extended?"

"About a thousand years."

"You've bought Nico and his aunt a hotel, haven't you?" Ruby said.

Gerald blushed. "It was the least I could do, after what we put Nico through," he said. "It'll set them up, and you just know that Nico will make the business a success. So much more satisfying to build your own fortune."

"More satisfying than what?" Ruby asked.

"Than inheriting it," Gerald said.

There was a pause in the conversation. The afternoon sun streamed through the tall windows, filling the games room with lethargic warmth.

Gerald looked up to find Ruby staring at him.

"School starts on Monday," she said. "For Sam and me, anyway."

"Yeah," Gerald said. "I know."

"So what are you doing?" Ruby asked. "Have your mum and dad decided?"

"They're talking about boarding school," Gerald said. "In some grim castle in Scotland, I think."

"It'd be nice if you were in London," Ruby said. She turned over the queen of hearts. "You know. Close by."

The room seemed to heat up a few degrees. Gerald's stomach did a backflip.

"Yeah," he said. "That'd be good."

There was an awkward silence.

Sam jumped out of his chair. "Oh for Pete's sake, let's go outside and do something. You two are making me nauseous."

He clipped Gerald over the back of the head and made for the stairs.

"I'll get you for that!" Gerald called after him. He pulled Ruby out of her chair and they set off after Sam, diving down the staircase in a helter-skelter dash to the front entry.

They skidded past Mrs. Rutherford and pitched through the door into the sunshine.

Summer may have been over.

But there was still fun to be had.

ΔΕΛΦΟΙ

Dear Gerald,

And so to the family legend. When I was a young woman, my father sat me down and told me a fantastical tale of ancient Greece. I had no reason to disbelieve him then, and you have no reason to disbelieve me now. You are the first and only person I have told this story to. But there are others who know of it. And that is the reason they are out to kill me. And you.

The prize they are seeking is the one that we must protect. That is our purpose and our promise.

The prize is in Delphi.

It is the very secret of the Oracle herself.

I will not bore you with the details of the Pythia: They are recounted in endless books. Get a library card and educate yourself, dear boy. But you need to know that you are her descendant—and that makes you special.

I visited Delphi in my younger days, sailing down from Turkey. It was truly wondrous. I wasn't looking for the Oracle's secret—I knew it was hidden well enough.

But I wanted to see the place, to feel its presence.

We must protect this secret, Gerald. The future is for all of us to create—not for any one person to control.

I have left a great trust to one so young, Gerald. Use this fortune to honor that trust. And to bring some happiness to others.

And buy yourself some ice cream. I wish I'd eaten more of it.

Wishing you eternal good fortune,
Geraldine

P.S. And for pity's sake, tell Mr. Fry that teaspoon collection I left him is extremely valuable—worth five million pounds to any decent collector. He's such an old fluff, he's probably sulking about getting a box of cutlery. I hope he doesn't give you a hard time about it. xxx

ACKNOWLEDGMENTS

A big thank you to:

Dr. Gilbert J. Price from the Center for Microscopy and Microanalysis at the University of Queensland, for advice on the fossilization of human skeletons; Jordan Brown in New York, whose unfailing good humor and patience has helped me chart new and sometimes bizarre territories; the many schoolteachers and librarians who have sipped coffee at the back of the room and allowed me to talk with their students about the wonderful world of writing; booksellers—I salute you; and Jane Pearson, whose vision I trust and whose skill, talent, and patience are beyond measure.